AN ENEMY OLDER THAN TIME

The Shadow used human minds for fuel and the bodies inside the Valkyrie suits were maimed humans. But was the Shadow a group of humans from another Earth time-line, pillaging and destroying other timelines? Dane had already traveled to several timelines where the human race had been wiped out by the Shadow in its quest for power, air, bodies, and water.

"I believe I can find a portal to the Shadow's world using the map inside the sphere," Dane said.

"But you have no power for the sphere," Earhart noted.

Dane had no desire to use humans as power again, the way they had just used the crew of the doomed USS *Nautilus* from another dying timeline. The nine crystal skulls were lined up in a cabinet, a macabre audience to this meeting. "We have the crystal skulls. They're drained, but maybe we can power them back up. They were powered up when we recovered them from Little Bighorn."

"So we need another massacre?" Earhart said.

"All I know is that I think I can find the portal to the Shadow's timeline using the sphere map."

"It's doubtful," Foreman said, "that the gate in the Shadow's timeline will be unguarded."

Dane didn't respond, knowing what Foreman had said was true . . .

BATTLE FOR ATLANTIS

Greg Donegan

BERKLEY BOOKS, NEW YORK

BATTLE FOR ATLANTIS

A Berkley Book / published by arrangement with the author

PRINTING HISTORY
Berkley edition / February 2004

Copyright © 2004 by Robert Mayer.
Cover art by Craig White.
Cover design by Judith Murello.
Interior text design by Julie Rogers.

For information address: The Berkley Publishing Group,
a division of Penguin Group (USA) Inc.,
375 Hudson Street, New York, New York 10014.

ISBN: 0-425-19453-1

BERKLEY®
Berkley Books are published by The Berkley Publishing Group,
a division of Penguin Group (USA) Inc.,
375 Hudson Street, New York, New York 10014.
BERKLEY and the "B" design
are trademarks belonging to Penguin Group (USA) Inc.

PRINTED IN THE UNITED STATES OF AMERICA

10 9 8 7 6 5 4 3 2 1

1

"Four score and seven years ago our fathers brought forth on this continent, a new nation, conceived in Liberty, and dedicated to the proposition that all men are created equal." The tall man with the dark beard and lined face paused and looked out over the crowd that listened to his speech. Soldiers, politicians, locals. And the dead. Acres and acres of dead in the cemetery he had come to dedicate. He felt the presence of the dead more than he did the living. He also sensed another presence, one he had known all his adult life.

He was in southern Pennsylvania, in a small town that few had heard of before the great battle of the previous summer that had taken place in and around this place called Gettysburg. It was just past mid-November and the *trees were bare of their leaves, making the terrain much different from what it must have looked like in July when the great armies clashed here.*

Lincoln continued. "Now we are engaged in a great civil war, testing whether that nation, or any nation so conceived and so dedicated, can long endure. We are met on a great battle-field of that war. We have come to dedicate a portion of that field, as a final resting place for those who here gave their lives that that nation might live. It is altogether fitting and proper that we should do this."

Almost fifty thousand men had been killed or wounded or were missing from the three days of battle. It was a number that had staggered a nation that had seen large numbers of casualties reported before. Many of the Union and Confederate dead still lay in their shallow battlefield graves and if one penetrated far enough into the surrounding woods, they would find those who had not even been buried, the bodies picked clean by scavengers, leaving skulls and bones to trip up the unwary.

There was an air about the place. It was more than hallowed ground. It was as if the battle still resonated in the very soil. Lincoln had walked most of the battlefield the previous day upon arrival. Visiting places that were already becoming legend: Little and Big Round Tops; the Peach Orchard; Culp's Hill; Seminary Ridge; and, most important, Cemetery Ridge and the long open field leading up to it. Mary had refused to come with him to the last place, and he had become ill shortly after walking along the stone wall on top of the ridge, peering out to the west where so many had charged across on the last day of the great battle.

"But, in a larger sense, we can not dedicate—we can not consecrate—we can not hallow this ground. The

brave men, living and dead, who struggled here, have consecrated it, far above our poor power to add or detract. The world will little note, nor long remember what we say here, but it can never forget what they did here. It is for us living, rather, to be dedicated here to the unfinished work which they who fought here have thus far so nobly advanced."

A slight breeze blew across the gathered crowd, and Lincoln felt a chill on his skin. He had made so many decisions in the past few years and so many people had died as a result of those decisions. And he knew there were more decisions to come. There was to be a final reckoning for which this was but a prelude. So he had been told.

"It is rather for us to be here dedicated to the great task remaining before us—that from these honored dead we take increased devotion to that cause for which they gave the last full measure of devotion—that we here highly resolve that these dead shall not have died in vain—that this nation, under God, shall have a new birth of freedom—and that government of the people, by the people, for the people, shall not perish from the earth."

Abraham Lincoln glanced down at the notes he had made on the way to Gettysburg from Washington and which he had honed the previous night in the local house at which he had stayed. There was another paragraph, one he had scribbled on the carriage ride from that house to this spot. One that he had spent many restless nights tossing and turning over, debating whether he even dare write it, never mind utter it. Mary, dear Mary, had told him not to. Had told him that the Truth was best left unsaid. That the apparent sacrifices that had been made were enough for people to know. That knowing more would be dangerous.

There was no applause as Lincoln stopped talking. The speaker before him, Edward Everett, has spoken for over two hours, eulogizing those who had died in the Battle of Gettysburg this past summer. Lincoln had just spoken only two hundred and seventy-two words in less than two minutes. There were many in the crowd who hadn't yet realized he'd begun speaking, never mind stopped. It didn't matter. The dead had heard.

President Lincoln looked out over the audience. At the right edge of the crowd he saw his wife's familiar face. He turned away, and then looked back and she was still there, peering at him intently, the face hidden beneath a black, broad-brimmed hat. The head bobbed slightly, as if indicating approval, and Lincoln shivered once more for several moments, despite the Indian summer warmness of the day. There were prices to be paid beyond that taken in battle. He took the envelope on which he had written the last paragraph, folded it in half and slid it inside a pocket on the inside of his long coat.

"God help us," Lincoln whispered to himself as he left the speaking podium. "God help all the worlds. We have done our part."

He made his way through the crowd shaking hands, edging his way closer to his wife. When he reached her, he looked into her dark eyes. She held his gaze.

"Mary," Lincoln said. Lincoln leaned his tall form toward her, like an old oak blown by a strong wind until his head was next to hers. "Did it work? Was it worth all the death?"

"I don't know yet. I am still waiting for the Voice to tell me."

"It's been months," Lincoln argued, a refrain that had been going between them ever since the great battle.

"Time in this war doesn't work like that."

Lincoln knew his wife wasn't referring to the War between the States. It had taken him a long time to accept that there was something at stake larger than even the Union.

Mary Todd Lincoln put a hand on his arm. *"I promise, I will let you know. As soon as I hear it."*

2

Custer

Colonel George Armstrong Custer stared at the blood on his hands in disbelief. There was no pain. He just felt very, very tired. He was aware that someone was walking next to his horse, holding him in the saddle. He looked down and saw his nephew Autie Reed guiding him. There were troopers all about, most mounted, some on foot, all heading up the draw toward higher ground.

That was good, Custer thought. Higher ground was always best.

He could hear firing and screams, but they seemed far away. Where was the village? Were the Indians running? He saw his brother Tom Custer off to his right and slightly ahead. He tried to call out but no words would come. They rode out of the draw and a knoll was ahead. Tom was deploying troopers in a defensive line, facing downslope.

Defensive? Custer thought. That was wrong. They should be attacking. Always attacking. Autie was helping Custer off his horse. Custer tried to stand but his legs were so weak, he sank to the ground. He was surprised when Autie pulled a pistol and shot his horse—his favorite steed. Why did he do that? Custer wondered as the horse collapsed next to him. Autie helped Custer to a seated position, with his back against the dead animal. He drew Custer's pistol and placed it in his hand. Custer could barely hold on to it. He tried to ask Autie what was going on, why were they on the defensive, but no words would come and his nephew turned his attention outward, pistol at the ready. There was blood on Autie's face. How had that happened?

Then Custer saw beyond the perimeter. Hundreds of Indians coming forward, up the draw like wolves to a downed buffalo calf. They were firing rifles and bows. A trooper trying to escape was swarmed by the wave of hostiles, disappearing. This couldn't be, Custer thought. It just simply couldn't be happening. Not to his regiment. Not to the Seventh.

Bouyer

Mitch Bouyer and Lieutenant Weir, with D Company behind them, reached a high point where they could see to the north.

"Oh my God," Weir whispered.

A small knot of soldiers were holding a perimeter about a mile away on a hill. And all around were Indians. At least a thousand, Bouyer estimated. And the Indians weren't charging, but holding back, pouring lead and arrow at the soldiers.

"We can't . . ." Weir didn't finish the obvious.

Bouyer understood, but he also knew he didn't have the luxury of choice. He had three skulls. He'd had to pad the satchels with his blanket to keep them from burning his horse. They'd been growing hotter with each passing minute mirroring the intensity of the battle.

Bouyer kicked his spurs into his horse's side and headed forward.

Weir wheeled his horse and pointed back the way they had come. His troop needed no urging. D Company raced back to the bluff that held the survivors of Reno's command.

Crazy Horse
Crazy Horse rode around to the left, two hundred of his mounted warriors following, putting the firing to his right. He knew the terrain and knew where the battle was taking place. He also knew that the other tribes would attack head on.

This was the great battle that his mother had foretold.

He and his warriors galloped along a draw, out of sight. Crazy Horse could sense the anxiety among his men, their desire to ride straight toward the shooting and join in the battle. But they followed his lead.

Gall
Gall strode back and forth along the front edge of the Indian line, holding them back from charging directly into the white men's guns. It was difficult, but his size and stature brought grudging obedience. They lay down in the waist high grass, along the edge of the coulees that

flanked the hill on which the white men had set up their perimeter.

Gall had warriors with rifles move forward so they could see. He directed those with bows back, out of direct sight, and had them fire up into the air, their arrows arching over and down into the whites. Gall had his hatchet in one hand, the satchel from the Sun Dance in the other. Inside of it was a crystal skull.

Custer
Autie placed something in Custer's lap. A leather satchel. With something hot inside. That woke Custer from his blood-drained stupor. He blinked, looking about. Arrows were coming down, almost as heavily as a summer squall. Some men had pulled saddles over their backs as they lay prone, firing. The ground was littered with arrow shafts like stalks of prairie grass.

Custer saw that the damned Springfield rifles were jamming as cartridges expanded in the heat of the chamber. One trooper, fifteen yards in front of the main line of the perimeter was on his knees, knife in hand trying to extract a round. Several braves saw this and charged forward. The man grabbed the barrel of his Springfield and jumped to his feet, swinging it like a madman. He knocked two of the braves to the ground before he was overwhelmed by the others.

Custer tried to lift his hand holding the revolver but he couldn't do it. Where was Tom? And Autie? And Boston? And Calhoun? His family? Someone came rushing up on the left and Custer twisted his neck. Tom. Bleeding from a wound in his chest.

"George—" Whatever he'd been about to say was cut off as an arrow punched in one side of his neck and out the other with a gush of blood. Tom's hands grabbed for the shaft as arterial blood spurted for several seconds. A bullet cut short that attempt, hitting Tom Custer in the side of his head, splattering his brother with his brains.

Custer could only stare in horror.

Bouyer

A soldier came galloping madly toward Bouyer, leaning as far forward on his horse as possible. It took Bouyer a second to realize why the man was in this uncomfortable and unusual position—he was trying to minimize his back as a target for the dozen braves on ponies chasing him.

Bouyer pulled back on the reins, halting. As the man raced past a bullet caught him in the shoulder, tumbling him from the horse. The man scrambled to his feet, looking about wildly. He saw Bouyer and raised his hands in supplication.

Bouyer forced himself to be still as the braves raced up, two jumping off their ponies. One of them smashed the back of the soldier's skull in with a stone-headed club. The other braves circled Bouyer, weapons held menacingly. Bouyer pulled one of the crystal skulls out of its wrapping. It glowed bright blue and was so hot, he could feel it sear his flesh, but he held it high.

The warriors pulled back, even the two who had been in the process of scalping the soldier. Then they were startled as a second glowing skull held high appeared over a rise to the west. And the hand holding it belonged to Sitting Bull.

"Powerful magic!" Sitting Bull cried out in Lakota.

"Yes," Bouyer agreed.

Sitting Bull turned to the left. Just over the next rise

lay the battlefield. They could hear the firing falling off from the crescendo it had been. Bouyer knew the end was close.

"We go?" Sitting Bull inclined his head toward the rise.

Bouyer nodded and put the stirrups to his horse. Skulls in hand the two rode toward the rise.

Custer

An arrow slammed into Custer's left thigh, piercing through flesh and muscle into the ground beneath. He didn't feel any pain. He didn't feel the burning heat from the satchel Autie had placed in his lap. All he felt was in his mind, disbelief and shock about what was going on all around him.

Gall

Gall saw Sitting Bull and the strange half-breed from the Sun Dance appear to the south, both holding up glowing skulls. He signaled, indicating for the warriors not to attack the half-breed. Then he reached into his satchel and grabbed hold of the hot skull. He almost laughed at the pain. The Sun Dance had prepared him for this. He held the glowing skull aloft and moved forward.

Buffalo Calf Woman

Buffalo Calf Woman slammed an awl into a dead soldier's left ear, pulled it out, and then jammed it into the right, piercing the eardrum. He should not hear in the afterworld. Because he had not heard clearly in this world. Not heard the Great Spirit warning the whites to leave the People in peace.

She looked up and saw mighty Gall striding forward, a glowing blue object in his hand. She opened the satchel she'd taken from the blue-coat. She blinked at the bright blue glow, and then reached in. She grabbed hold with both hands and held it aloft. Then she headed in the direction Gall was going.

Walks Alone

The boy who had shot Custer as he tried to cross Little Bighorn, Walks Alone, saw Gall and Buffalo Calf Woman. Where was Crazy Horse? he wondered, as he pulled out the skull the great warrior had given him. He stood up, ignoring the warnings from the braves around to stay down. There were still soldiers alive on the hill, firing.

None would hit him, Walks Alone knew. He headed up the hill.

Two Moons

Two Moons notched an arrow and fired it high into the sky, firing a second before the first impacted. He paused as he noted the people moving forward with the skulls. He put down his bow and opened the satchel he'd taken from Bloody Knife. He removed the skull, gasping as it burned his flesh, and moved forward.

Crazy Horse

Crazy Horse turned to the south. Toward the firing. His warriors spread out on either side. He could hold them back no longer. Their vengeance against those who had invaded their land, killed their families, brought disease and death, was unstoppable now.

Crazy Horse reached into the satchel tied to his pony and pulled out the talisman given by his "brother." He kicked his pony in the side and raced forward.

Sitting Bull

Sitting Bull halted, fifty yards short of the last stand being mounted by the whites. He could see the Son of the Morning Star, still alive but wounded in several places, leaning back against the saddle of a dead horse.

Bouyer saw Custer also. He stopped next to Sitting Bull as Buffalo Calf Woman and Walks Alone joined them. The skulls seemed to sense each other's presence, their glow becoming brighter, unbearable to gaze on directly.

And then Crazy Horse and three hundred warriors crested the hill behind the last stand and swept down.

The Space Between Worlds and Times

The dolphin Rachel leapt out of the dark water and landed with a splash directly in front of Eric Dane and Amelia Earhart. The Space Between was the name Earhart had given to this strange place—a transit point for the portals between parallel Earth timelines and time itself, consisting of a circle of black land surrounding the Inner Sea which they were on, enclosed inside what appeared to be a massive semicircular cavern.

"Let's go," Dane said. He didn't wait for a reply as he moved forward in the Valkyrie suit, floating ten feet above the water, following Rachel's dorsal fin. The dolphin paused, arched her back so she could see that they were following, and then continued ahead. They were both ensconced in the hard, white suits that they'd stolen from the Shadow's emissaries.

Dane saw their destination. A narrow portal column,

streaked with red, flickering to solid black, then gray with red, then black, still filled with the red lines.

"That's not a locked-in portal," Earhart said.

Dane didn't respond. He moved forward, hit the portal and disappeared.

Earhart followed.

Little Bighorn

"Angels," Custer whispered. "Come to rescue me." He dropped the pistol he couldn't fire and reached up with both hands toward the white figures that had just appeared in front of him. All around the dying colonel were the dying remnants of half of the Seventh Cavalry.

· · ·

Dane saw the massacre all around as a wave of several hundred warriors washed over the vestiges of Custer's command. But all veered away from the strange vision of he and Amelia Earhart in the Valkyrie suits and Custer nearby with a glowing skull in his lap.

Dane slowly turned and saw a handful of people approaching, glowing blue skulls held in their hands. He raised his white arms wide, welcoming them, spreading out the metal net he had taken from the sphere.

The screams of the last dying soldiers echoed in his ears. He didn't want to believe he'd become jaded to death; he wanted to believe that this battle had been inevitable anyway and he was here to cull something good out of a futile massacre.

Sitting Bull walked up and dropped the glowing skull into the net. Then Buffalo Calf Woman. Walks Alone.

Crazy Horse. Gall. Two Moons. And then Mitch Bouyer with two skulls.

Eight.

"Eric."

Dane had almost forgotten Earhart was with him. He turned.

George Armstrong Custer was looking at him. His face was pale, his body wounded in several places.

"The ninth," Earhart said. Custer was the only one of his command left alive. And on his lap was the ninth skull.

Dane felt Custer's shock and confusion. "Take it," he ordered Earhart.

With a clawed hand she reached down and lifted the skull from Custer's lap. Dane wanted to say something to those around, but he knew the portal might not last. He turned to it, hit the blackness and disappeared.

Behind him Amelia Earhart hesitated. Her thoughts and feelings were jumbled. She saw her lines in Bouyer's face. Her son, but not her son. Standing on a hillside littered with bodies. He was half of one people, half of the other. What would happen to him, she wondered? He didn't even know who she was.

The portal flickered and she entered it.

. . .

Dane went directly to the sphere's power room carrying the skulls.

Earhart took her place in the control room, entering the command pod. There was no need for them to talk, to discuss what came next.

Staying in the Valkyrie suit, Dane removed the nine glowing skulls and placed them in the alcoves that were on the same level as the portal map. When he was done, he went to the center and exited the suit. The power flowing in from the skulls was intense, much stronger than what he had just experienced from the crew of the doomed submarine *Nautilus* from another Earth timeline who had given their lives to get him this far. He let his hands flow among the portal strands, letting his own timeline attract them with its draw.

His hands wrapped around a strand that felt familiar in a way he couldn't explain. Then he realized he'd touched this one before, when he'd cut off the portal the Shadow had been using to drain power from his world, this sphere had come through.

"I've got power," Earhart said. "I see the portal. It's big enough. You're sure it's the one back to your timeline?"

"I'm not sure of anything," Dane said. "But, yes, this is the one."

The sphere hit the portal, rocked, bounced and then Dane almost fell off the pedestal as the craft canted hard right.

"Whoa!" Earhart called out. "I've got it." The floor leveled. "Deploying panels and releasing the ozone."

. . .

On board the FLIP, Foreman, Dane's CIA boss, was one of the first to get the reports of the massive sphere reappearing. A dozen military and research aircraft from various countries were within range of the craft and they immediately vectored in.

. . .

"What are we going to do about the radiation?" Dane asked.

"We're heading north now," Earhart reported. "You

just keep the power coming. I'll take care of it. We've discharged all the ozone we picked up. And keep that gate open."

. . .

At McMurdo Station in Antarctica the surviving scientists couldn't believe the data their instruments were recording. It wasn't just a reprieve for them; it was a reversal of the damage to the ozone layer that had been done for decades previously. The Shadow's attempt to destroy this Earth timeline by completely stripping the atmosphere of ozone had failed.

. . .

Moscow was a ghost town, millions having fled the inevitable wave of radiation from Chernobyl being born by the winds. The front edge had passed through the suburbs and now threatened the city itself. A handful of dedicated soldiers stayed at their stations, manning the nuclear launch control center, the air defense monitoring station, and other key facilities which had NBC protection capability. They would stay there as long as they could remain buttoned up and survive.

The air defense monitoring station was the first to pick up the image of the sphere as it approached from the south. The size of the image was so overwhelming the general in charge had no idea what to do.

. . .

Earhart brought the sphere and its miles of deployed panels down to a level where they wouldn't hit the highest object. "How's the power?"

Dane looked at the nine skulls. Five had already gone

blank, while four still glowed. "We're under fifty percent."

"Damn." Earhart knew the controls of this ship. It was something she hadn't wanted to discuss with Dane because she didn't know how she knew. Whether the Ones Before had planted the knowledge in her somehow or, more darkly, she had piloted this craft sometime in the past and didn't remember, she had no idea.

She pushed a button to her extreme left.

The panels crackled with energy, drawing the radiation in the air toward them. The sphere and panels swept through the sky above Russia in long, fast S-turns, cleaning the air of death, heading toward Chernobyl which the Shadow had completely destroyed after draining all the reactor cores of their power.

"We're getting hot inside the cargo bay," Earhart informed Dane.

"We don't have much power left," Dane replied. "How much longer?"

"I think we got it," Earhart said, checking the displays. "Most of it at least. I'm heading back toward the portal and bringing in the panels so we can go faster."

As the sphere accelerated, the panels began folding on themselves.

Eight of the skulls had been drained of the energy put into them at such cost. Only one still glowed. Dane was staring at it as if he could keep the power flowing from it with simply his will. Perhaps he could, he suddenly realized. He was one of the chosen. He realized he had the power if he was willing to make the sacrifice.

He had asked others to make sacrifices.

"Eric."

He lifted one hand out of the portal map and extended

it toward the line of blue power that flowed from the skull to the map.

"Damn it, Dane. We're almost there. What are you doing?"

He put his hand into the flow. His head snapped back as if he'd been shot in the forehead. He was only kept from falling by his one hand still gripping the portal end of his Earth timeline.

The sphere hit the portal with a jar that knocked Dane to the other side, pulling his hand out of the power flow. Unconscious, he let go of the portal map and collapsed to the floor.

"We made it," Earhart's voice echoed inside the Valkyrie suit. "Dane? Eric, are you there?"

Little Bighorn

Sitting Bull

There was firing to the south, where Reno and Benteen's troops were dug in on top of a knoll. They didn't have access to water and Sitting Bull knew it would only be a matter of a couple of days before they became dehydrated and desperate.

They were not his immediate concern. He looked over the battlefield strewn with the dead blue-coats and crowded with his people. All had gathered round, staring up at him. The two ghosts had just disappeared into the black with the glowing skulls. Such a thing none here had ever seen, and all knew they had witnessed powerful medicine.

For the first time in his life, Sitting Bull was at a loss

for words. He could see Crazy Horse and the strange half-breed who had brought the skulls whispering together.

"My people—" Sitting Bull began, but he still could not summon the words that had always flowed so easily. Thus he gave way when Crazy Horse surprisingly came forward. The one who never spoke in front of groups. Who let his actions speak.

Crazy Horse stood next to Sitting Bull looking around at the thousand faces looking back. Warriors, squaws, children. Many covered in white man's blood. He too heard the shooting to the south where warriors kept the other blue-coats trapped. This was a great victory indeed, but—yes, even Crazy Horse could finally accept the but—they had destroyed only half of the Seventh Cavalry. And there was another column of blue-coats coming from the north with even more men than Custer had. And there were more, an ocean of soldiers to the east ready to sweep west. For the first time in his life, Crazy Horse saw the truth, the reality.

"What happened today," Crazy Horse said, his powerful voice easily carrying over the crowd, "the magic you have witnessed, must never be spoken of. Even among us. And you would be wise not to speak of this battle at all to the whites. For they will come thirsting for vengeance for the Son of the Morning Star and the others who lie here." He swallowed, looked at his "brother" who met his gaze steadily, then continued. "We must leave. Separate and go our own ways. And make peace with the whites when they offer it."

There were no cries of dissent. The magic all had witnessed had been too powerful, too full of portent.

"If we continue to fight," Crazy Horse continued, "we will all die. We will become as extinct as the great buffalo.

We used to see the plains covered with them as far as the eye could reach. They would pass by our encampments for days on end. Now we must search long and hard for a small group. If we continue to fight we too will come to an end."

He waved toward the west. "Go. Separate. Hide from the whites. And when they offer peace, take it. It is not a good thing. It is not what I or you would want. But it is what will happen."

Crazy Horse walked down, past the horse against which Custer lay dead, up to his "brother." "Go in peace. Talk to the white chiefs. Tell them it is over."

The Space Between

Earhart floated into the power chamber which was lit only by a dim gold glow from the portal map. She saw Dane lying at the base of the portal pedestal. "Eric?"

Dane slowly opened his eyes.

"Are you all right?"

Dane nodded, grimacing with pain. "We must take the fight to the Shadow."

"How do we do that?"

"First, we find the Ones Before." Before Earhart could ask the same question, Dane continued. "I sensed something in the portal. I think I can get us to them."

"And then?"

"We find out the truth about this war and who the Shadow is. And we end the war and the Shadow."

3

EARTH TIMELINE—THE PRESENT
The Devil's Sea Gate

"How do we do that?" Foreman asked Dane. The elderly
CIA agent was seated in a swivel chair in the control
room of the FLIP, a research vessel two hundred meters
long with the capability of submerging its bulbous bow,
which contained a muonic probe, to keep track of gate activity. The ship was currently holding position two miles
from the Devil's Sea Gate, out of which Dane had just
brought the Shadow sphere, which now bobbed in the
water just off the bow of the FLIP. The Devil's Sea Gate
was a triangular area off the coast of Japan, which like
the Bermuda Triangle, had been the scene of numerous
unexplained disappearances over the centuries. Disappearances they now knew were the work of the Shadow.
Dane had just repeated to Foreman what he had told

Earhart in the sphere about finishing the war and the Shadow.

Foreman had been in the CIA over fifty years, from the very beginning of the organization. He had tanned, rough skin, with a sharp nose like an eagle's beak. His hair was pure white, some of which Dane attributed to his experiences around the gates. His fascination—more obsession—with the gates had begun during World War II when his brother's aircraft had disappeared into the Devil's Sea Gate that lay nearby. Foreman had also watched on radar as Flight 19 disappeared into the Bermuda Triangle Gate in 1946, one of many famous disappearances over the centuries in that region.

Dane was seated across from Foreman, with Earhart to one side and Ahana, the Japanese scientist who was now in charge of the FLIP to the other. Once more Dane had managed to stave off disaster, but he knew the assaults would not end as long as the Shadow, the unknown malevolent force that attacked through the gates, existed. Dane had first encountered the Shadow when he entered the gate at Angkor Kol Ker in Cambodia during a mission while assigned to Special Forces in the Vietnam War. He'd been sent by Foreman to recover the black box of a U-2 spy plane that Foreman had sent into the gate to gather data as he struggled to figure out what the gates were.

Who or what the Shadow was remained a mystery, although they now knew that the Shadow used human minds for fuel and the bodies inside the Valkyrie suits were maimed humans. The thing that preyed on Dane's mind ever since making the discovery of the humans inside the Valkyrie suits was whether the Shadow was a group of humans from another Earth timeline, one that was pillaging and destroying other timelines. Dane had already traveled to several other Earth timelines, some where the human race had been wiped out by the Shadow in its quest for power, air, bodies, and water.

"I believe I can find a portal to the Shadow's world using the map inside the sphere," Dane said.

"And then?" Foreman pressed.

Dane leaned back in the seat, exhausted from recent events. "We have the sphere. We can travel through portals safely."

"But you have no power for the sphere," Earhart noted.

Dane had no desire to use humans as power again, the way they had just used the crew of a doomed USS *Nautilus* from another dying timeline. The nine crystal skulls were lined up in a cabinet in the control room, a macabre audience to this meeting. They were clear, drained of power. He nodded toward the cabinet. "We have the crystal skulls. They're drained, but maybe there is a way we can power them back up. They were powered up when we recovered them from Little Bighorn."

"So we need another massacre?" Earhart said.

Dane couldn't judge her tone, whether there was disapproval in it or resignation. There had been so much death already.

"There are many massacres throughout history," Dane said. "Little Bighorn was just one of them. And not necessarily a massacre, either, but rather an intense battle where the minds of the men involved generate the power evoked by dire straits."

"The skulls drained pretty quickly when we came back," Earhart noted.

"Maybe they weren't charged with as much power as they are capable of," Dane said.

"Even if you had power," Foreman said, "what would you do when you got to the Shadow's world?"

Dane had been thinking about that while returning to the FLIP via the Devil's Sea Gate. Given the ability of the Shadow to manipulate power at a level beyond that of scientists in Dane's Earth timeline he doubted there was anything he could bring from his own timeline, even nuclear weapons, that would be able to defeat the Shadow. For all he knew any power source he brought to the Shadow as a weapon could be appropriated and used by it.

"We're getting too far ahead," Earhart interjected.

"Where should we be?" Dane asked, grateful for the reprieve from focusing on a problem for which there was no immediate solution.

Earhart lifted a single finger. "We know that what are inside the Valkyrie suits are people, humans, right?" She didn't wait for an answer. "Maimed people, damaged people, but humans nonetheless. Much as we don't want to admit it, I think we have to assume that the Shadow is an Earth timeline; a timeline raping and destroying other timelines to keep itself going. Most likely an Earth timeline from what would be the future, even for you people, and most definitely for me."

Ahana broke in. "Not necessarily the future. Perhaps a timeline that simply developed more quickly than we did."

Dane rubbed a hand across his forehead. He didn't want to hear what Earhart was saying but he knew, could sense, that it was the truth. It had all been more palatable when he had considered the Shadow to be some alien force bent on destroying Earth. We have met the enemy and they are us, he thought.

"I've heard what happened after I was kidnapped by

the Shadow on my around-the-world flight in 1937,"
Earhart continued. "World War II. I've heard what the
Germans did in their camps. The Japanese in the places
they conquered. Even what we Americans did in the name
of ending the war at Hiroshima and Nagasaki. I think we
cannot underestimate the power of mankind's inhumanity
to itself. I have no doubt that an advanced timeline of
humans—and we know that not only do the portals lead
to parallel Earths but that they can also move one forward
or back in time—would not hesitate to destroy other
Earth timelines to sustain itself. We live on the same
planet and we do it to each other. It would be even easier
to do it to another planet.

"They take the basics. Power. Air. Water. And people. I
think they use people from other timelines for spare
parts." Earhart looked at Dane. "We know what they do in
the Space Between in their Valkyrie cavern. Removing
hearts, lungs, skin—whatever they need from those they
capture. From what we saw of the people inside the
Valkyrie suits, the people who make up the Shadow are
damaged. They're willing to do whatever it takes to get
what they need. That means they're ruthless," Earhart
summarized. She held up a second finger. "The thing that
intrigues me, though, is the group we're not talking
about."

"The Ones Before," Dane said.

Earhart nodded. "Yes. They've tried to help us. And we
definitely need more help now. Who are they? Why can't
they do more?" She didn't wait for an answer. "Before we
go after the Shadow, I think we need to find the Ones Before. We need to learn exactly what we're up against.
Also, and this is just my feeling, I think there might be a
larger plan that we are part of. After all, there are more

timelines than ours being affected, or will be affected, by the Shadow. It would be helpful if we knew what our part is and what the overall plan is."

Dane tapped the side of his head. "The Ones Before send the messages I hear and the visions I see. But I don't control when I receive them. And I've gotten nothing to show me the path we should take now or, if there is a plan, what it is. All I know is that I think I can find the portal to the Shadow's timeline using the sphere map."

"It's doubtful," Foreman said, "that the gate in the Shadow's timeline will be unguarded."

Dane didn't respond, knowing what Foreman had said was true.

Earhart turned to Dane. "Do you think the Ones Before have a plan or are just reacting as we are?"

Dane didn't stop to think. He felt the answer, and it surprised him that he had not felt this so strongly before. "I think we're part of something larger. There are others—have been others as we just saw at the Battle of Little Bighorn—who have roles to play."

Ahana spoke up. "You've acted as if there were some mystical power behind these visions and the voices you hear—and that others like you, such as Robert Frost, also heard. But I think we need to look at it in terms of science. If these visions and voices are real then we should be able to do something just as we use this boat to track the activity of the Shadow."

"What do you mean?" Dane asked.

"What happens in your head, what you get from the Ones Before, *is* real, isn't it?" Ahana asked.

Dane nodded. There was no doubting the visions and voices now.

"Then it's something we should be able to track down,"

Ahana said. "Like we did with the muonic emissions from the gates and the Shadow's lines of power."

"Do you have any theories about how we can do that?" Dane asked.

"It took us years to track down the correct frequency for the Shadow's muonic emissions that come through the gates," Ahana said. "We learned quite a bit doing that. I suspect that the Ones Before are sending on a very similar frequency and in a similar manner."

"Why haven't you uncovered it then?" Dane asked.

"Because we haven't looked," Ahana replied. "We've been so focused on the threat posed by the Shadow and the gates, we never put any effort into looking at the Ones Before."

"Then do it," Foreman ordered.

Dane held up a hand. "Wait. We—you"—he amended looking at Ahana—"zeroed in on the muonic frequencies by focusing on the gates the Shadow was using. Wouldn't it be easier to figure out how the Ones Before are transmitting if you found what gate they use to send their messages through?"

"Certainly," Ahana agreed.

Dane stood. "I think I might be able to find the portal line they use."

"The sphere map?" Earhart asked as she also stood.

Dane's response was to head for the door, then along the deck to the launch that could take him over to the Shadow's massive sphere floating nearby. As the launch took them over, they failed to notice the sleek gray form swimming off the port bow, slicing through the water with ease and watching them with one dark eye rotated in their direction.

New York City

Manhattan Island was part of a massive slab of granite that encompassed parts of nearby Connecticut and New Jersey. Its top surface had been scoured by water, particularly cut through by the Hudson River flowing to the ocean, but the slab was many miles thick and very stable.

Deep underneath the southern tip of Manhattan, though, was something very strange. Approximately six miles down, just below the slab, was a large cavern, cut out of the planet. Over three miles wide, the walls of the cavern were perfectly smooth, and the slab had been used as the roof, given some support from long black metal buttresses and beams.

In the exact center of the cavern there was a tall derrick with drilling equipment. A start had been made on the floor, with a hole excavated about fifty meters down, but it appeared as if the work had been interrupted and never resumed.

There was one opening in the wall of the cavern—a tunnel one hundred meters in diameter that went off to the east straight as an arrow. If a light were shone in that tunnel, it would show no immediate end as it ran for over a thousand miles to the middle of the Atlantic Ocean where it ended at a metal door. On the other side of that door there was another large chamber, but that one was full of debris and had been flooded by the ocean long ago.

The tunnel and chamber were all that remained in our Earth timeline of the civilization of Atlantis other than the myth that had been passed down through the ages. And the few people who had survived its destruction by the Shadow.

4

EARTH TIMELINE—VIII
Antietam, MD, 16 September 1862

"We will make our stand on these hills," General Robert
E. Lee told his three senior officers as they looked out
over the Maryland countryside in the waning light. He
was flanked by the three corps commanders of the Army
of Northern Virginia: Generals Longstreet, Jackson, and
A. P. Hill.

Lee was an imposing figure, a man who commanded
respect wherever he went. His father had been Light-
Horse Harry Lee of Revolutionary War fame and the military had been Lee's focus since he was a young boy in
Virginia. He went to the relatively new Military Academy
at West Point and graduated in 1829, second in his class.
He fought, and was wounded, in the war with Mexico. He
eventually returned to West Point and was superintendent,

thus becoming responsible for training many of the men who would be commanders on both sides in the Civil War.

When war broke out he was in command of the Department of Texas. He'd been offered command of the Union forces by President Lincoln on the advice of his generals, but Lee had turned him down. Three days after Virginia seceded, he resigned from the Union Army and became the military adviser to Confederate President Jefferson Davis, before taking command of the Army of Northern Virginia.

He had been leading the Southern army in Virginia for two years and his string of successes was becoming almost mythlike. He had an uncanny ability to anticipate the actions of his opponents and for understanding their weaknesses. He stayed true to the tactics he'd learned and taught at West Point—particularly using interior lines of communication and presenting his enemy with a convex front so that his supplies, messages, and reinforcements had a much shorter distance to travel than his enemy's. His greatest tactic though was the use of entrenchments. Heretofore battle had been considered simply maneuvering one's force against the enemy, and then both sides stood in the field blasting away at each other until one or the other gave way.

Lee believed, and put into practice, that a smaller body of men, which he invariably had when up against Union forces, could hold against a much larger force if it were properly entrenched. While this happened, he would send another element of his army in a flanking maneuver to hit the fixed enemy from the side or rear. This was a radical military concept, one that would not be fully appreciated until the bloody reality of the World War I.

Now he was in the North, with his army. Stonewall

Jackson had led the way for the Southern forces into Maryland, arriving in the nearby town of Sharpsburg earlier in the afternoon. With Harpers Ferry having surrendered to his rear, Lee felt he was in a strong position to weather a Union assault, especially as he found this ground favorable. He deployed his army, taking up defensive positions along a low ridge stretching from the Potomac on his left to Antietam Creek on his right. As usual, his front curved back on the flanks, giving him interior lines and forcing the Northern forces to curve concavely.

Lee placed cannon on Nicodemus Heights to his left, the high ground in front of Dunkard Church, the ridge just east of Sharpsburg, and on the heights overlooking the Lower Bridge. He directed infantry to fill in the lines between these points, including a sunken lane less than a half mile long with worm fencing along both sides. A handful of Georgia sharpshooters guarded the Lower Bridge over Antietam Creek on one flank. This attention to detail and deployment was a trademark of the leadership that Lee had displayed in two years of nonstop victories. Despite all those victories, though, the war was dragging on.

Across the creek, his spies told Lee that the Union Commander, General George McClellan had about sixty thousand troops ready to attack—double the number available to Lee. Still, the Confederate commander felt confident. They had yet to lose to the Yankees, and these positions were strong. At West Point, he had been taught that the attacker should outnumber the defender three to one at the point of attack and he doubted George would be able to focus his large forces for a concentrated assault.

McClellan had been a cadet at the academy while Lee had been superintendent.

This was General Lee's first invasion of the Union. He'd gone North for several reasons. First, he wanted to earn recognition from the European powers that thus far had stayed on the sidelines of the Civil War being fought on the North American continent. Britain and France were both potential allies, and Lee felt a strong military showing by the Confederacy could swing one or the other to his side and perhaps force the North to sue for peace. Lee was the only cadet ever to graduate the Military Academy without a single demerit, and he knew that the longer the war lasted, the shorter the odds of a Southern victory grew.

Lee also went North to take the battles out of his beloved Virginia, which had seen most of the fighting so far. The Second Battle of Bull Run had just ended with another Southern routing of Union forces, and he'd felt the time was right to march North. He was beginning to feel that the North could keep sending army after army into the South and take defeat after defeat with little effect. As he went to sleep in his tent on the evening of the 16th, Lee felt secure in his positions and happy that the battle the next day would take place on Northern soil. Even though he had seen much war, Lee had no frame of reference for what the next day would bring.

The fact that he was fighting against the country he had taken an oath to defend when getting sworn in as a cadet at West Point disturbed Lee at times, but it was a thought and feeling he fought hard to keep at arm's distance. For him, the war was not about slavery, but about freedom. The freedom of states from a strong central government. The same type of freedom his father had fought for in the Revolutionary War against England. For him, Virginia would always take precedent over the United States.

He was a realist who knew the longer this war lasted, the smaller became the odds of the South winning. The North was simply too big, too populated, too industrialized for the rural South to expect to outlast. He needed a victory, a bloody one, to make the North howl and cause the European powers to take interest. He planned to have it tomorrow.

. . .

The battle opened on a damp, murky dawn when Union artillery on the bluffs beyond Antietam Creek began a murderous fire on Stonewall Jackson's lines. In an attempt to roll up Lee's left flank, McClellan sent troops toward The Cornfield north of town. Confederate troops hidden among the stalks rose up and delivered a murderous fire into the Union lines as they tried to deploy for the assault, driving them back. The Federals responded by withdrawing the infantry and training their artillery on the field, unleashing a brutal barrage. The fire was so intense that every stalk of corn was cut down as neatly as if by a massive scythe. The effect on the Confederates who had been in the field was less neat, tearing bodies apart and soaking the ground with blood.

The Union forces assaulted and drove the Confederates from the field, only to have a reinforced Jackson drive them once more out of it. The Union counterattacked again, and the two lines stood less than two hundred yards apart among the blood-spattered corn and mutilated bodies and fired into each other for over half an hour. Loading and firing, creating a man-made cloud from powder that hung close to the ground. All day long, the battle for this piece of field went on, the terrain changing hands over fifteen times and the harvest of bodies growing deeper and deeper. The ground became so soaked with blood and bodily fluids that it turned into a nasty mud.

Pushing his Union forces farther to the north, still desiring to turn the flank and recognizing the bloody stalemate in The Cornfield, McClellan sent a division of troops into the West Woods, but they in turn were hit on their flank by Confederates who decimated the Federals with point-blank fire, killing and wounding over half the two-thousand-man division in less than fifteen minutes. It wasn't warfare, it was slaughter.

An attempt to bolster the attack on the flank went awry when Union forces were misled and actually hit the Confederate center. As Lee had predicted, McClellan was having trouble coordinating the movements of his massive army. The Rebels were hunkered down in an eight-hundred-yard-long sunken road that had been made by years of heavy wagons taking grain to a nearby mill.

Four times over the course of three hours, the Union forces charged across open fields toward the road and four times they were thrown back. By one in the afternoon, over fifty-six hundred men lay dead or dying in the vicinity of the road, which had now earned the name Bloody Lane.

Finally, two New York regiments managed to penetrate the Confederate lines and lay down a withering fire along the length of the sunken road, turning the defensive position into a trap and sending the Rebels into headlong retreat. The center of Lee's line was now open for the assault and disaster loomed for the South.

Unfortunately for the North and for those who would

die in the next three years, McClellan decided not to throw his reserves into the attack. Perhaps the carnage of The Cornfield and Bloody Lane caused him to pause. Regardless, that decision did not end the day's fighting or the battle as it had taken on a life of its own, out of the control of the generals who had only a vague idea of what was playing out across the fields and woods of Maryland.

On the south end of the battlefield, Union General Burnside had been trying to cross a twelve-foot-wide bridge since the morning, getting thrown back time and again by the Georgia sharpshooters on a bluff overlooking the bridge. The fact that the creek the bridge spanned could be waded was something Burnside never seemed to take into account as wave after wave of Union soldiers charged across the stone bridge, finally getting a foothold on the far side in the early afternoon only to be pinned down at the base of the bluff, now unable to retreat without facing the same withering fire they had charged into.

Between this bitter success on the left and the opening in the center, General Lee appeared on the verge of defeat as Union forces closed on Sharpsburg, whose streets were crowded with retreating Confederate forces.

Then, as so often happens in war, luck intervened. General A. P. Hill's division, which had been left behind at Harpers Ferry to salvage captured Federal property, arrived at the battlefield after an amazing forced march of seventeen miles in eight hours. They unexpectedly struck the Union's left flank, catching the Federals by surprise and driving them back across the bridge they had crossed earlier that day at such great cost.

As the day came to a close, both sides were exhausted

and bloodied beyond anything they had experienced in the war to that date. The battle was over and neither side had won.

It was the bloodiest one-day battle of the Civil War. Federal losses were approximately 12,410, while Confederate losses were around 10,700. One in four men engaged in battle that day had fallen. This was a level of loss greater than even Napoleon and other European generals had ever experienced in their campaigns.

The sun was setting on the bloodiest day in American history, a record that would stand far into the future, outstripping even the casualties of June 6, 1944, in Normandy. For this timeline, the numbers—twenty-three thousand casualties in one day—would not be topped until the final assault of the Shadow over two hundred years in the future, at which time life on the planet, in this timeline, would come to an end and there would be no one around to count the billions of dead.

On the following day, Lee began to withdraw his forces back to Virginia, and McClellan failed to press the battle against his retreating foe, resting his bloodied and weary army. Lee's wagon train carrying his wounded stretched for over fourteen miles.

. . .

It was not a victory. Abraham Lincoln knew that as he sat at his desk in the Oval Office and read the tersely worded dispatches from Sharpsburg. There had been no victories since the Rebels fired on Fort Sumter in Charleston Harbor in 1861. A few minor skirmishes here and there won, of course, but every major battle had been a Union defeat.

And the Europeans were waiting on the sidelines like vultures, staring across the Atlantic, waiting for the opportunity to wade in. It was about economics and cotton for them and a chance to get their feet back on the continent. Lincoln knew that. And he knew that he had to change the playing field. Take it all to a higher level to keep the Europeans at bay.

And the dead and wounded laid out in the cold numbers in the telegrams—the numbers were staggering. And if his experience with such dispatches was to be trusted, they were understated. The truth would not be revealed for weeks, but already the newsmen were saying it was the bloodiest day of the war so far.

It was also not a defeat, though. Lee was retreating. And, truth be told, the North could accept high casualties more than the South could.

Lincoln put down the telegraphs and leaned back in his chair, stretching his long legs out so that the tips of his worn boots appeared on the other side of the desk bottom. He heard a door open to his left and he twisted his head. He got to his feet as he recognized his wife's diminutive form. Just two inches above five feet, Mary had clear blue eyes and light brown hair that was now beginning to show hints of gray. They'd met when she was twenty-one, living with her sister in Springfield. She was beautiful, but it had been her sharp wit that had captivated Lincoln on their first meeting.

She was from high society and he, as he liked to tell friends when recounting the tale of their courtship, was a poor nobody. Their courtship lasted three years. There were aspects to it that Lincoln never related when speaking of the past. The first time she'd come to him after hearing the voices. The time he broke off the engagement in dismay, only to be drawn back to her by a force greater than his fear. In a way, they were the perfect match, as she had an unshakeable belief in his abilities and his gentle demeanor allowed him to tolerate what others politely called her excitability.

Their early years of marriage had been difficult because his circumstances brought her down quite a few notches in the social circles. The war had not made things easier, as Southerners claimed she was a traitor, since her family came from Kentucky; Union papers assailed her attempts to bring the White House up to what she considered an acceptable level for the leader of a great country.

"Mary." Lincoln strode across the room. "Are you all right?" He wrapped her in his large arms and led her over to a couch.

"I hear them," Mary Todd Lincoln whispered. "I hear them."

Lincoln placed a hand on the back her neck, massaging. "The voices?"

"Yes."

Lincoln closed his eyes and counted to ten before speaking, a habit he had begun early in their courtship and maintained ever since. "And what are they telling you?"

Mary turned her clear blue eyes toward her husband. It had been those eyes that he had first noticed so many years ago in Illinois, looking at her across a room full of people. They had been a magnet that had drawn him to her and kept him at her side all these hard years. This past year had not been easy, especially with the death of their son Willie earlier in the year. Mary had always heard voices, but the strange thing was that Lincoln had learned to separate out the different types she heard, because some of them were very accurate about the future. Some he knew came from a part of her brain that she could not be held accountable for. She had told him the first time they spoke that she knew he was bound for greatness. Then she had been told he would be president, at a time when he had never even considered running for any office and was just trying to eke out a living as a lawyer in Springfield. Such a bold, and apparently outrageous, prediction coming true had certainly made him take her much more seriously.

"You should sign the proclamation," Mary said. "That's what they tell me."

Lincoln frowned. He had penned the preliminary proclamation in the spring but kept quiet about it, showing it only to Mary. In July, he had finally read it to Secretary of War Seward and Secretary Wells. Both men had been shocked speechless for over a minute, and then Seward had voiced his protest, while Wells seemed too confused to say anything.

Slavery was a difficult issue that had to be handled delicately. In the early days of the war, large numbers of slaves had fled to Union lines. Technically, according to the law of the time, even though the two sides were at war, those slaves should have been returned under the Fugitive Slave Law on the books in the federal government. Lincoln had managed to dodge that issue by getting the Fugitive Slave Law annulled. Then he'd gotten a law passed allowing the federal government to compensate owners who freed their slaves—this allowed all the slaves in the District of Columbia to be freed in April of this year.

Then he managed to pressure Congress into passing a law forbidding slavery in U.S. territories which flew in the face of the infamous *Dred Scott* decision by the Supreme Court. Despite all this, the core issue of slavery was still being skirted by the Union, thus Lincoln had sat down and written the proclamation.

The curious thing about the proclamation was that it freed slaves only in specifically named states—all parts of the Confederacy. Those border states that the Union was trying to keep in the fold were not affected.

"It's a dangerous thing, Mary," Lincoln said.

"Everything's dangerous. But the time is now. Call this battle a victory"—she raised a hand to stifle his protest—"Lee is retreating, is he not? So many men died. I've seen the papers. And we both know the truth will be far worse than what the reporters scribble in their dispatches. Don't let them die in vain. Sign the proclamation." She put her hand on his arm. "And it will keep the Europeans at bay. It will raise the war to an entirely new level. A moral level at which they cannot get involved on the side of the Southerners. It will identify any who side with the South as siding with slavery."

Lincoln stared at his wife, surprised that he was surprised. She had had so many great ideas over the years, but it still amazed him at times the way her mind worked. He had just been thinking along the same lines but she had cut right to the core of the matter. He walked over to his desk and pulled out the document that had so disconcerted his two secretaries. He set it on top of the desk. He considered it some of his best writing.

"And change the name," Mary added.

"To what?"

"Call it the Emancipation Proclamation."

EARTH TIMELINE—XIV
Zulu Territories, 22 September 1828

A million dead in the Zulu nation. And that was just the estimate. No one knew the real number. A rough estimate could be made of those killed in battle, but the hundreds of thousands who died after the battles of starvation and disease could only be guessed. There were so many dead that one could not travel without feeling the presence of ghosts all about. The *mfecane*, the warfare and forced migrations that was being enforced by the king on his people, was destroying both the land and the people.

Had it been only twelve years since his half-brother Shaka had been crowned king of the Zulus? Dingane wondered. For him it had been an eternity. He sat in the darkness away from the fires that marked the king's *kraal* (encampment), his *iKlwa* across his knees. It was a wide, heavy-bladed thrusting spear, an invention of Shaka's. Most warriors carried it now, instead of the traditional *assegais,* the long, thin throwing javelin that had been the weapon of choice of the Zulu before Shaka. The *iKlwa,* in combination with the heavier cowhide shields Shaka had also developed, allowed mass formations of Zulus to smash their lighter armed enemies into submission. That, along with the ironclad discipline and innovative tactics with which Shaka had molded his army, made them the most potent military force in Africa.

Before Shaka, battle had been mostly a ceremonial event, with both sides posturing. Some blood was drawn, true, but few deaths occurred. Shaka had changed all that. Now battles were fought to the point of annihilation. Dingane knew of entire tribes that now ceased to exist, that had been wiped out to the last man, woman, and child.

While he had little sympathy for those the Zulu had vanquished, he was dismayed to see Shaka turning that same deadly focus against his own people.

Dingane was discontent, as were many. For years, they had tried to get Shaka back on the path of light, away from the dark path of the *mfecane*. But to no avail. The last straw though, was the white men. They'd arrived four years ago and at first had been treated with suspicion by Shaka and all around him. But then the king had been wounded in battle and the Europeans nursed him back to health—and things had never been the same. Shaka had signed over vast amounts of Zulu territory to the whites, something Dingane saw as ultimately only bringing great trouble to the land. Yes, the whites were few in number now, but like the dung beetle, he had a feeling they would multiply. And they had different, powerful weapons that could kill at great ranges, beyond even the range of an *assegais* thrown by the strongest warrior.

Also, the way of the whites was different. Dingane and others saw them as a corrupting force with their religion, which they did not hesitate to press on those who were willing to listen to them. He did not see the path the whites called "Christian" and the path of the Zulu warrior heading in the same direction. And if the Zulu warrior lost his edge in battle, there were many all around their territory who could not wait to wreak revenge on the Zulu.

Shaka was—had been—a great leader, of that Dingane was one of the first to admit. But the last several years, particularly since the death of Shaka's mother, had seen the great man deteriorate. Shaka had had seven thousand people put to death when he'd heard his mother was gravely ill, in the hopes such a sacrifice would bring her back to health. And then, after her death, had ordered a nationwide fast that had lasted three months and almost destroyed the tribe with starvation. It had only been when Dingane and the other war chiefs had begged Shaka for several days straight, that the king had lifted the fast. But then he kept the army on the move, attacking, always attacking, even when there was no need. Even when the next opponent threw open their *kraals* and begged for mercy, still Shaka attacked and killed as if blood were a salve for his grief.

Dingane heard movement in the bush and sprang to his feet, the *iKlwa* at the ready. His nostrils flared as he sniffed the air and his eyes darted about, trying to see in the dark. A slight figure ran by, less than two feet away and Dingane stuck out his leg, tripping the intruder. He had a knee on the person's chest and the tip of the *iKlwa* against the throat in a second.

In the moonlight, a young woman's scared face looked up at him, eyes wide. "Please, great warrior, spare me."

She was holding something tight to her chest, a bundle wrapped in a blanket. Dingane poked at it with the tip of the *iKlwa* and was rewarded with a baby's yelp of pain.

"I know you," Dingane said as he saw her features more clearly in the moonlight. "You belong to Shaka's *seraglio*." He knew he should return her to the *kraal,* but he truly could not blame her for trying to get away. Just two days earlier, Shaka had had twenty-five members of his *seraglio* (cluster of wives) executed because he'd found a locust in his sleeping mat.

"Please," she repeated once more, getting to her knees, the baby held tight against her chest.

"Whose child is that?" Dingane demanded.

She lowered her head. "It is Shaka's daughter."

"You lie." Dingane put the sharp tip of the *iKlwa*

against her throat. "Shaka does not have intercourse, only the *ukuHlobonga*." The latter, external intercourse, was the only sexual contact allowed among unwed couples, and Shaka had always been adamant that he would not father a child, given his own horrible childhood. Dingane also knew that Shaka feared bringing a son into the world, because that would automatically be a threat to his own rule. As long as there was only Shaka, with no clear heir, he felt his position to be safe.

The woman met his gaze, not flinching at the added pressure of the blade at her throat. "I do not lie." She held out the baby. "This is Shakan, daughter of Shaka. And I am Takir, princess of Butelezi and possessor of the Sight."

Dingane pulled the blade back. The Sight was a rare thing, and those that possessed it very dangerous. Some said Shaka himself had it, and Dingane thought it might be true. Certainly, the king had made many wise decisions, particularly in combat, when the way to be taken had been anything but clear.

"This is not about Shaka," Takir continued, "or about me. This child, my daughter, Shakan, will one day, many years from now, do something very important. Something more important than Shaka or even the Zulu people."

Dingane felt the power of her words. He pulled back the *iKlwa* as he remembered what he had been contemplating alone here in the dark before Takir and the child stumbled by. "Apparently the Sight does not help to see in the dark," he muttered.

To his surprise, Takir laughed. "No, it does not. It is not very useful at times."

"Tell me something," Dingane began, but then he halted.

"You want me to tell you of Shaka and what the future

holds," Takir said as she got her feet, holding the bundle tight.

"Your Sight told you this?"

Once more Takir quietly laughed. "No. I just speculated what Shaka's half-brother would be doing sitting alone in the dark with a weapon in his hands. Even one without the Sight knows there is much trouble about."

"Does your Sight see Shaka's future?"

Takir looked down at the *iKlwa*. "Shaka's future is in your hands."

"What do you—" Dingane halted as he realized he was gripping the *iKlwa* so tightly his fingers were screaming with pain.

"You are doing the right thing for the people," Takir said. She turned and then was gone into the darkness.

Dingane waited a few moments, and then turned toward the *kraal*. He hefted the *iKlwa* and headed to meet Shaka for the last time. He paused as he heard the rumble of thunder to the south and west, then continued to his half-brother's tent.

．　．　．

Isandlwana. The rocky outcrop near the border of Zulu territory was so named because its outline resembled a wrist and clenched fist. It was a place of little interest to the Zulu except that it lay along the main route from the center of their nation to neighboring Transvaal.

It was, however, of interest to others.

Three miles below the rocky outcrop was one of the world's largest concentrations of pure diamonds. They were suspended in rock in a curious latticework formation, present nowhere else on the planet except on a large scale at the very center.

While Dingane was going to visit his brother for the last time, a storm was raging over the Isandlwana area. Dark clouds covered the moon and stars, and bolts of lightning streaked across the sky. At the highest point of Isandlwana, a small dark circle appeared. The circle grew wider until it elongated to eight feet high by three in width.

A figure shielded in a pure white suit of some kind of armor appeared, stepping out of the gate. Two more followed it, taking up flanking positions with strange spears at the ready.

The center Valkyrie, as they had been named so long ago by the first Vikings to see the creatures, was not armed with a spear, but with a gold, glowing tube five feet long and six inches in diameter. It placed one end of the tube against the stony ground. On the other end was a small display, and the creature watched the display as it sent a pulse of subatomic particles called muons into the planet. The muons reached the diamond field and confirmed its presence and arrangement—as expected.

Satisfied, the creature made an adjustment on the buttons along the top side of the tube. Then it fired another pulse, a stronger one into the rock, penetrating the planet to the lattice field. The tube went dead, all its energy having been sent out in that pulse.

The thousands of diamonds that made up the lattice field began to glow ever so slightly.

The Valkyries turned and disappeared back into the gate, which snapped out of existence.

In the lattice field not only were the diamonds now charged but ever so slightly the charge was extending from one to another. The process was so slow, it would take decades, but the Shadow was patient. It could wait decades to reap the crop it had just sown here.

EARTH TIMELINE—III
Antarctica, July 2078

Colonel Joshua Lawrence Chamberlain IV knelt next to the fledgling plant, marveling at it, not daring to touch it with his armor-gloved hand. He had not seen green outside of the hydrofarms for over twenty years. He was, of course, in full battle kit. One could not be on the surface without it. Standing orders that had been drilled into Chamberlain since he was seven and taken from his parents to live in the *agoge,* the barracks where he had lived ever since.

The suit he wore was painted flat black, the external material a ceramic polymer that provided protection against both weapons and weather. Beneath the armor, the suit was cutting edge technology, the result of decades of work. Battery-powered strips of ionic polymer metal composites added power, magnifying the wearer's own strength when activated by movement.

The inner layer was airtight, fitting against the skin. The suit was designed to be used in all terrain, even under water. A backpack contained both the computer that operated the various systems and a sophisticated rebreather that could sustain oxygen for over twelve hours when operating on total seal. If operating in a safe environment, a valve in the back of the helmet could be opened to allow outside air in.

The helmet was the most advanced part of the outfit. It had a visor to the outside world, but when the visor was shut to block either outside light or for protection, flat screens on the inner front portrayed whatever direction the wearer ordered. Numerous minicams were on the external armor, from the two on the side of the helmet pointing forward to give a normal front view with depth, to ones pointing straight up, down, and back. They were necessary because the helmet fit onto the body of the suit tightly, allowing no movement. The display not only relayed the view from the cameras but also could have an overlay display with various tactical and technical information.

The suit was moved by the person inside moving. The suit's special qualities were voice activated by the wearer, who gave commands out loud, which were picked up by the computer.

The only time Chamberlain had been on the surface without full battle kit was for two weeks when he had been sent out of the city naked for survival training. Hiding during the day from the fierce rays of a sun unblocked by ozone, freezing at night here at the bottom of the world, despite the ice cap having melted, the temperature still dipped below zero at times.

One out of three sent on survival training never returned. Only one of twenty who entered the *agoge* graduated it with the tiny flaming sword tattoo on each temple, a sign of being one of the First Earth Battalion.

Chamberlain had come back from his two weeks of surface survival training covered in dried blood from a seal carcass he stole from underneath the less than observant nose of a mutated polar bear, one of the few creatures that still walked the surface of the planet: its white fur reflected the rays of the sun, but its eyes were blinded by the solar radiation and thus it relied on the sense of smell to hunt.

Chamberlain stood, the articulated micromotors of the full-body suit fighting the effort. He had the suit set to train, which meant instead of amplifying his movements, the suit's inner gears worked against him, forcing his muscles to fight their action and develop. He put the suit in combat mode only during full-force training maneuvers and then only because he knew he had to keep his nerves attuned to the suit's capabilities for the day he, and his men, would actually be in combat.

A day that many said would never come.

He leaned, looking down through the clear blast-glass face shield built into the helmet that covered his head. It was indeed a plant. Could the seed have been brought by a bird? No one had seen a bird in over ten years, but it was possible, wasn't it? Could life be coming back to a planet the scientists, and every observable piece of evidence, insisted was dying?

But here was life where there should be none.

A glow on the horizon warned him that the sun was coming. Reflexively he dropped the outer face shield over the blast-glass, sealing him from the outside world. Projected on the reflective layer on the inside of the shield, his external cameras relayed the various views of his external world.

"Thermal," Chamberlain whispered and the display changed to a spectrum of colors. The plant was cold and Chamberlain frowned. He reached down with armor-plated fingers and dug, pulling out the plastic facsimile of a plant. He felt no disappointment as he had lived almost his entire life on a dying planet and hope was a concept neither taught nor encouraged.

How long had it lain here? Fallen from some resupply to a research station years ago, perhaps. Decoration for an underground base most likely.

There was no life coming back on the surface of the planet.

"Day mode," Chamberlain ordered. The thermal imaging stopped and the screen displayed the outside view with the dangerous rays of the sun filtered out. The terrain around Chamberlain was desolate, black sand with numerous rocks tumbled about as if a giant had let loose a barrage onto the surface. Over two miles of ice had covered this land as recently as fifty years ago. The melting of both ice caps had been swift and dramatic after the Shadow sphere had stripped the planet of its ozone layer. The sea level rose over three hundred feet in less than a year, inundating coastal areas around the world.

Between that and the radiation, over two billion people died in the first ten years after the final Shadow assault. The survivors struggled to live as crops failed and livestock died. The human race burrowed into the planet to escape the unshielded rays of the sun. Hydrofarms— massive greenhouses with the most dangerous rays of the sun filtered out—were built. Deep wells to tap the fresh water the Shadow hadn't siphoned off were dug. Still the human race dwindled, another billion dying in the second decade after the last assault from the Shadow as society spasmed with violence and despair to adjust to a raped planet.

In the face of such devastation and the battle for survival, the barriers between countries, between religions, between races, were eventually dropped. The elite of what was left of each countries' military forces was sent to Antarctica to form the First Earth Battalion. Along with the remainder of the top scientists not involved in survival technology.

Their goal was simple. To develop weapons to fight the Shadow.

It seemed a strange task, given that they had already lost the war with the Shadow and their planet was dying. Plus, there were no more known gates, the Shadow apparently shut them down here, isolating this timeline.

Chamberlain turned to the south and ran across the terrain, fighting the suit that tried to slow him, his muscles straining with the effort. He crested a ridge and came to a halt on top. A valley covered with jumbled rocks lay ahead with no sign of life. Chamberlain scanned it on protected vision, then on low-level thermal, then on infrared. Nothing. Excellent.

Chamberlain activated the secure, frequency-jumping radio in his suit. "Alpha, Six, Five. Return to base. Over."

The valley exploded with over two hundred black, human-shaped forms, bursting upward from their hide positions in the sand. Weapons at the ready, the soldiers of the First Earth Battalion made huge hundred-meter bounds using their suits on combat power as they headed back to their home base. They moved tactically, squads leap-frogging and providing cover for each other. Heavy weapons set up fire spots, ranging their weapons out until the forward scouts passed their limits, then moving forward. Flankers raced along the high ground on either side, protecting the main axis of advance.

Chamberlain watched his men and women with pride. Their world was dying, but they were prepared for one last battle with the Shadow. And according to the Oracles, they would be given the opportunity for it. How, when, and where, the Oracles couldn't say, but one thing they all agreed on: There was to be one final assault.

One thing the Oracles didn't say, and no one talked about, was whether the assault would be in the form of the Shadow coming back to this timeline or whether they would take the battle to the Shadow's timeline or some other timeline.

Sometimes, in the middle of the night usually, Chamberlain would lay awake on his bunk and wonder if the prophecy was real or had just been a way to unite people and give some hope to their doomed existence. Always he ended up back at the same conclusion—it didn't matter. Only time would tell if the prophecy was true.

5

EARTH TIMELINE—THE PRESENT
The Devil's Sea Gate

The sphere map rested on the column in the center of the room, the surface dull and void of power. There were faint markings etched in the gold, the outlines of the strands that marked portals between worlds and times. Dane and Earhart had entered the large black sphere that the Shadow used to travel through portals and descended to the map room.

"Can you activate it?" Amelia Earhart asked Dane as he approached the sphere.

In response, Dane placed his hands on the sphere. The material was cold to the touch at first. He closed his eyes and focused his mind. The events of the past several months had left no doubt that he was different from other humans and that the core of that difference rested in his brain.

Sin Fen, Foreman's agent who had worked with him during the mission into Cambodia, had explained as much as she knew to him. She herself was descended from a long line of priestesses who traced their lineage back to Atlantis. A civilization had thrived there ten thousand years ago, one that was far advanced in technology because the humans there were different from those in the rest of the world.

Sin Fen had told Dane he too was descended from the Atlanteans and his brain bore the same differences. The normal human brain is bicameral, consisting of two distinct hemispheres that are largely redundant. For most people, the speech center is present in both hemispheres but active only in the left side and dormant in the right. Dane's right side speech center was active but not tied to normal speech. It was the place where he received his visions and heard voices. Some of those came from the Ones Before, the mysterious group that was trying to aid them in the war against the Shadow. Some came from sources he couldn't identify. He also had had a telepathic link to Sin Fen who'd told him she suspected the original Atlanteans had an even more pure connection between the hemispheres of the brain, allowing them to be fully telepathic and also to develop a written and verbal language. The Atlanteans could use their telepathy to get concepts across without the limitation of the spoken or written word, but then they could use the latter to work on the details of what they were doing, the specifics.

As Dane stared at the sphere map, he considered what Sin Fen had learned about the Atlantis civilization and its development thanks to an ancient computer they discovered on an Atlantean boat trapped in one of the graveyards of vessels caught by the gates. Unlike our civilization, the Atlanteans had focused inward, rather than outward. They had harnessed the basic powers of the brain and its connection to the outside world.

That is until they came into contact with the Shadow, which first appeared out of the Bermuda Triangle Gate. To battle the Shadow, they developed a kind of shield that tapped into both the power of the mind and the planet itself. Unfortunately, the best the shield could do was stop the Shadow's encroachments, not attack and defeat it. In the war, the continent of Atlantis was destroyed, and the few survivors were scattered around the world.

Although the legends of the gates—the Bermuda Triangle, the Devil's Sea, and others—had been with humankind for millennia, Dane didn't know why the Shadow had decided recently to step up its assault against our Earth timeline. He had helped the planet avert disaster several times, but he knew they were about out of time and chances. The most recent assault, which had stripped the ozone layer and destroyed Chernobyl, had come very close to fatally crippling the planet.

Dane opened his eyes and glanced at Earhart. She was watching him, waiting. He reached out toward her with his mind and saw the surprise in her eyes as his mental probe touched her.

"What are you doing?"

"Give me your strength," Dane said.

"What strength?"

Dane looked back down at the sphere. "The feeling you had when you were flying, free of the Earth, at the controls of your plane. The power."

It had been so long for Earhart since she'd flown, having been captured by the Shadow during her attempt to fly around the world and then freed by the Ones Before to survive in the Space Between. She had no idea how long she'd existed in the Space Between as there had been no way to tell time there. She searched her memory, bringing back images of being in her Electra, taking off, climbing into the sky at full throttle.

Dane felt the mental connection with Earhart grow more vivid, and a slight surge of power came from her to him. The sphere under his hands became to grow warm. The strands began to become distinct from each other. His fingers slipped between them, delving into the map, as if he had pressed his hands into a ball of warm, writhing snakes.

Visions flashed into Dane's mind as he touched different strands. An image of a desolate Washington, DC, the buildings smashed and deserted. The Eiffel Tower with two flags flying from it—a Nazi swastika and the rising sun of Japan, but with several modern skyscrapers in the background. The ill feeling from that vision caused him to let go of that particular strand immediately. He saw a planet, he had to assume it was Earth, that was endless ocean, with no sign of land.

Dane knew he was seeing parallel Earths, where history had taken different forms. Ahana had speculated that there might be an infinite number of such timelines, but Dane didn't agree with her. After all, there were a finite number of strands in the sphere. Perhaps there were an infinite number of parallel worlds but only a certain number were connected by portals.

There were gates on either end of each portal line. Most gates went from a world and time to the Space Between which seemed to be a transit area. Some went from one time and world directly to another, but there were not many of these.

Dane frowned, never having really thought about what exactly the portals were—did all the parallel timelines exist in the same space, with only some slight variable that current physics didn't yet understand separating them?

He tried to focus on the Ones Before, on the messages they had sent him. His fingers flitted over strands as he searched. Energy was still coming in from Earhart, standing close by his side. His left hand brushed a strand and he heard a faint clicking noise, something that was familiar in some way, but he couldn't place it. He wrapped his fingers around the strand.

The clicking noise grew louder. One end of the strand was a portal, here on this planet and now in this time, Dane realized. He tried to pinpoint the location. There was something very strange about the portal for the Ones Before, though. Its space on one end was somehow different from all the other portals in some manner that Dane could not understand. The clicking increased, then abruptly surged, sending a spike of pain through Dane's brain and causing him to release the strand. He staggered back, the connections with both the map and Earhart broken.

"What's wrong?" Earhart asked as she placed a hand on his shoulder to steady him.

"It's been there right in front of us the whole time," Dane said.

"What has?"

"The way the Ones Before send messages. The relay on our planet." He headed for the exit. He said nothing to her about the strangeness of the other end of the portal, the one whose space felt different, because he wanted to have time to think about it. "Let's get back to the FLIP."

. . .

Thirty minutes later they were on board the research vessel. Dane had Foreman call Dr. Martsen, Rachel's handler, from her cabin. She came into the control room with her laptop computer, as Dane had requested.

"What's going on?" Martsen asked.

Dane indicated the computer. "Can you play the clicking, the echo noise that Rachel makes?"

Martsen accessed her database, then pushed enter. Dane had to listen for only a few seconds to realize this was the same noise he'd heard when he grabbed the last strand.

"They're using the dolphins to send the visions and the voices."

"Who?" Foreman.

"The Ones Before," Dane said as he pointed to the laptop. "I touched the portal they channel through and that's what I heard."

Martsen frowned. "That noise is Rachel's sonar. She uses that ability to echo-locate, to navigate, and to find prey, not to communicate. The language I've been working on is her squeals and whistles, which are different. She makes the clicks with her blow hole and emits them through her forehead. She then gets the bounce-back in her jaw bone. Her brain analyzes the information and forms a picture of her surroundings, much like a submarine uses sonar to get an idea of what's around it in the water. We've even run studies where dolphins have used the emitter to send high-frequency bursts to stun prey."

Dane turned to Foreman. "When you sent my team into

Cambodia so many years ago to recover that black box, you were running an experiment using high-frequency transmissions through the gates, weren't you?"

Foreman nodded. "I had a U-2 spy plane fly into the Angkor Kol Ker Gate at the same time the submarine *Scorpion* went into the Bermuda Triangle Gate on the other side of the world. Then I had them transmit on HF. They were able to communicate with each other, even though there was no way the signal could travel around the planet, so I had to assume the signal was being relayed through the gates."

Ahana had been listening from her workstation. "High-frequency bursts would be an efficient way to send a piggy-backed message through a portal. I can scan the gates to see if any of them are emitting high frequency."

"Do it," Foreman ordered.

"You need to scan high up," Martsen said. "Rachel can emit and hear up to one hundred and fifty kilohertz, beyond even what a bat can pick up."

Earhart was by the hatchway, looking out at the dark wall of the Devil's Sea Gate, which lay two miles away. She caught a glimpse of Rachel about fifty yards off the bow, swimming smoothly through the water. "How smart is Rachel?"

Martsen ran a hand across her chin. "That's a hard question to answer because Rachel's environment is so different from ours. First, she lives in water, while we live on land. Second, she doesn't have hands so she really can't manipulate her environment. Dolphins live in harmony with their world, unlike humans."

Something about what Martsen had just said struck Dane as significant but before he could analyze it, Martsen continued.

"The strange thing I've always wondered about dolphins is that they went in the opposite direction evolutionwise than we did. We came out of the water and stayed on land. Dolphins are mammals also, but sometime during their evolution they went back into the water."

Martsen had mentioned that before, Dane remembered. "Maybe, as you said, they did it to get away from us."

"It's possible," Martsen said.

"Who is 'we'?" Dane asked Martsen.

"Excuse me?"

"You said 'we' earlier," Dane said. "I assume you don't work alone."

"I work at the Space and Naval Warfare Systems Center outside San Diego," Martsen said.

Dane sat down in one of the hard plastic chairs. "Why is it called that?"

Martsen shrugged. "It's had a lot of names over the years. The program with dolphins actually started in 1960 and was called the Marine Mammal Program. They started with one Pacific white-sided dolphin. At first, the primary goal was to test the animal under the auspices of hydrodynamic studies. Scientists at the time had heard accounts of incredible efficiency exhibited by dolphins; and since the navy had the task of developing better and faster torpedoes, it made sense to check out whatever special characteristics dolphins had that they might apply to their underwater missiles."

Dane could sense that Foreman considered this a waste of time, but Earhart and Ahana were focused on what Martsen was saying. He knew there was a thread here that needed to be pulled and followed—and at the end, he had a strong suspicion, there would be the Ones Before.

"Unfortunately," Martsen continued, "the first dolphin,

named Notty, exhibited no unusual physiological or hydro-dynamic capabilities. One of the scientists believed that was because of the restrictions of the long testing tank in which she was being held and tested in. The decision was made to move the testing to the ocean, the dolphin's nat-ural habitat. The facility moved to Point Mugu, Califor-nia, where the Pacific Missile Range and Naval Missile Center was located."

"That's odd," Dane said. "Why move it to a missile test facility?"

"It was on the water, and space was available," Mart-sen said. "And a group of scientists in the Life Sciences Department of the Naval Missile Center was also in the process of studying underwater life, including porpoises."

Dane wanted to ask why, but he decided to hold back.

"Starting in 1963, the two groups of scientists began investigating and testing dolphins. In the beginning, their research was two pronged—to study how dolphin's in-herent systems and capabilities, such as sonar and deep diving, worked, and to see if dolphins could be used for various underwater tasks, especially ones that were dan-gerous for humans, such as detecting mines and planting explosives.

"Their first major success came in 1965 when a bot-tle-nosed dolphin named Tuffy operated untethered near Sea Lab II, carrying tools and messages between the surface and the inhabitants of the lab underwater. That year the lab moved from Mugu to San Diego and study intensified.

"That was when they began to try to figure out how the dolphin brain functioned, with the startling realization that as a mammal, its brain was not that much different from a human's."

That caught everyone's attention.

"Neurophysiological studies, using behavioral and noninvasive techniques were the first steps in this process. Brain-wave activity was charted, along with hearing tests and investigation into how dolphins made noise"—she tapped the computer—"That was when we first began to realize how they used sonar. A project originally called Quick Find, and later renamed under top-secret classification the Mark 5 Marine Mammal System, used dolphins to locate and attach hardware to inert ordnance.

"They also continued research on dolphin hydrodynamics with the same goal: to determine if the dolphin possesses drag-reducing characteristics that can be applied to underwater hardware. The capabilities for undertaking this work are now greatly improved and include instrumentation for measurements that previously were impossible. Among the possible drag-reducing mechanisms being studied are skin compliance, biopolymer secretions, and boundary layer heating, which may work synergistically and in combination with other drag-reducing processes.

"Other research used sophisticated psychophysical experiments to determine how dolphins process target echoes to make difficult detections and fine discriminations. This information was modeled to aid human sonar operators in identifying targets from clutter. When I came on board, my focus was on trying to understand their language, which most scientists in the field said they didn't have. I've proven they do communicate."

"And what classified work is being done there?" Dane asked.

Martsen paused. "I have a Q clearance, but—"

"No 'buts,'" Foreman stepped forward. He looked at Dane. "What are you looking for?"

"If the Ones Before are using dolphin high-frequency sonar to send the visions," Dane said, "then we need to know what else dolphins can be used for." He looked at Martsen. "What are the space guys using dolphins for? You said the facility was called the *Space* and Naval Warfare Systems Center. I don't see the connection."

Martsen pressed the tip of her fingers together. "Dolphins are capable of diving to depths of over six hundred meters for over fifteen minutes. Think of the pressure they can withstand and how long they can go without breathing."

"And they can do tasks," Dane added.

"Right," Martsen affirmed.

"And they can communicate," Dane continued.

Martsen simply nodded.

"What are you getting at?" Foreman demanded.

"They're evaluating dolphins for space travel," Dane made it a statement, not a question.

"They're beyond that," Martsen said, drawing everyone's eyes to her. "Last year a dolphin went up on one of the shuttles in the cargo bay, inside a specially built water tank. It was a highly classified experiment."

"So they can function in space?" Dane asked.

"It—the dolphin's name is Proteus. And he's still up there. In the International Space Station."

"Doing what?" Dane asked.

"Being evaluated."

"For?"

"Further missions."

Dane was getting irritated with Martsen's brevity. "What's planned?"

"I'm not privy to that," Martsen said.

Dane stood. "We're going to California."

"Why?" Foreman demanded.

"To find out what the future holds," Dane said.

6

Lincoln stared at the map spread over the desk in the Oval
Office with mounting frustration while Secretary of War
Stanton stood in front of the desk, shifting his feet ner-
vously and with some degree of anger. The secretary of
war did not like answering to a civilian, but even worse,
he did not like having to accept that his generals had been
failing quite miserably for quite a while now.

The North and South had been at war for over two
years, with no end to the horrible conflict in sight. Initially, the South had won several victories, including the
two battles at Bull Run. Lincoln has claimed the bloody
battle at Antietam as a victory, when in reality it had been
a stalemate. However, Lincoln had been forced to seize on
even a whiff of good news to issue the Emancipation

Proclamation, which served the purpose of elevating the conflict to a higher moral level and kept the European powers, which had been leaning toward helping the South, on the sidelines, hamstrung by the moral issue of helping the side in favor of slavery.

Despite this ethical and political victory, the Union defeat at Fredericksburg followed shortly afterward. A battle report on top of the map revealed the most recent disaster, at Chancelorsville, just west of Fredericksburg where newly appointed General Hooker had tried to take the fight to Lee.

"Fighting Joe," Lincoln said.

"Excuse me?" Secretary of War Stanton asked.

" 'Fighting Joe' Hooker. That's what you called him." Lincoln slammed a fist on the desktop. "Where's the fight? Where's the attack? This"—he picked up the telegram—"says he's retreating."

"He's reconstituting—" Stanton began, but Lincoln cut him off.

"I don't care what word you use, General Lee of Virginia holds the field, does he not?" Lincoln read further and raised an eyebrow. "Stonewall Jackson's dead?"

Stanton nodded. "Yes, sir. By his own men. An accident."

"If only Lee would do us the same favor and get himself killed," Lincoln mused. He leaned back in his high-backed chair. He'd offered Lee command of all Federal forces at the beginning of the war. Lee had politefully declined, feeling his call of duty was stronger to Virginia than the United States. It made Lincoln question the effectiveness of the Military Academy at West Point given that so many of its graduates had chosen to side with the Rebels. So much for duty, honor, and country.

Secretly, Lincoln also often wondered if the war was dragging on because the vast majority of senior officers on both sides were graduates of the academy. Not only did they know each other but they had been taught the same things. Sometimes Lincoln thought of the war as a man fighting his own image in a mirror.

He was the sixteenth president of the United States and many thought he would be the last. He was also an example of the uniqueness of America. There was no country in Europe where a man born in a log cabin could rise to such a high position. Sometimes Lincoln himself was amazed at the path he had taken to arrive in the White House.

Lincoln's childhood had been hard as he'd spent most of his time working. He had less than a year of formal education. He'd seen his father lose his farm in Kentucky due to confusion over land titles, and the family had been forced to move to Indiana with only what they could carry with them. They'd spent the winter of 1816 in a crude, three-sided shelter with a fire at the open end, giving meager warmth as they waited for spring when they could build another cabin. Two years later his mother died. The casualty lists from the battlefields appalled Lincoln but not as much as it did many from the East. He'd seen much death and suffering on the frontier, losing several siblings in childhood to various diseases that swept the frontier.

As a young man he'd moved to Illinois and helped his father build another log cabin. Shortly after that, he hired on a flatboat on the Mississippi taking a load of cargo to New Orleans. That was where he saw his first slave auction, something that affected him deeply. The following year, he ran for a seat in the Illinois House of Representatives. It did not seem a fortuitous decision at the time because a month after the announcement the store he was clerking at went out of business and Lincoln lost the election.

Out of work, and just defeated, Lincoln eagerly signed up when the Illinois governor called for volunteers to put down a rebellion of Native Americans—the Fox—led by Chief Black Hawk. Lincoln enlisted as a private but was so well liked that he was elected captain of his company, a pretty common practice that continued to the present day in the current conflict at lower unit levels. Men preferred to serve under someone they respected and liked rather than some stranger thrust over their heads.

Although Lincoln saw no action, he had always been proud of his time in uniform. From private to captain it was still a big jump to the White House. Lincoln became a postmaster next, a job that gave him a lot of time to read. It also allowed him to meet most of the people of his county and when he next ran for the Illinois legislature, he won. While serving he also began to study law on his own and eventually started his own practice.

In 1840 he met and married Mary Todd, who foretold his future with uncanny accuracy. The previous night she had told him more of what she heard, and he knew she was right.

It was raining outside and the atmosphere inside the Oval Office was dark and gloomy, befitting the report. Lincoln closed his eyes. "It's coming, Stanton. Can't you feel it?"

"What's coming, sir?"

"The great battle." Lincoln opened his eyes. "What does Fighting Joe Hooker plan on doing next?"

Stanton waved a hand, indicating the report. "He doesn't say. He's on the north side of the Rappahannock."

"The more important question, I must reluctantly add," Lincoln said, "is what does Lee plan?"

"Hooker has him fixed—" Stanton cut short what he was going to say at Lincoln's snort of derision.

"Hooker has nothing fixed. Lee is a ghost. Who knows where he'll pop up next?" Lincoln leaned forward and looked at the map. Washington and Richmond were not far apart. At least in miles. But in blood spilt over the last two years they might as well be a continent away. There were many in Washington who believed that Lee would one day show up outside the city with his army behind him. This despite the fact that there were thirty thousand troops with heavy artillery dug in deep, guarding the approaches into Washington, making it the most heavily fortified city in the world.

Lincoln's eyes went vacant, as if he were peering off in the distance at something only he could see. Stanton had seen the president do this before and knew a decision was coming.

"He's coming North," Lincoln concluded, agreeing with what Mary had told him the previous evening. The logic of Lee's situation agreed with the voices she had heard.

"Sir?"

"Lee. He'll be coming North again."

Stanton shook his head. "Mister President, that would leave Richmond exposed."

"Richmond isn't the key," Lincoln said. "The Army of Northern Virginia is. And Lee has no fear of Hooker attacking. Why should he?"—he glared at Stanton—"Try to find me a general who understands that Lee and his army is the key to winning this war, not Richmond."

"Yes, sir."

As soon as Stanton was gone, Mary came in from the room on the left. She didn't say a word, walking over to her husband and taking a position behind him. Lincoln leaned forward, placing his head on the desktop, too weary even to keep his body upright. A tic at his left temple jumped uncontrollably. He pressed his hands to either side of his skull, as if by doing so he could block something from entering his head. Mary put her hands on top of his.

He saw the vision that invaded his mind from hers. Wave upon wave of men in gray charging forward into withering fire. Being mowed down with cannon and musket fire by the thousands.

It appeared to be the start—or finish—of a Union victory, but Lincoln could feel from Mary that it was much more than that. For in the midst of the Confederates' line was a case, and inside it were crystal skulls that began to glow blue and grew stronger as the carnage grew more deadly and the gray line forged forward into the hail of deadly fire.

Lincoln moaned in agony. "If only this burden could be taken from us," he whispered. But he knew from Mary's continued touch it was not to be. He felt another presence. He lifted his head and turning his chair looked at the windows. Across the garden and lawn there was a solitary, tall figure standing near the street, staring back at him. All Lincoln could make out was shiny black skin underneath a black, broad-brimmed hat and deep penetrating eyes. He realized with a start that the figure was an old woman.

Lincoln blinked, and when he opened his eyes once more, the woman was gone.

"Did you see her?" Lincoln asked his wife.

Mary nodded. "Yes. It was a vision. She wasn't really there. She is another like me. One who can see. And she will be part of it when the time comes. In her time and her world."

Lincoln looked up at his wife. "I don't understand this, Mary. Different worlds. Different times. This dark force you speak of, the Shadow, and its threat. The visions and voices. I've trusted you, but . . ." his voice trailed off.

"I know it's hard for you," Mary said. "But this war was inevitable. You knew that when you were running for office. The battles are inevitable. You saw the numbers from Antietam. We used that battle for the Emancipation Proclamation. There will be more battles that we must use. Especially one. A great battle that is coming soon. I sent the vision to you just now. It's a true one. Those men will die. But you can give it a greater reason also."

It still made no sense to Lincoln. It never did, no matter how much they talked about it. But he knew what she said was true as strongly as he knew his love for her was true. He would do what he could to make things happen in the way they must be. Whether the other players involved would do their part was something he could not control.

EARTH TIMELINE—VIII
Virginia, Spring 1863

General Lee was ill. His stomach rumbled and beads of sweat dotted his high forehead just below the magnificent mane of white hair. His hand shook slightly as he ran it over the map, the gesture carefully watched by his three corps commanders.

To his right was Longstreet, his war horse. "Old Pete," Lee sometimes called him when they were alone. Solid, dependable, and steady in action. But unimaginative. And sometimes slow to the assault, preferring to dig in and hold the defensive if given the opportunity. But he had held the stone wall at the base of Marye's Heights at Fredericksburg and taken the best the Union had to throw at him. He'd been a rock there, and without him the day and battle would have been lost.

And then next to Longstreet was the second corps commander, General A. P. Hill. A pragmatist who had been feuding with Stonewall Jackson for over a year. Two more opposite, yet capable men, one could not find. And now Jackson was dead. Along with approximately thirteen thousand of Lee's men at Chancelorsville. While the North had suffered almost half again as many casualties, the Union could more easily afford losses. Another battle that led nowhere. A. P. Hill was steady but impetuous. Hill had begun the Seven Days' offensive by attacking Union forces because he had grown bored sitting in his defensive positions. He had saved the day at Antietam with his forced march from Harpers Ferry and fortuitous arrival on the battlefield at the critical juncture.

In Jackson's place as the third corps commander was General Ewell. With his wooden leg replacing the one of flesh that he'd lost at the Battle of Second Bull Run. His men called him Old Bald Head and would follow him anywhere. An excellent division commander, but now he had a corps, and Lee knew some men had their levels where they excelled and when moved from their comfort zone, they floundered. Ewell worried Lee, who missed

Stonewall Jackson more than he would ever let on, particularly to the man who had replaced him.

Jackson had been the one of his three corps commanders willing to take calculated chances, and Lee knew how important that was in the ebb and flow of battle. Following orders was fine, but once the first shots were fired, orders had a tendency to be outdated. Hill would act and take chances, but he did so blindly with little calculation, which was as dangerous sometimes as doing nothing.

Lee stopped his hand from shaking by placing a blunt finger on their current position on the south side of the Rappahannock in Virginia. Without saying a word he slid the finger to the west and then north, up the Shenandoah Valley, through Harpers Ferry, into Pennsylvania and then eastward toward Philadelphia and southward to Baltimore and then Washington.

"Gentlemen, I propose we bring the war to the Union."

Lee saw Ewell and Hill glance at Longstreet, a subtle acknowledgment that the senior corps commander should be the first to comment on the proposal.

"And Richmond?" Longstreet asked. They all knew that Jefferson Davis and the pack of politicians who ran the Southern government would complain if Lee moved the army too far away from the capital and left the Army of the Potomac sitting in Virginia.

"Hooker is beaten for now," Lee said. He'd known Hooker at the Military Academy and he did not fear decisive action from the man. "It would take something very great to get him to move. Leaving a proper feinting force in place along the river, I believe we could be in Pennsylvania before he even knows we're gone. And then he would not advance on Richmond, but rather turn to the North after us. He has no daring, and the newspapers of the North and their politicians would not allow him that daring even if he had it."

Longstreet nodded while stroking his gray beard. "True. But Philadelphia is fortified. As are Baltimore and Washington."

"Philadelphia might or might not be our objective," Lee said with a shrug. "My main goal is to draw the Union Army out into the open. Destroy it. And then our options are open. Perhaps the Union will sue for peace." Unsaid was the acknowledgment that European support was no longer a possibility. Not since Lincoln had issued that blasphemous proclamation. For Lee, the war was not at all about the issue of slavery. It was about state's rights. But not everyone saw it that way.

"The Union might want to sue for peace," Longstreet said, "but not Lincoln. That's a hard man."

Lee had met Lincoln and he would never admit out loud that he admired the Union president. The man had an air about him that Lee, who had the same air, understood. Lincoln was a leader. A man who would do whatever it took to achieve his goals. Fortunately for Lee, Lincoln had yet to find a general in the same mold.

"They have a congress in the North," Lee said. "Lincoln may be president but he is not all powerful. They've had draft riots in New York City. There are many in the North who grow weary of the war and the casualty rolls."

Lee felt a spasm of discomfort and pain ripple from his stomach to his lower intestines. He had been ill now for several days and it was not getting any better. The soldier's curse. "Gentlemen, we don't have much time. Prepare your corps for movement."

The abrupt order startled all three commanders. "Sir"—Longstreet protested—"this is a bold and—"

He was cut off as Lee headed for the door. "Gentlemen, please do as I requested." And then Lee was gone.

Within six hours, the Army of Virginia began to move North.

EARTH TIMELINE—XIV
Southern Africa, December 1878

"I am Shakan, daughter of Shaka Zulu."

King Cetewayo, ruler of the Zulu people and their allies, stared at the tall old woman who stood in front of his throne, so proudly proclaiming to be direct kin to the founder of their nation. It had been fifty years since Shaka was assassinated by his half-brother Dingane with no apparent successor.

Cetewayo was the latest king in a line of ruthless men who had seized the throne of the most powerful nation in Africa. He pondered whether to have this upstart who had managed to find an audience with him immediately executed or tortured. She wore a black robe that went from her neck to the dirt floor. Her dark curly hair was sprinkled with gray and was cut close, with just barely a quarter inch left. Her skin gleamed in the torchlight with high cheekbones and dark eyes that bore into the king. She was a woman to be reckoned with, of that he had no doubt. Few looked him in the eye so steadily.

They were in his lodge, set in the center of his *kraal*. He had over a thousand warriors close at hand. His principal war chiefs sat on lesser benches to either side of his throne. They had been discussing the latest problems with the British when the old lady who called herself Shaka's daughter had made her appearance, making her way to the middle of the lodge before anyone even knew she was there.

"Great King of the Zulu," Shakan continued, "I know you think me foolish to be in front of you claiming the bloodline of Shaka, but I do not come here to claim a throne or power. I come to warn you of the British."

Cetewayo's laughter was echoed by those of his council of warriors. "I know of the British. I do not need an old hag to come here and tell me anything. And a woman can never claim the throne or gain power."

The British in neighboring Natal were indeed a problem, of that there was no doubt. The previous year, two wives of one his senior warlords, Sirayo, ran away with their lovers to Natal and were pursued by Sirayo's sons demanding justice, because adultery was a capital crime in Cetewayo's kingdom. The wives were captured, returned, and executed as decreed by Zulu law. However, this precipitous pursuit had violated the boundary of British claimed land. The British governor had demanded that the culprits, along with five hundred cattle, be handed over as a fine; instead Cetewayo apologized and offered the British five hundred pounds as restitution, a price he felt most fair but had not really appeased the British.

Following that incident, events along the border escalated. What Cetewayo found particularly galling were the missionaries who entered his territory without permission, seeking converts. The white man's religion he saw as being very dangerous because it subverted the iron-clad discipline of the army, which was the backbone of the Zulu nation. There were missionary stations all around the border, and even over the border, of his lands. He had ordered his warriors to refrain from attacking these representatives of the white man's god because he suspected they might be a deliberate ploy by the British to draw him into war. Still, there was only so much he would tolerate, and the British were pushing him harder and harder. Then there were the Boers, who fought with the British. The blood feud between Zulu and Boer went back at least a generation.

Cetewayo began to raise his hand, to indicate for his guards to take the woman away and slit her throat, when Shakan took a step forward and knelt, hands upraised in supplication. "I have the Sight as my father had the Sight."

All the men present went silent, eyes shifting from Shakan to Cetewayo. The Sight was a powerful thing and it had been years since any of the Zulu had been able to show they had it. Some believed it was not real and that Shaka had simply been a master warrior who had a string of luck in battle until he was assassinated by Dingane. Then there were the whispers that Shaka had had the Sight, but lost it in the insanity of his later years. Still, there was no record of Shaka ever having a child by any of his wives.

"Who was your mother?" Cetewayo demanded.

"Takir."

Cetewayo's senior adviser leaned forward and whispered in his ear, informing that Takir had indeed been a wife of Shaka, but she had disappeared just before the Zulu king's assassination.

"What does your Sight show you?" Cetewayo asked, waving for his guards to stand back for the moment.

She pulled open the neck of her robe, revealing a glittering crystal on a leather thong tied around her neck. "I have been to a strange place where I received this," she said, indicating the crystal. "And I have seen in my vi-

sions strange things. I have seen three columns of men
dressed in red along with Boer and native levies invading
during the next cycle of the moon. One column along the
coast to the Nyezane River. One to the south. And one in
the center headed straight for this place. The other two
columns will also turn and head here with the plan to
bring three spear thrusts directly at you."

The dispute with the British was serious, but not at that
level yet, Cetewayo knew. Or so his spies told him. But
before he could say anything, she continued.

"The center column is the key. It will encamp at Isandlwana Mountain." Shakan raised her eyes to Cetewayo's
and her voice took on a deeper tone. "There you will meet
the British in battle. A great victory will be yours."

Cetewayo smiled. Predicting a victory in battle was always a smart move. But still—

"However," Shakan continued, "while you will win
that battle, you will eventually lose the war with the
British."

Several of his senior warriors leapt to their feet, brandishing their *iKlwas*. Predicting defeat in war was not a
smart move for a seer, but Cetewayo waved the warrior's
back to their places, intrigued by both her bravery and her
prediction. "Why do you tell me this?"

"Because great glory will unfold," Shakan said, "and in
our defeat we will sow the seeds of a greater victory." She
stood. "So I have seen."

* * *

At the very top of Isandlwana the black hole opened once
and three Valkyries appeared. The two guards took up
their flanking position while the center one placed the

green tube on the ground, watching the display on the other end.

All had developed as planned. Deep underneath Isandlwana, over 98 percent of the diamond lattice-field was now connected with a low level of power.

It was just about ready to be harvested.

EARTH TIMELINE—III
Antarctica, July 2078

Colonel Joshua Lawrence Chamberlain IV was the latest in a long line of warriors. Over three hundred years earlier his ancestors had fought in the American Revolution, then the War of 1812, then the little known Aroostoock War of 1839 with Canada and most famously, his great-great-great grandfather, Colonel Joshua Lawrence Chamberlain I had made his mark in the American Civil War.

Chamberlain IV had been a second lieutenant, fresh out of West Point, when the Shadow made its last assault, stripping his timeline of its ozone, most of the fresh water, and causing great devastation around the Pacific Rim as it drew power from the core of the planet, destabilizing the Ring of Fire. In desperation, military forces from various countries made forays into the black gates through which the Shadow attacked, but no one ever returned from any of those attacks. Still they continued to assault as the situation grew more dire. Chamberlain was with the Eighty-second Airborne Division onboard an aircraft carrier that was preparing to go into the Bermuda Triangle Gate when all the gates abruptly closed, leaving behind a dying planet.

Chamberlain then participated in the evacuation of

Washington, DC, as it flooded when the ice caps melted. Then he fought in the brutal food riots of 2062 and 2063 and helped restore law and order to what remained of the United States. When the call came for volunteers for the First Earth Battalion he didn't hesitate, even though the unit's mission was classified and no one really knew what it was.

He'd been here fourteen years, rising through the ranks until he took command the previous year. They trained constantly, always ready, for exactly what, though, no one was quite sure. There had been encounters during the Shadow War with Valkyries and some of the suits had been captured. They were the basis for the combat suits Chamberlain and his soldiers now wore. Their weapons were designed to penetrate the Valkyrie armor, something scientists had been able to develop only after the war was over and the gates shut.

Chamberlain was currently on board an MH-90 Nighthawk heading toward the coast of Antarctica. The First Earth Battalion was not the only group of people who were waiting, and he was on his way to visit the other critical component in their readiness.

The coastline of the seventh continent was not much different—unlike the coastlines of the other six continents—despite the rise in ocean levels with the melting of both ice caps. Antarctica had actually had the most interesting transition of all, as the mile-thick layer of ice that had covered it had melted. The land beneath, freed of the massive weight, had actually risen as the ocean levels around the world also rose.

Chamberlain looked over the pilot's shoulder and saw the remains of Mount Erebus directly ahead. As part of its assault along the Pacific Rim, the Shadow had made numerous volcanoes become active, Erebus one of them. Half the mountain was gone, blown away during its initial eruption. Long strands of dark, cold lava stretched from the volcanic cone to the sea.

As they got closer, Chamberlain could make out a cluster of pod buildings on one of the strands that poked out into the ocean, just above the pounding surf. A wharf extended out onto the ocean with a tower at the end. New Delphi was the name of the station and it had been established just before the First Earth Battalion was formed. Indeed, it was the place where the concept for the First Earth Battalion had been launched.

The craft flared to a landing on the edge of the small center, and Chamberlain exited. He wasn't in battle gear, wearing a one-piece pale blue jumpsuit and full headgear to protect his skin and eyes.

A woman waited for him, dressed in a similar outfit. Although he could not see a single square inch of her skin, he knew exactly what she looked like underneath the protective clothes. Chamberlain acknowledged her salute with a touch of his right hand to his protective visor.

"Anything, Captain Eddings?" He knew it was a stupid question, because if there was any news, he would have heard about it already. Thus he was momentarily stunned at her answer.

"Yes. We've had activity."

"What? What happened?" After all these years of nothing.

Eddings put a hand on his shoulder. "Easy, Colonel." She turned toward the pier. "Come with me and see for yourself."

They walked along the steel decking out to the tower. Eddings punched in her access code to the door, and it slid open revealing an elevator. They entered and then immediately descended over fifty feet to the underwater headquarters of the Oracles.

The doors opened and they entered a circular chamber, completely enclosed in blast-glass, the ocean pressing against it in all directions. A dozen high-backed chairs were evenly spaced around the chamber, facing outward. Eleven of the chairs were occupied. Chamberlain knew the twelfth was Eddings'. She was the liaison between the Oracles and the First Earth Battalion. She'd also been his lover for the past year. In the very center of the chamber, less than five feet from the elevator entrance, on a black throne, sat the High Priestess Oracle.

Eddings went to one knee in front of her superior. "Colonel Chamberlain is here."

The Oracles had a very different system than the military and Chamberlain had long ago learned the truism of when in Rome do as the Romans. He also went to one knee in front of the old lady occupying the throne. "High Priestess," he said, bowing his head.

"Colonel. Captain. Please stand. Are your warriors ready?"

Chamberlain pulled off his helmet, tucking it under one arm as Eddings did the same. "Yes, ma'am. Always."

The old lady fingered a crystal charm that hung around her neck. "The time we have waited for is coming."

So they had said years ago, Chamberlain thought. He glanced around the chamber. "What has happened?"

The old woman raised a hand and pointed a bony finger past him, just over his shoulder. "Look. Sentinels."

Chamberlain turned. Two orcas—killer whales—swam into view and came to a stop just inches from the glass, their black eyes peering in. When the Shadow had conducted its final assault, the Valkyries had not been the only force coming through the gates. Strange, mythical creatures had come through the gates on land. And kraken had poured into the oceans from the sea gates, killing all they encountered. Similar to giant squids, but possessing mouths on the end of each tentacle, they were horrible creatures, who had homed in on killing dolphins for some strange reason that none of the scientists had been able to figure out.

The sentinels had been the answer. Orcas, trained by the U.S. Navy to do recovery work, had been unleashed to fight the kraken. The most amazing thing was that only a half-dozen orcas had been in the Navy program, but those six had spread out and immediately swam to their fellow whales and gathered them. In the dark depths of the world's ocean, terrible battles were fought. Kraken versus dolphin and orca. The carcasses of the dead washed up on shores all over the planet, most of the bodies being dolphin.

The orcas were the vicious cousin of the dolphins. The largest member of the dolphin family, they were more widespread in the world's oceans than dolphins. Males could grow to over thirty feet in length. They ate pretty much anything they ran into and could catch including blue whales and squid.

Like dolphins, they also used echo-location to check out their surroundings and locate prey. They also could communicate among themselves with high-speed clicks that sounded like rasps and screams. However, when they needed to be quiet to draw in prey, they could remain silent for days on end.

The strange thing about orcas though, was that once mated, male and females stayed together for life. A remarkable display of fidelity for a species with the moniker "killer." Mothers bore their young for over sixteen months and then nursed them for another year and a half. They were a strange combination of lethality and love.

By the time the Shadow closed the gates, all of the world's dolphins were dead, but the orcas finished off the last of the kraken left behind. And then the Oracles found something most fascinating. Even though all gates were closed, the orcas were picking something up, something from beyond this timeline.

It was the Sentinels, through the Oracles, who delivered the message to form the First Earth Battalion from the Ones Before. And to be ready. That they would be needed and have one last chance to avenge the slow death of their planet.

"What are the Sentinels sending?" Chamberlain asked.

It was Eddings who answered. "Nothing specific. Just a sense of"— she searched for the word—"anticipation."

Chamberlain found that an odd choice of words. "What do you mean?"

The High Priestess Oracle answered. "For years we have sat here and listened. And all we have heard are whispers. Of a great battle to come. To be ready for a final assault. But now. It's not a specific message from the Sentinels as Captain Eddings noted. It's a feeling."

"Captain Eddings said 'anticipation,'" Chamberlain noted. "Is that what it is?"

The old woman turned her eyes to him and smiled, the first time he had seen her smile in all the years he'd known her. "No. Not anticipation. Not exactly."

"What then?"

"Hope."

7

EARTH TIMELINE—THE PRESENT
Space and Naval Warfare Systems Center,
San Diego, CA

Throughout the long flight from the Devil's Sea Gate to
San Diego, Professor Ahana had kept in contact not only
with the crew aboard the FLIP but with her comrades
manning the Super-Kamiokande in Japan. Dane had taken
the opportunity to catch up on much needed sleep. Earhart
did the same, both not knowing when the next opportunity
for rest would come.

When they were under an hour out from the West Coast
of the United States, Dane cracked open one eye and
looked about the inside of the navy transport aircraft.
Ahana had two laptop computers open, one on each seat
next to her and wore a headset that was linked to the

plane's secure MILSTAR communications system. Earhart was nowhere to be seen.

Dane stood and stretched, then walked forward to the door leading to the cockpit. He opened it and wasn't surprised to see Earhart in the co-pilot's seat, her hands on the controls, the crew watching her respectfully. It wasn't every day you had a legend of aviation—one supposedly long dead—in your cockpit.

Dane stood there for a while watching as the pilot showed her the latest gadgets the plane was outfitted with. He supposed that other than the controls, everything in the cockpit was pretty much new to Earhart, but she seemed a bit unimpressed with the technology.

"Having fun?" Dane asked.

Earhart glanced over her shoulder. "Too much stuff. Hell, all my navigator had when I did my round the world attempt was a basic radio set with which he tried to raise whatever transmitter he could pick up to try to triangulate our position. We'd be lucky to figure it out within a hundred miles. That was flying. Now you've got this GPR thing that updates a gazillion times every second and locates you to within three feet. Where's the challenge to that?"

"Takes some of the fun out of it?" Dane asked.

Earhart smiled. "No. I knew from the first time I went up in a plane that this was where I belonged. That hasn't changed. And flying will always be dangerous."

Dane jerked his thumb toward the rear of the plane. "We probably ought to see what Ahana has come up with before we land."

Earhart reluctantly let go of the controls as the pilot took over. She thanked the crew then headed back with Dane. They sat down across from Ahana and waited as she completed another radio call. The Japanese scientist then took off her headset and glanced down at first one and then the other of her computers before lowering both screens closed.

"You say you sensed from the sphere map that there is a gate near San Diego?" she asked Dane, never one to waste words.

"That's what I sensed when I held the portal strand— that the clicks were coming from there. Or going to," he added as he realized he really didn't know in which direction, if not both, they were being transmitted.

"And the other end of that strand?" Ahana asked. "To the Space Between?"

Dane shook his head. "No. The other end was"—he searched for the word, then shrugged—"blocked I guess. When I tried probing in that direction I hit darkness. Like a solid wall of black."

"Well," Ahana began, "the Super-Kamiokande has nothing, no muonic transmissions anywhere near San Diego."

The Super-Kamiokande was a device buried three miles below the planet's surface, in northern Japan, in an abandoned mine that had opened into a natural cavern. There was a control room at the top of the cavern where Ahana's cohorts worked, their computers, desks, and chairs set on a steel grate that covered a highly polished stainless steel tank, sixty meters wide by sixty deep and filled with water. The walls of the tank were lined with twenty thousand photomultiplier tubes—PMTs. The tubes were very sensitive light sensors that could pick up a single photon as it traveled through the tank's water. The Super-Kamiokande was essentially a ring-imaging water Cerenkov detector. Cerenkov light is produced when an electrically charged particle travels through water. The reason the Super-Kamiokande was so far underground was to allow the miles of earth and rock above it to block out the photons emitted by human devices on the surface of the planet. While they knew little about the gates and the Shadow, they did know that activity by the Shadow produced muon emissions, which the Super-Kamiokande could trace. During the last several battles with the Shadow, they had used the Super-Kamiokande to try to anticipate attacks. It could read muonic activity throughout the planet.

"It would make sense that the Ones Before are transmitting in a somewhat different mode than the Shadow," Dane said. "You don't want to transmit on the same frequency as your enemy."

Ahana nodded. "I agree it would make sense. Muons are part of the second family of fundamental particles. Most of what we are used to here in our timeline is in the first family, consisting of electron, up-quarks, and down-quarks. The second family consists of muons, charm quarks, and strange quarks. And all these things are not single points according to string theory but rather tiny one-dimensional loops that are vibrating, which gives them several characteristics that allow us to merge relativity and quantum mechanics."

"So have you checked the charm and strange whatever you call them?" Earhart asked.

"Yes," Ahana said. "Nothing so far. However, let us take this to a deeper level."

Dane exchanged a glance with Earhart. He'd listened to Ahana and her late-professor Nagoya discuss the cutting edge physics with which they were trying to understand what was going on with the gates and the Shadow and he'd had a hard time, especially considering the two scientists themselves didn't completely understand what they were dealing with and most of the time were just theorizing out loud.

"There are four base forces in nature," Ahana said. "Gravity, electromagnetic, strong, and weak. Each has a force particle. For electromagnetic there is the photon. For gravity it's postulated that there is a particle called the graviton but only because of effect, as we've never seen one. For strong the particle is the gluon. And for weak we have weak gauge bosons.

"Professor Nagoya believed the Shadow can manipulate the strong and weak forces," Ahana said. "We can do so, but only in a rudimentary fashion. For example a nuclear weapon explodes when atoms are suddenly split and the strong forces are released in a very short amount of time. When uranium decays in a reactor, we are using weak forces, releasing the power in a slower mode. We are nowhere close to controlling these forces like we do electricity. But I think—and so did Professor Nagoya— that the Shadow can control those forces quite readily."

"And the Ones Before?" Earhart asked.

"We've been searching," Ahana said, "but nothing so far."

Dane frowned. "What about high frequency?"

"We've checked high frequency," Ahana said. "Nothing there either."

Dane knew a little about radio transmissions from his time in the military and doing rescue work. "A radio transmission is just frequency modulation on an energy wave, correct?"

"Basically," Ahana agreed.

Earhart picked up on that. "You haven't said anything

about gravity," she noted. "The fourth power." She pointed out the window at the wings. "Gravity is something every pilot is very concerned with."

Ahana sat back in her chair and shifted her focus from the two computers, even though they were closed, to the two people. "As Professor Nagoya would advise if he were here, we must look at the basics first. Sir Isaac Newton proposed his law of gravitation in 1687. He said that every particle in the universe attracts every other particle with a force that depends on the product of the mass of each particle divided by the square of the distance between them. The exact formula is F equals G times mass one times mass two divided by the square of the distance between them. G is the universal constant of gravitation, which Newton had no clue as to the value of.

"According to this theory, gravity is a linear force, directly between the two centers of gravity between the two masses. As I said, the one thing Newton wasn't able to figure out was the value of G. An apple falling from a tree is fine, but not exactly scientific data. Over a century after Newton, the English physicist Henry Cavendish finally managed to measure G and it was a very, very small number."

"So gravity isn't very powerful in a way," Dane said.

"It's a strange force," Ahana said. "You can look at it as the force between two objects, but you can also look at it as a field. As Ms. Earhart notes, the gravitational force around the earth produces a downward force on objects near the surface. Also, objects can affect each other across distance. This is the essence of the how the solar system stays in balance around the sun. In fact, before anyone ever saw Neptune, scientists were able to postulate it existed by noting unexplainable variations in the motion of the planet Uranus due to Neptune's gravitational field."

Dane had closed his eyes as he listened to Ahana. They were in transit with nothing else to do and he had learned that golden nuggets of vital information were often mixed among the deluge brought forth by scientists. In his gut he knew they were on the right path and that what Ahana was saying was important in a way he would only understand after other pieces of this puzzle fell into place.

"A problem with Newton's theory," Ahana continued, "involved relativity. According to his theory, two observers making measurements of the speed of an object will end up with different numbers depending on their own motion relative to each other. For example, a person standing on a platform observing a stationery ball on a train passing by will measure the speed of the ball as the same as that of the train, while a person on the train will measure the ball's speed as zero. Thus Newton would say there is no constant, fundamental speed in the physical world because all speed is relative. However, near the end of the nineteenth century this came under attack and the Scottish physicist Maxwell proposed a complete theory of electric and magnetic forces that contained just such a constant which he called c. He estimated this to be one hundred and eighty thousand miles an hour. That was how fast electromagnetic waves, including light waves, traveled. This feature of Maxwell's theory caused a crisis in physics because it indicated that speed was not always relative.

"The scientific community struggled with this until Einstein came up with his theory of relativity in 1905. An important aspect of Einstein's theory was that no object could travel faster than c. This conflicted with Newton's gravity theory, which implied gravity moved at infinite speed."

"But no one's been able to find this particle that is the essence of gravity," Earhart noted. "So how can anyone know it moves at infinite speed?"

"A good point," Ahana said. "We can measure light waves directly but not gravity—only the effect. Einstein did see the discrepancy, and in 1915 he formulated a new theory of gravity in which he said the force of gravity moves at speed c. Another important difference between Einstein and Newton was that Einstein described gravity as a curvature of space and time, not exactly a linear force."

"The portals," Dane said. "Could they be curves that cross time and space?"

"It is possible," Ahana admitted, "that the portals are some effect of the manipulation of the force of gravity at levels we cannot comprehend. Einstein proposed, in his general theory of relativity, that space and time are united in a single, four-dimensional geometry consisting of three space dimensions and one time dimension. This geometry is called space–time, and particles move from point to point as time progresses along curves called world lines. If there were no force of gravity, then the particle lines would be straight, but gravity causes the curvatures."

Dane looked out the plane's window. All he could see was water so he knew they were still a distance out from San Diego. He felt very isolated contemplating trying to take a war to an entity that could control forces the best minds of his timeline were still struggling to understand.

Ahana continued. "Einstein proposed that gravity's effect should not be represented as the deviation of a world line from straightness, as it would be for an electrical force.

Gravitation changes the most natural world lines and thereby curves the geometry of space–time. In a curved geometry, such as the two-dimensional surface of the earth, there are no straight lines. Instead, there are special curves called geodesics, an example of which are great circles around the earth. These special curves are at each point as straight as possible, and they are the most natural lines in a curved geometry. The effect of gravity is to influence the geodesics in space–time. Near sources of gravitation the space is strongly curved and the geodesics behave less and less like those in flat, uncurved space–time.

"The problem is that even using our most modern technology we still find it very difficult to test these theories with experiments and observations. But Einstein's theory has passed all tests that have been made so far. Einstein's theory of gravity revolutionized twentieth-century physics.

"Following it another important advancement that took place was quantum theory, which states that physical interactions, or the exchange of energy, cannot be made arbitrarily small. There is a minimum interaction that comes in a packet called the quantum of an interaction. For electromagnetism the quantum is called the photon. Gravity has also been quantized. We call a quantum of gravitational energy a graviton.

"What scientists have been searching for lately is the T-O-E—the theory of everything in which all four of the fundamental forces are just different aspects of the same single universal force. We have made some progress unifying electromagnetism and weak nuclear forces and strong nuclear forces. But gravity, with its complex math and geometry has been more difficult to unify."

"But it will happen," Dane said.

Ahana nodded. "I would assume so. If we have the time."

"I think the Shadow either is a timeline that is also in the future," Dane said, "or a timeline that advanced much more quickly in the field of physics than us."

"It is most likely," Ahana said.

Dane could see land ahead, the shoreline of California. He had a little better understanding of the big picture of what they were involved in, but he knew theory would do them little good.

The plane banked and swooped down toward a military airfield on an island just off of San Diego. Dane could see the warships in the harbor, then he closed his eyes and began to search outward with his mind. He dimly felt the plane touch down and the deceleration as they went down the runway.

"Do you feel it?" Dane asked Earhart, opening his eyes.

Earhart shook her head. "What?"

"There's a gate nearby," Dane said.

Ahana was looking at her computers. One of them was linked to a portable muonic detector that could pick up activity in the immediate area. "We're not picking up anything."

"There's one close by," Dane said. "But it's different than the other gates. I don't get the bad feeling I've always had in the past when I got close to a gate."

The door to the plane opened and two military policemen escorted them without a word to a waiting car. They drove from the airfield toward the waterfront. Dane noted the armed guards at the doors to the building they pulled up to and knew they weren't rent-a-cops, but professionals. That, in combination with the other obvious security

measures around the facility, told him that whatever the
Space and Naval Warfare Systems Center was working on
was highly classified. Dr. Martsen led the way through the
gates, Foreman having called ahead and gotten them au-
thorized access.

The facility was located inside the Naval Base in San
Diego and Dane felt strange to be on a military post after
so many years as a civilian. Two guards escorted them to
a typically drab three-story military building next to the
harbor.

While the exterior was unimpressive, the inside was a
totally different matter. Martsen led them along a white-
painted corridor to a pair of steel doors that slid open
when she placed her eyes against a retina scan. They entered an elevator and it descended, taking them below sea
level in a matter of seconds. They remained still for a few
seconds as air was pumped in.

"We're equalizing pressure," Martsen said. "We're
down forty feet, deep enough so that our work can't be observed by satellites. We need to equalize the pressure—
well, you'll see."

When the doors opened once more, Dane took one
step, then halted, staring about in amazement. The facility
was a melding of air and water, with clear glass tunnels
crisscrossing the room and there were several open places
in the floor that gave access to the water below—the reason the atmosphere needed to be pressurized. There were
about fifteen humans in the room, doing various things,
and a half dozen dolphins, either in the tubes or at the access points.

However, what caught everyone's attention was in the
center of the complex. There were two large, clear, vertical tubes. A man in a white coat stood next to them giving

some idea of the dimensions. One was about fourteen feet high by six in diameter. The other eight feet high by four in diameter. In both there was a thick-looking, greenish liquid inside. And floating inside the larger tube was a dolphin covered with a black body suit. Various lines and leads went to the creature's body. The dolphin's head was totally enclosed in an oversize black helmet out of which ran several tubes and wires. The dolphin floated freely, back slightly hunched over. In the other tube there was a human, also wearing a black suit and with head covered by a black helmet. Numerous wires ran from the tubes to a console between them.

A tall black man in navy whites walked up to greet them. "Dr. Martsen," he said, acknowledging her. Then he turned to Dane, Ahana, and Earhart. "I'm Commander Talbot. Welcome to Dream Land."

8

EARTH TIMELINE—VIII
Washington, DC, June 1863

"He comes."

Lincoln turned in surprise to his wife next to him in the carriage. "Who?"

"Lee. He's coming. And he's bringing the terrible storm of death with him." She looked at her husband. "It's coming. As the voice told it would. This summer."

The carriage was bringing them back from dinner with a group of generals at the War Department. Lincoln could smell raw sewage, the odor of Washington in the summer. To his left, along the Mall, were rows and rows of tents. Soldiers, just arrived from New York, via the Baltimore railroad. In both cities, the soldiers had been attacked by mobs. The eastern cities were boiling over with resentment at the draft. Which the rich could buy their way out of for three hundred dollars. Lincoln had fought against the practice and lost. There were simply too many rich contributors to Congress who did not want *their* sons sent into the cauldron of battle.

Lincoln understood, to an extent, the desire of these men not to lose their sons. His and Mary's firstborn, Edward, had died in 1850 at the age of four. Willie had died. These deaths had caused Mary much grief, and there had been times in public where she'd grown hysterical.

Washington had never been a good place for Mary. They'd first come here in 1846 when he was elected to Congress. They'd come with high expectations, which had been quickly dashed by the reality of the situation. Lincoln had thought he could make his mark quickly, only to find that he was one of many unknown freshmen congressman and the inner sanctums of power were closed to him. The social life Mary had been looking forward to was as equally distant and closed.

He served one term, before heading back home. He'd been offered the governership of the new Oregon territory but he'd turned it down to return to practice law, having seen his first foray into politics on a national level end discouragingly.

It took the passage of the Kansas-Nebraska Act to energize him in 1854. This act had created the territories of Kansas and Nebraska and said that each territory could be admitted as states with or without slavery, as dictated by the people of the state at the time of admission. Lincoln felt this went against what had previously been determined and would spread slavery, something he was strongly opposed to. This led him into direct conflict with the author of the Kansas-Nebraska Act, Stephen Douglas, and their famous series of debates that brought Lincoln into national prominence.

For Douglas, slavery had been a political issue. For Lincoln, there was a moral level to it all—slavery was incompatible with democracy. Although as he had campaigned, Lincoln had kept himself distant from the strong abolitionist views, preferring to work within the system to solve this festering problem. That approach, obviously, had not worked.

"Do you hear anything else?" Lincoln asked his wife as they turned up the drive to the White House.

Mary nodded. "Meade."

Lincoln was confused. Was she referring to beer? His wife drank rarely, and he was always fearful when she did as it upset her delicate disposition.

"The general," Mary said, sensing his confusion. "Fifth Corps commander. He's the one."

Virginia, Summer 1863

It was hot and humid, not good marching weather, but Lee's men had covered many miles so far in this war, and the fact that they were moving North served to give their step an extra spring.

Jubal Early's division, part of Ewell's corps, was in the lead and made forty-five miles in two days, surprising the Union garrison at Winchester. A. P. Hill's corps was still in the vicinity of Fredericksburg, which meant Lee's army was stretched over one hundred miles, not exactly sound tactics as he had been taught at West Point.

Lee was not unaware of the danger, but he felt his position to be reasonably secure. He had a screen of cavalry to his east, between him and Hooker's troops, and he had the cover of the Rappahannock and the Blue Ridge mountains also on his flanks. Lee's spies told him that Hooker was finally reacting, albeit several days too late, doing as expected, and pulling back North, as the Union commander was uncertain of Lee's objective. Given that Lee himself was a bit uncertain about his specific objectives, he could understand Hooker's uncertainty. Hooker was reacting, which meant Lee could maintain the initiative.

Winchester fell quickly, and the Union forces that didn't surrender fell back in disarray toward Harpers Ferry on the Potomac. It became almost a race between the retreating Union forces and the front edge of Lee's army for the crossing.

Meanwhile Lee's cavalry under Jeb Stuart fought pitched battles with Union forces along the eastern flank. Crossing the Potomac certainly raised the morale of the troops, but it troubled Lee that he was losing touch with Hooker's army. He had enough respect for the Union Army to know that he needed to fix his enemy's position before venturing too much farther North.

On June 24, Lee called Jeb Stuart to his headquarters, even as his advance troops entered Chambersburg in Pennsylvania, sending the countryside into a panic. Still feeling the effects of his recent illness, Lee was quick with his orders to Stuart.

Too quick as events would show. On the evening of the 24th, Stuart rode off with the majority of the Southern Cavalry to the East. Lee would not see him again until it was too late.

Feeling he still had several days' lead on Hooker, Lee ordered his subordinate units to spread out to forage the bountiful countryside. A secondary goal of this attack was to resupply his army, and his men took the orders to heart.

Washington, DC, Summer 1863

"Everyone knows Lee is in Pennsylvania, it seems, except Hooker."

Secretary of War Stanton had nothing to say to Lincoln's statement. The president held up a copy of a newspaper, whose headline screamed of plundering Confederate troops. "I am sick of editors being more informed than my commanding general."

Stanton cleared his throat.

"Yes?" Lincoln folded the newspaper and placed it in front of him as he waited for his secretary of war.

"Hooker is—ahh—"

"Say it," Lincoln ordered.

Stanton glanced at the telegram in his hands. "Displeased that General Halleck refuses to send him more reinforcements. He threatens to resign his position unless I order Halleck to do as he requests."

Lincoln rubbed his temples. "Take his resignation. Effective right now."

"Yes, sir," Stanton said.

Everyone waited as Lincoln continued to rub his temples as if trying to push out bad thoughts. "General Meade, the Fifth Corps commander, is from Pennsylvania, is he not?"

"Yes, sir," Stanton said.

"Your opinion of him?" Lincoln asked Stanton.

"Solid. He did a good job at Antietam and Fredericksburg. His men held their own."

"Which is more than we can say about most others," Lincoln said.

"Yes, sir. But he is not the senior corps commander."

"Let's see how he is at defending his own state's soil," Lincoln said as he scratched out the order putting Meade in command on a piece of parchment.

Pennsylvania, Summer 1863

Hard marching had taken a toll on the Army of Virginia in a way most would not think of. That is those who were not infantry would think of.

Shoes.

More than half the army lacked them. And those who were shod had worn the leather on their soles down to paper thin, making every footfall on a stone or pebble a painful experience.

Early's division of Ewell's corp force-marched to Gettysburg, a sleepy little town mostly known for its Lutheran seminary on a ridge nearby. They arrived on June 24, even as General Meade was being roused by an aide with Lincoln's order putting him in charge of the Army of the Potomac.

Reaching Gettysburg, Early demanded ten thousand dollars worth of goods from the town's inhabitants, but most had fled, and those who were still there had hidden their wealth. As they passed through the town, Early did notice something of interest, though. A shoe factory.

Early scribbled out a note to A. P. Hill, telling him of the fact, before marching on to occupy York.

The few remaining citizens of Gettysburg were thankful the Confederates had passed through and life got back to normal. There was movement all around the town, but no soldiers from either side in it. Gettysburg seemed to be free of the coming storm. Calm settled over the inhabitants. Just like the calm at the eye of a hurricane.

EARTH TIMELINE—XIV
Southern Africa, January 1879

Three columns of British forces crossed in Zululand on January 6, exactly as Shakan had predicted. They were under the overall command of Lieutenant-General Lord Chelmsford, whose expertise leaned more to the lord and less to the general side of his titles. He led six thousand regulars and colonial volunteers along with nine thousand levied natives. He felt the core force of British regulars more than enough to deal with any African force, even though experienced officers and the Boer advisers on his staff made dire warnings about the capabilities of the Zulus.

Besides, his troops had twenty field guns and ten rocket launchers, a potent mix of firepower that he believed should cow any dark-skinned foes, who were armed with spears and ox-hide shields. Chelmsford saw no possible way such a foe could offer a threat to a British regular.

Chelmsford had never heard of Custer, even though that battle had taken place less than three years earlier on the American continent. If he had known the details of the Battle of the Little Bighorn, he might have been startled to see the similarities between his plan of splitting his force into three columns and Custer's ill-fated plan. Then again, Chelmsford was a man whose imagination was limited to his field of vision, so the similarities would most likely have escaped him.

The British movement did not go unnoticed by the Zulus. Cetewayo had been sufficiently impressed by both Shakan's vision and by the reports of his spies in the Transvaal of British preparations so that he sent out reconnaissance patrols along the border. His immediate concern was the column that posed the most immediate threat, the central column.

Nominally under the command of Colonel Glynn of the Twenty-fourth Regiment, the central column crossed the Buffalo River near the Swedish missionary at Rorke's Drift. The command was only nominally Glynn's due to his misfortune of having Chelmsford and the general's staff accompanying him. Not content with being in overall command, Chelmsford also issued orders to Glynn's men as if they were his own and the central column his specific command.

It was a long formation of almost five thousand men, eighteen hundred of which were European. Using oxen to pull their wagons limited the rate of advance to that of the lumbering beasts.

They moved in a thick mist and drizzling rain that did little to keep morale up. Mounted troops from the local militia led the way, into the Buffalo River. Trouble struck the column immediately at the river as several of the mounted troops, up to their necks in the water, were swept away and drowned. The column was delayed as Chelmsford ordered flat-bottom pontoon boats brought up to move his less expendable regulars of the regiment across the river. Chelmsford left behind a small force of infantry at Rorke's Drift before pressing forward into Zululand.

Sitting on his mount, watching the troops file past,

Lord Chelmsford felt quite confident that he would soon
have the African nation under British rule. Which was
only appropriate. After all, the sun never set on the British
Empire.

Noting that it was early afternoon and knowing how
long it took to make an appropriate camp and get his tent
erected, Chelmsford ordered the column to halt, only a
few miles into enemy territory, overruling Glynn's
protests that they should push on farther to maintain the
initiative. It was tea time and a civilized man always paid
attention to such details. He also overruled Glynn's orders
to prepare a proper encampment with barriers and outposts.

.   .   .

Shakan climbed to the top of Isandlwana. She shivered,
feeling a chill in the air, one that cut to the bone and that
no amount of clothing could alleviate. She felt some
warmth on her collarbone, pulled away her robe, and
looked down, noting that the crystal amulet around her
neck was glowing very faintly.

This was the place she had seen in her visions. Besides
the chill, there was a distinct feeling of evil about the hill.

Shakan knelt down and began to pray as her mother
had taught her. Not prayers to a God, but prayers for
courage from within.

EARTH TIMELINE—III
Antarctica, July 2078

The MH-90 Nighthawks came in high and fast from the
east toward the operational area. The MH-90 was the di-

rect descendant of a program from the early twentieth century called the Osprey, which had failed. Each craft was over sixty feet long and capable of holding forty combat-equipped troops in the cargo hold. Each stubby wing had a powerful jet engine mounted on it and could rotate from horizontal to vertical to allow take-offs and landings just like a helicopter. When the wings rotated back to horizontal the craft could fly at just over the speed of sound just like any other jet. On top of all that, the fuselage and engines were pressure sealed, and the craft could operate for limited amounts of time underwater.

In the rear of the lead Nighthawk, Colonel Chamberlain had his suit on night vision and full combat power mode. He'd done one hundred twenty-seven combat equipment drops, but each one brought a level of anxiety. He was the rearmost soldier in the plane, right next to the back ramp. His chute was rigged to the back of the combat suit at four contact points.

"Six minutes." The pilot's voice was flat, emotionless over the secure command frequency.

Chamberlain echoed the command on the platoon net to the men and women on board. Then he continued with the jump commands. While at the academy, Chamberlain had attended the Airborne School at Fort Benning, Georgia, one of the last classes to graduate there before the post was destroyed in the final phase of the Shadow War. He imagined that the Black Hat instructors who had taught him so many years ago would have approved of similar jump commands being used for this operation, even though they would have not recognized the technology.

"Get ready," Chamberlain called out. A red light began flickering in the rear of the plane, just above the ramp.

"Outboard personnel, lock in," he ordered. He took a step toward the center of the plane, where two steel rails ran from the forward bulkhead to the tail. He straightened and the locks on the top of his helmet slid into the two rails securely. "Inboard personnel, lock in."

The rest of the platoon attached themselves to the rail. The red light stopped flickering, confirming that all the soldiers were securely fastened. Still, Chamberlain followed procedure.

"Confirm lock in."

From the front-most soldier toward the rear of the plane, each man and woman counted off, confirming they were in place and ready.

"Three minutes," the pilot announced. "Depressurizing in thirty seconds."

"Check suit pressure," Chamberlain ordered. Again, all confirmed their suits were sealed and they were on internal oxygen.

Secure in his suit, Chamberlain noticed no change as the cabin was depressurized. He did a quick switch of views on his internal screen, tapping into the cockpit's display, getting a view of the terrain ahead. Through swirling snow, he saw mountains to the left and right, with a narrow valley in between, just as planned. The winds were high, beyond normal safety parameters, but it did not occur to Chamberlain to call off the jump.

"Two minutes," the pilot announced, and Chamberlain relayed it to the platoon.

The plane jerked hard right, then left. Locked into the rail, the soldiers weren't really affected, but each knew something wasn't right.

"Incoming," the pilot's voice had yet to change in affect.

Checking the pilot's view, Chamberlain could see red bursts come from the high ground to the left, arcing toward them.

"One minute," the pilot said.

Chamberlain changed his view to his own. A crack appeared in the rear of the plane as the back ramp began to open. Cold air swirled into the cargo bay. The red light was a steady beacon above the opening.

"Ten seconds. Lock down."

Chamberlain tensed, keeping his breathing steady. He locked down his arm, neck, and leg manipulators.

"Stand by."

The light turned green and Chamberlain barely heard the pilot as an electromagnetic surge ran down the two steel rails, accelerating the line of jumpers out of the plane.

Chamberlain hit the plane's slipstream and tumbled about for several seconds. They were dropping at four thousand feet, but he immediately realized something was wrong. The plane's evasive actions had taken them too far to the left and they were partly over the ridgeline.

"Unlock," Chamberlain ordered his suit as he glanced at his above ground level—AGL—display. Fifteen hundred feet, not four thousand. And he was free-falling. The numbers were winding down swiftly.

Chamberlain spread his arms and legs, trying to get stable. The tumbling slowed as he passed through eight hundred feet. Too low.

"Deploy," Chamberlain shouted.

A drogue chute popped out of the pack on the top of his back, immediately pulling out the main chute. Chamberlain was jerked backward, even as the AGL indicator went below four hundred feet. The ground was rushing up.

Chamberlain's training took over as he brought his legs together, bending his knees, just as he had in the fields of Fort Benning so many years ago. He rotated his armored arms in front of his helmet.

He hit hard, harder than he ever had. The suit's micromotors took most of the impact, but he was on the side of the ridge and instead of coming to a halt, he tumbled downslope.

"Disconnet," Chamberlain ordered, but it was too late, as he was getting wrapped up in the lines leading to his canopy. His cameras were covered by nylon and he was effectively blinded as he still slid down the side of the ridge. He came to a halt when he crashed into something that sent a jarring spike of pain into his left rib cage.

"Blade," Chamberlain ordered through gritted teeth. A knife snapped out from its case on top of his left wrist and he sliced through lines and chute, freeing himself. The chute fell away as he got to his feet, automatically scanning the immediate area.

He could see other Nighthawks coming in, dropping their complement of soldiers.

He accessed his tactical display and he knew right away the drop was a disaster. The pilots had reacted to the incoming fire and their evasive maneuvers had spread the battalion across not only the valley but both ridgelines on either side. The battalion frequency was full of calls for medics from soldiers injured on the drop. There were also seven small flashing red dots on tactical.

Seven dead. Seven who had hit the ground too fast. And at least three times that many injured.

Chamberlain watched as platoon and company commanders organized their units and the casualties were tended to. Chamberlain moved into place in the formation, his three-member battalion staff falling into place surrounding him.

"Seven dead," his adjutant reported. "Twenty six injured, five serious. Med Evacs are in-bound."

He could hear the reproach in her voice. A high price for a training jump. He went up to her and touched his helmet to hers so that only she would hear what he had to say. "Lieutenant, I ordered that simulated fire on the planes. I wanted to see how we—and the pilots—reacted to the unexpected. And we did not do well. So we will do this again and again until we do react well. Because I can assure you one thing. When we hit the Shadow, whatever is waiting for us is going to be something we can never expect."

He pulled his head away and went to the Battalion Command Net. "Reform." Then he ordered the Nighthawks to come in and pick them up. "We're jumping again."

9

EARTH TIMELINE—THE PRESENT
Space and Naval Warfare Systems Center,
San Diego, CA

Dane could see that Commander Talbot was looking at Earhart strangely—it wasn't every day you met someone you'd read about in history books. Talbot spread his hands wide in invitation. "I've been ordered to extend you every courtesy and answer any question you have."

The question everyone had was what was going on with the dolphin in the tank, but instead of asking it, Dane walked over to the closest free dolphin. Its head was slightly turned and one dark eye returned his gaze. As Talbot was about to say something else, Dane held up a hand, indicating quiet. He stood still for several minutes. Gradually, all work in the lab died down and everyone was watching him but he was unaware. His entire focus was on the creature in the water, which was as still as he was. Earhart was at Dane's side. Ahana stood in the background, waiting.

"Do you track your dolphins?" Dane finally asked.

Talbot nodded. "They're all tagged with transponders that are picked up by satellite, and the computer keeps a record of their movements."

"Can you show me the tracks of all your dolphins in the last twenty-four hours?" Dane asked.

"Don't you want a briefing first on what we're doing here?" Talbot seemed a bit put out. Dane imagined that he had briefed others on his project, and it was a great source of pride to him.

"In due time," Dane said. "There's something else I need to know first."

Talbot led them over to a large screen and gave instructions to one of his technicians. A flurry of lines appeared on the screen.

Dane walked up the screen and tapped a spot where all the lines intersected. "Where is this?"

"Coordinates," Talbot said to the tech.

The man rattled off some numbers that made no sense to Dane, but obviously did to Talbot.

"About three miles from here. There's a small fault line off the coast. That spot is right on top of the fault line."

"Take us there," Dane ordered.

Talbot looked surprised at such a blunt order, but he obliged, and within short order they were back on the surface and onboard a boat heading out to sea.

"It's getting stronger," Earhart said.

Dane nodded. "I know. What did you pick up back there?"

"Just a feeling."

Dane leaned closer to her. "And that feeling was?"

"Hope."

Dane nodded. "I felt the same thing."

Ahana looked like she was going to say something, but didn't. She was opening up a large plastic case that contained some of her monitoring equipment.

The boat slowed and then came to a halt, the helmsman using his engines and rudder to keep them in place against the current. Dane could feel it now—a low-level flow of power through his body, pulsing hypnotically, in a rhythm that Dane found familiar but could not place.

"There's a gate near here," he announced even though there was no black wall that normally indicated a gate.

Ahana was looking at her instruments. "I'm not picking up anything."

"You won't," Dane said. "The signal is piggy-backed, and the gate is more of a window than a door."

"What is the signal piggy-backed on?" Ahana asked.

"Give me a second." Dane sat down on the deck in the lotus position and closed his eyes. He shut down his external senses one by one until there was only the inner world of his brain. He could feel the stream, more a trickle, of power passing through his body.

Dane's eyes flashed open.

"What is it?" Earhart asked.

Dane pointed up. "It's coming from there. Not from the ocean. From up there coming down to the ocean." He kept his hand up, finger extended, and closed his eyes once more. He moved his hand ever so slightly, trying to make his body an antenna for the power. The variances were so slight that it was very difficult. Several times he thought he had the power line locked in, but then he would lose it.

The sun was going down and a slight chill came with the evening breeze, but Dane didn't notice.

The power line was getting stronger, of that he was certain. After slightly over thirty minutes, he realized that one of the problems was that the power line was shifting. Moving ever so slightly.

Dane froze his hand and opened his eyes once more. He looked up, along the line of his arm toward where his finger was pointing, just above the horizon to the east.

"There."

Everyone turned and looked. A full moon was rising over the mountains beyond San Diego.

"It's being broadcast from there," Dane said.

"The moon?" Ahana was skeptical.

Dane understood part of it now. "There's a gate here and the other end of the portal is there. The transmission is coming from the Ones Before to a gate on the moon and then being broadcast to this spot where the dolphins pick it up. Then they retransmit in the form of the visions and voices those of us with the Sight can pick up. I knew I felt something strange about the other end of the Ones Before portal when I touched it in the sphere map."

Dane felt a sharp spike of pain through the left side of his head and he staggered. Earhart grabbed his arm, steadying him. "Are you all right?"

Dane looked over the side of the boat. A dolphin floated there, gazing up at him. Another piece of the puzzle fell into place. "That's my—" he whispered, searching for the right word. The pain was a little less intense now and he tried to focus his thoughts.

"What?" Earhart asked.

"That dolphin." Dane pointed. "She's"—he shook his head, frustrated that he couldn't conjure up the word he needed. He tapped the side of his head where the pain was receding—"She's the conduit through which I get my visions. Through which the voices reach me. We each have one. Each of us with the Sight. That's why you haven't had any visions in this timeline," he said to Earhart. "You don't have a dolphin counterpart here."

"I don't—" Ahana began but Dane shushed her as he leaned over the boat, close to the dolphin, which used its tail to lift its body a third of the way out of the water. For several seconds the tableau was frozen—the dolphin partly out of the water, Dane leaning over. Then Dane reached out and touched the dolphin's forehead.

It was like touching a live wire. But he maintained the contact for several seconds, until, with a flip of its powerful tail, the dolphin splashed back into the ocean and disappeared into the dark water.

Dane sank to his knees, leaning against the side of the boat. Earhart, Ahana, and Talbot knelt next to him in concern.

"Should I get a Med Evac?" Talbot asked.

Dane slowly shook his head. "No. I'm all right. I see most of it now. Not all. But I know what I have to do next."

"And that is?" Earhart asked.

"Go to the Ones Before." Dane got to his feet.

"Can you make it through this?" Earhart asked doubtfully.

"I'm not going there physically," Dane said. "They've barricaded their end of the portal to prevent anything physical from coming through. Commander," Dane said to Talbot. "Please take us to shore."

"So how will you get there?" Earhart pressed.

"How else?" Dane didn't wait for an answer. "With my

mind." He looked at Talbot. "When we get back, you can brief us on your project."

The rest of the ride was made in silence.

Talbot led them down into the complex. The same dolphin was in the tank and in the exact same position. Talbot led them past the tank, down a short corridor and into a room with rows of chairs. He stood at the front, next to a screen.

"Ladies and gentlemen, this briefing is classified top secret, special compartmentalization."

Dane felt a surge of anger. After all that had happened in the war against the Shadow, more secrets. From whom he wondered? He knew Foreman had gotten them access to this, but he also resented the CIA man for all he represented. All the deceptions and lies had played into the Shadow's hand over the years and now the Earth was reaping the results.

"Just get to it," Dane snapped, earning him surprised looks from Ahana and Earhart.

Talbot glared at Dane for several seconds.

"Gentlemen." Amelia Earhart stood up. "If we could do without the pissing contest, maybe we could get to the facts?"

Dane leaned back in the chair and stretched his legs out. He put his hands on the arms of the chair and nodded. "Go ahead, Commander."

"Have you ever heard of Operation Grill Flame?" Talbot asked.

Dane realized that Talbot was one of those people who could not adapt, who could not change to the situation. He was going to give this briefing the way he had in the past no matter what.

"No," Dane said.

"Grill Flame was the code name for a Defense Intelligence Agency operation using remote viewers," Talbot said.

"Remote viewers?" Earhart asked.

"Psychics," Talbot explained. "People who could see things at a distance just by using their minds. Grill Flame was what it was first called in the sixties. It was renamed Bright Gate in the eighties. They used it to search for the hostages in Beirut. With no success. Something was lacking."

"Then you got involved," Dane said, surprising Talbot.

The Commander nodded. "Yes. To be honest, it was just damn luck. We were running a search and recover training mission with one of our dolpins in the Gulf of Mexico, near an oil rig. Bright Gate was running a remote viewing exercise, trying to get one of their operators to see the oil rig and describe it."

"They connected," Dane said.

"Yes." Talbot stared at Dane, re-evaluating. "We found the dolphin was the one doing the transmitting. The remote viewer was just a receiver. So Dream Land came into being."

Dane wondered if things would have been different if he had known about Dream Land. He had only just realized he received his visions and heard the voices via a dolphin. Here, they'd known for years that dolphins transmitted. Connecting the two might have made a difference.

"We worked on both transmitters and receivers," Talbot continued. "Trying to increase both capabilities. We also tried to channel the process into remote viewing."

Talbot picked up a remote and clicked a button. A slide appeared, showing a single tube with a man inside. The man floated freely, his arms and legs akimbo, a breathing tube leading into a black helmet covering his head along with numerous leads.

"We started with men because we knew more about the human brain. Plus"—here he glanced at Dr. Martsen— "there was the problem that dolphin couldn't exactly tell us what they were seeing. We eventually realized that it was better to ramp up the dolphin's transmitting power, along with a human's receiving power, so we began working on dolphins in the isolation tubes. The results have been interesting to say the least."

Talbot paused, and Dane knew they were crossing the line now, moving from what Talbot and his scientists knew to what they could only guess about. He had picked up the same thing from Ahana and Nagoya when they started discussing the theoretical physics they thought might apply to the Shadow. He had a moment of doubt, wondering if they were so far behind the Shadow's knowledge base that his vague plan of assaulting the Shadow's timeline was an extremely naive one.

Talbot began. "The science we are dealing with here is on the psychometric or virtual plane. While we have little actual understanding of how this works, our philosophy here has been to focus on what works, rather than how it works. What we've managed to do is not only remote view but to project an avatar onto the psychometric plane."

"The what plane?" Earhart asked. "Project what? You'll have to excuse me, Commander, but my science is several decades old compared to yours."

Talbot tapped the side of his head. "The psychometric plane is the one that exists in our heads. What is reality?" He didn't wait for an answer to the question he posed and

Dane knew he had had to answer this question before. "What we perceive it to be. Even though we are all in this room, we are experiencing everything in a slightly different manner as our brain processes the input from our senses.

"An avatar is a form that represents the original in the virtual plane," Talbot continued answered. "If you play a computer game, whatever form you take in the game is your avatar. We've found avatars to be important because it allows the remote viewer to orient oneself in the psychometric plane."

Earhart shook her head. "I don't understand. How can reality be different? There is one reality in this timeline."

Talbot considered her for several seconds, and Dane could almost sense him counting back the years to when she had disappeared into history. "We—scientists—in the last hundred years or so have been digging deeper into the physics of what makes up reality. If you'd asked a scientist a hundred years ago what he thought reality was, he would have said pretty much the same thing you just said.

"For centuries, the most learned men of their age believed that matter and reality consisted of four basic substances: fire, earth, water, and air. We've come a long way since then, but it is foolish to believe we have reached the end of that path of knowledge. In some ways, people two hundred years from now may look at us as we look at those who believed in the four base elements composing all matter."

"That's if there is anyone around two hundred years from now," Dane interjected.

That gave Talbot a brief pause before he got back on track with his briefing. "Early in this century, we believed that the atomic level was the basic building block of matter, and thus of reality. But with the subsequent discovery of quarks and further research into quantum physics, the realm of reality has been extended further into levels that couldn't even be conceptualized by the early atomic scientists."

Dane glanced over at Ahana. He half expected her to jump in the fray, but she was quiet, her dark eyes on Talbot, her mind probably somewhere very far away.

"We at Dream Land," Talbot continued, "believe that the psychometric plane is beyond the plane of quantum physics, which scientists are still groping to understand, although there are *some* proven laws of physics we can connect to it."

"Such as?" Dane pressed.

"Think of the psychometric field like a magnetic field," Talbot suggested. "The Earth's magnetic field is all around us, yet we don't feel it. We need something special, like a compass, to indicate its existence. In a somewhat different manner gravity is all around us, but we can't see it, only its effects.

"We call these invisible fields hyperfields. Quantum physics, with its quarks and wave theory, is a hyperfield. But there are others. They are around you all the time. In fact, there is a concurrent hyperfield to the quantum physical one. A psychometric field. Existing side by side at times with the real plane, at other times existing very separately from the other. It is the boundary between these two planes that is the entire focus of our efforts at Dream Land, where we can project into the psychometric and see into the real plane. Without getting into the philosophy of it, a mental field—what you perceive in your brain—is a virtual field. If you perceive something to be with your mind, then it exists in the psychometric field."

Ahana finally spoke up. "But not in reality."

"Most physicists would say no, not in reality as it is currently defined," Talbot agreed. "But if our thoughts are not reality, what are they? Everything humans have ever invented or done has come out of our thoughts. So they are real in some way. Or become real at some point. So there is definitely a link between the psychometric world and the real world. The line between the two is constantly being breached. And that line, with the proper equipment and training, we are able to breach at Dream Land."

If only they could have linked up Ahana and Talbot at the beginning, Dane thought to himself. He had a feeling this is what the Shadow had managed to do—combine physics with mental power in some fundamental way. As Talbot had said, Dane had seen the results of the two fields meeting when Sin Fen shut the Bermuda Triangle Gate using the abandoned Atlantean pyramid and the power of her mind.

Dane could still see Sin Fen's skull changing from flesh and bone into crystal and channeling the power coming out of the pyramid against the darkness of the expanding gate. Between that experience and what happened on the Nazca Plain, Dane believed there was a connection between a powerful force deep inside the planet and the ability of the mind to tap into and use that force.

Talbot brought up a new slide. On one side was the label "Real Plane" and on the other was "Psychometric Plane." There was a line linking the two.

"These two planes exist inside each of us. We have our minds, which operate on the psychometric plane, and then we have our bodies, which operate in the real plane. And they are connected through the nervous system. We can take ideas from the psychometric plane of our imagination and make them real in the physical world, say in a painting or a computer program or a book. And we can process things from the physical world into our brains, remember them, even change them with our thoughts. You have to consider the fact that a memory is not really what happened in real terms, but how we processed what happens. No two people remember things exactly alike."

"That's not true," Ahana said. "Everyone in this room would agree that two plus two is four."

"That's not a memory," Talbot said. "That's a concept that exists on the psychometric plane and resides in our minds. We can share the same concepts but no two memories are alike, much like snowflakes are all different."

Ahana frowned, but didn't say anything as she digested this.

Talbot continued. "What we are doing here is trying to shut down—as much as possible—the physical part so we can focus on the mental. Then we link our man with the power of the dolphin's natural transmitter."

"What have you achieved?" Dane asked.

"We've been able to remote view anywhere on the planet with a high degree of accuracy."

"Does your man go where he wants to or where the dolphin wants to?" Dane asked.

"That's an interesting question," Talbot said. "Most of the time, the dolphin doesn't seem to"—he searched for a word, then shrugged—"care. Our RVer can tap into its power and project toward a target area. But once in a while, the dolphin seems to be doing, thinking, something else, and the RVer has no control."

"Where do they go then?" Dane pressed.

Talbot shrugged once more. "We don't know. That's

what we call a blackout situation. The RVer sees nothing. We usually shut those down pretty quickly as there's no point in continuing."

"Can you hook me up?" Dane asked. "To a dolphin?"

"I have trained people who can RV," Talbot said. "Tell me what you want my men to do, and we'll get it done."

"I don't think they can go where I want to go," Dane said.

"And where is that?"

"To the Ones Before. And they're not on this timeline or on this planet."

10

The bridge across the Susquehanna had been burned by the locals, which halted the Confederate advance toward Harrisburg. General Lee received this news without comment. His concern was no longer advancing, it was consolidating. His forces were stretched out over a seventy-mile swath of Pennsylvania, and while there had been minimal resistance so far from the local militia, he knew that Hooker had to be moving toward him. He felt he still had several days to prepare, but then came further bad news: Hooker was no longer in command of the Army of the Potomac.

Lee sat on his horse on the side of a dirt road, watching a column of infantry go by as he pondered this latest development. Another general to face. Lee knew Meade, who was to be next in command, the latest in the line that had taken command of the opposing army. Lee absent-mindedly returned the enthusiastic greetings of the soldiers as they filed past. He did note that it was Pickett's division, a relatively new unit overall, most of the men untested in battle. They were Virginians, every single man, and they straightened their backs and lengthened their steps when they saw Lee on the side of the road.

"General."

Lee turned, surprised to see Longstreet sitting solidly on his horse, like a sack of potatoes. Longstreet had never been an imposing figure in the saddle and out of deference, Lee dismounted. Longstreet did the same.

"How goes the march?" Lee asked Longstreet.

The corps commander tugged on his long beard. "The men are well fed. This is good country for commandeering provisions. They have not seen war here."

Lee nodded. He'd issued strict orders for his men regarding appropriating supplies. Civilians were to be paid for everything taken—the fact that the pay was in the AA form of Confederate script, practically worthless even in the South, was not a concern to him.

Longstreet let out a long sigh from deep in his barrel chest, and Lee waited. He knew Longstreet was working himself up to discussing something unpleasant, and Lee had found waiting to be the only way to allow the other man to do it. Prodding Longstreet only made him more reluctant to speak.

"Meade's taken over the Army of the Potomac," Longstreet finally said.

"I know."

"Meade's a solid man. I served with him before." There was no need for Longstreet to say before what, as they both knew. The days of wearing blue in the regular army of the

United States seemed forever ago to Lee. "He'll move," Longstreet said. "And Lincoln will be on him to move."

"Yes."

Longstreet straightened and looked his commanding officer in the eyes. "Do we know where the Army of the Potomac is at the moment?"

So that was it. Lee was not surprised. He empathized with Longstreet's concern because it was his own. "No, general, we do not."

"And Stuart? Our cavalry?"

"I fear that General Stuart is off on one of his long rides," Lee said. "I have sent couriers to find him, but none has returned with news, so I must assume he has ranged a bit farther afield than I had wanted." Or ordered, Lee thought, but refrained from saying.

Both remembered the last time Stuart had gone off with the cavalry on a long ride, completely encircling the Union Army. It was spectacular and daring but also militarily unsound as the cavalry was Lee's eyes. Without Stuart's men pulling reconnaissance for the army, the Confederates were operating almost blindly.

"If Meade is moving quickly—" Longstreet left the rest of the sentence unsaid.

"The Army of the Potomac has never moved quickly," Lee said, realizing even as they came out the danger in such words. "But," he added quickly, before Longstreet could also point out the same realization, "I am tightening the column. I've ordered Ewell's corps to pull back from York."

"To where?" Longstreet asked, somewhat relieved to hear the advance was halting, even if only for a day or so.

"A small town called Gettysburg. I've received a report that there is a warehouse of shoes there."

"The men need shoes," Longstreet said approvingly.

Both men turned as a dashing figure galloped up to them. General Pickett was mounted on a sleek black horse and wore a small blue cap, buff gauntlets, and matching blue cuffs on the sleeves of his uniform jacket. He held an elegant riding crop in one hand. Oddest of all, he wore his hair in long ringlets that dangled about his shoulders, and he perfumed his hair each morning before taking to the field, something Lee found distasteful but had refrained from commenting on, especially as, for some strange reason, Longstreet was very fond of his youngest division commander.

Pickett brought his horse to a halt and dismounted with a flourish. "Generals." Pickett bowed at the waist, which brought a slight smile to Lee's face and a frown to Longstreet's.

"Magnificent, aren't they," Pickett said, indicating his men marching by. "They are ready, sir, most ready to join the fray."

"The fray will come," Lee said. He found Pickett too eager to throw his men into the fray. Pickett had seen combat in the War with Mexico where he had been the first American to scale the walls of Chapultepec, a feat for which he had been widely praised. Pickett had graduated West Point with an undistinguished record in the same class as McClellan, the first commander of the Army of the Potomac, and as Stonewall Jackson. Pickett had been wounded in the shoulder at Gaines Mill, which kept him out of the war for a considerable period of time—too long some whispered. Lee had held Pickett's division in reserve at Fredericksburg as it was filling out with new soldiers after earlier losses when Pickett had not been in command. Both those latter two issues had gotten under

Pickett's skin and he was determined that in the next fray his division would be in the forefront. Lee knew such a thing was more determined by fate than decision, but he refrained from telling Pickett that.

Pickett lifted a gauntleted hand and idly stroked one of his locks, apparently unaware that he had interrupted the two senior officers. "Do you think the Yankees will fight?"

"Those people"—a term Lee often used to describe the Union Army—"will have to fight now that we are on their soil."

"Good," Pickett said.

A sudden feeling of weariness passed through Lee, draining him. He still had a touch of the soldier's curse and this was not the place to be so afflicted. He threw a boot into a stirrup and pulled himself onto his horse, taking Longstreet by surprise. The corps commander obviously still had something on his mind, perhaps a more vocal complaint about Jeb Stuart and the cavalry being missing, but Lee had not the energy for it nor did he wish to discuss such with Pickett present.

"Good day, gentlemen," Lee said, as he pressed spur to horse flank and rode off.

• • •

Meade inherited an army that had known only defeat, not the most comfortable situation. Indeed, so startled had he been to be awoken at three in the morning with the orders putting him in command, that at first he though the courier had come to arrest him and he had racked his brain trying to remember what infraction he might have been guilty of. There were other corps commanders senior to him, so he was uncertain why this task had fallen to him.

Regardless, he knew two things: one was that he had to

stay between Lee's army and the Washington/Baltimore area, and then, second, he had to fix and fight the Army of Northern Virginia. To accomplish the first, he immediately issued orders pulling the bulk of his army North out of Virginia. Hooker might not have been the most aggressive commander, but he had trained the staff and the army well, and he was cooperating fully with Meade. To work on the second, Meade decided to ignore the Confederate cavalry force to his rear and send the bulk of his own cavalry to the northwest to see if they could pinpoint Lee's exact deployment. He knew it exposed his supply line, but he felt his men had enough provisions and ammunition to fight at least one major engagement. Besides, they would be in Pennsylvania, on Union soil, where he could count on some local replenishment of his supplies.

As he rode North with his staff among the long columns of blue troops, a courier rode up to him with a letter. Meade stiffened when he saw the wax seal—it was from the president and the handwritten scrawl on the envelope also indicated it was for his eyes only.

Meade pulled off to the side of the road, getting out of the cloud of dust that traveled with every marching army. With trembling fingers he broke the seal and opened the letter inside. It was short and to the point:

> *General Meade,*
> *The army is yours. Your goal is Lee and his army. In Virginia we attacked and were always thrown back. In Pennsylvania turn the tables. Let him attack. Throw him back.*
> *A. Lincoln.*

· · ·

Lincoln could see the rows and rows of tents of newly arrived troops camped within view in Washington. A far cry from the city he had been forced to sneak into three years previously.

Lincoln knew he had earned the White House almost by default. He'd been nominated by the Illinois Republican state convention as their choice for president in 1860. During the national convention in Chicago, he earned the nomination by maintaining a very careful position between proslavery and antislavery platforms, which doomed his major competitors. The platform he adopted was one that tried to please both North and South, saying that slavery should not be expanded but should not be abolished where it already existed.

Like most compromises, it pleased none of the extremists on either side.

Fortunately for Lincoln, and the Republicans, the Democrats made the mistake of holding their convention in Charleston, South Carolina. The Northern and Southern delegations were at odds from the very beginning. Stephen Douglas was eventually nominated, which so incensed the Southern delegates that they stormed out and decided to hold their own convention, at which they nominated their own candidate, effectively crippling the party's effectiveness.

Lincoln easily won the electoral votes, but had only 40 percent of the popular vote, not exactly the strongest mandate for a leader. He also failed to win a single electoral vote from any Southern state.

The victory was bittersweet for Lincoln and the country, as the Southern militants had been threatening to secede from the Union if Lincoln was elected. In December 1860, even before he could take office, South Carolina

seceded. It was followed shortly afterward by Mississippi, Florida, Alabama, Georgia, Louisiana, and Texas.
These rogue states formed the Confederate States of
America. The lame-duck president, Buchanan, did nothing to stop the secessionist movement, and Lincoln remained silent on the issue, seeing no point in saying
anything until he had the power to back it up. He also
hoped, against what Mary predicted, that Union senti-
ment might reassert itself in the South and the lost states
would come back into the fold voluntarily.

When he headed to Washington to assume office, there
were threats of assassination, so he was spirited into the
city under the cover of darkness, something the opposition
ridiculed once it was found out.

He'd tried, Lincoln thought as he looked out at the soldiers camped in the capital. His inaugural address had
been aimed specifically at the South, to try to allay their
fears and reconcile. He'd flat out said he felt the federal
government had no right to interfere with the institution of
slavery where it already existed. However, he'd also
thrown down the gauntlet, saying he also believed a state
did not have the right to secede from the Union. However,
he'd ended the speech by saying that the government
would not assail the South. He hoped with this speech to
at least keep the wavering states of Virginia, North Carolina, Tennessee, and Arkansas in the Union.

The South, of course, took matters into its own hands
in the place where the Democratic Party had failed to
bring forth a strong enough candidate to challenge Lincoln.

Fort Sumter was fired on, the war was begun, and the
last five states seceded from the Union and joined the
Confederacy.

Pundits in 1861 had said the war would last no more than ninety days and end with Union victory. Mary had disagreed, and Lincoln had privately had his own doubts. Over two years later, Mary's prediction and his doubts had been confirmed. The war had gone more horribly than anyone on either side could have predicted.

And if Mary were to be believed again, it was going to get worse before it got better. How many of those boys out there, Lincoln wondered, would not see the end of the year?

It was a dark thought, something he was prone to, and he went to the couch and lay down on it, his long legs sticking past the edge, and descended into a pitch black pit of depression.

EARTH TIMELINE—XIV
Southern Africa, January 1879

"The Zulus are more dangerous than you think. You must deploy spies far from your front and flanks."

General Lord Chelmsford looked up from the splendid meal laid out on the Twenty-fourth Regimental china with irritation. The man who had just uttered this warning was splattered with mud and wore an amalgamation of uniforms—a British cavalryman's riding pants, a leather coat similar to what the militia wore, and a black hat with a single feather tucked in the brim. There was no indication of rank or even unit. A damn militiaman, one of the local Boers, Chelmsford guessed. He found the locals boring and unsophisticated.

The army was still less than five miles from the Buffalo River despite having crossed it several days earlier.

The track was in bad shape, and Chelmsford had sent his engineers forward to improve it to a state where the artillery could traverse it. The forward elements had already fought a brief engagement with the Zulus, routing them out of a *kraal* that overlooked the track. The position had been taken easily, and a large quantity of sheep and cattle had been captured, several of which had been slaughtered to provide the meal Chelmsford was about to partake of. The feeble resistance put up by the Zulus at the *kraal* had not done much to impress Chelmsford with their martial capabilities.

"And you are, sir?" Chelmsford demanded.

The Twenty-fourth's adjutant hastened to make the belated introduction. "This is Mr. Uys, General. He is a scout in the Boer militia and has much experience fighting the Zulu."

"And do you have much experience leading a column of British regulars?" Chelmsford demanded of Uys.

Even under his deep tan, Uys flushed in anger.

"If your people had done a better job with the Zulu, my people would not have to be here now," Chelmsford added as his steward brought out a covered dish.

Uys nodded, as if he knew something the general did not. "Good day to you, sir." He turned on his heel and exited the tent without another word.

As Chelmsford went back to his meal, Uys paused outside the flap and looked about. Chelmsford's tent was pitched on a small knoll, where the artillery, still hitched to their oxen, should have been deployed. Peering to the north and east, Uys could see a high escarpment—Isandlwana Hill—several miles away. He stiffened. He could swear there was someone up there, highlighted by the almost horizontal rays of the setting sun that came from behind him.

. . .

Shakan saw the militia man leaving the large tent. She felt his gaze touch her even at this distance. The man turned and went to his horse, galloping to the southwest and the Transvaal. Shakan knew he would not return. She was standing on the edge of the Nqutu Plateau to the north of where the British were.

She was worried. The British were moving slowly. Too slowly. She did not know the exact day the battle was to be joined, but she sensed it needed to be soon. She had had the voice in her head all her life, sometimes louder, sometimes just the tiniest of whispers that she could choose to ignore if she wished.

She was alone except for Cetewayo, the Zulu commander. Cetawayo had issued strict orders. The only Zulu south and west of the Nqutu Plateau were those who had put up the token fight at the *kraal* and retreated quickly as soon as they were engaged, a time-honored Zulu tactic to draw the enemy in. It was so time-honored that Cetewayo had hesitated to use it, until Shakan assured him that the British commander would not know of it.

Shakan had spent most of her life alone. Her mother had taken her far to the north, out of the Zulu territories and beyond the reach of any who might want to harm the daughter of Shaka if they learned she existed. They lived simply, off the land, having little to do with the people in the area. Takir had died when Shakan was twelve, leaving her alone. But just before she died, Takir had led Shakan on a strange journey.

To a cave four months' journey away, in the very north

of Africa. A cave where another old woman had been, as if waiting for them. A woman with white skin. But also with the Sight. Shakan had known that as soon as she entered the cave. The old woman had taken Shakan into darkness and beyond, a journey that had both frightened and thrilled the young girl. That was when she had received the first of her instructions from the voice.

Standing here on this escarpment with the king of the Zulus was near the end of a long journey, one that she knew needed to be over with soon. Beyond the coming battle, she could not see nor had she been shown or told anything.

"They are slow," Cetewayo said, echoing her thoughts.

"But they will keep coming," she assured him.

"There is one good thing about their slow movement, though," Cetewayo said.

"And that is?"

The Zulu king smiled. "They will not be able to retreat quickly either."

EARTH TIMELINE—III
Antarctica, July 2078

Two more soldiers had been killed on the second jump, colliding in midair and becoming entangled in each other's chutes. Chamberlain had reluctantly decided that enough was enough. He wasn't even sure their assault would be an airborne operation. The Oracles had never been very specific about exactly what form the Final Assault would take. For all he knew, they might have to walk into battle.

Before he brought the Battalion back to quarters, there

was one last thing they needed to do, a time-honored practice for soldiers about to go into battle: prepare their
weapons.

When the final battles against the Shadow had been
joined, the human armies had been dismayed to find that
their projectile weapons did not work well against the
Valkyrie armor. Bullets, even large caliber, bounced off.
The Valkyries' own spears could cut through the armor,
but to get the spears, they had to first kill a Valkyrie,
something that occurred rarely. By the time they managed
to capture some of the Valkyries and investigate the
armor, the war was over and the gates were closed.

They'd discovered, too late, that the Shadow used nanotechnology in the makeup of the armor, and that projectiles fired at high velocity actually imparted energy to the
molecules that made up the armor, giving them the power
to stop the projectiles. A slow-moving projectile—almost
a contradiction of terms to a traditional weapons expert—
however, could penetrate. The problem was how to make
such a projectile?

The answer was a weapon that had to be able to do two
things: fire a projectile to hit the Valkyries and then con-
tain a secondary load that could penetrate the suit armor
slowly.

Attached to each member of the First Earth Battalion,
on the shoulder of their firing side, was the M-6. Each one
was three feet long, cylindrical, going from six inches in
diameter where the circular magazine was, tapering to a
two-inch-thick barrel from which the rounds exited. The
gun itself slaved to receptors on the suit forearm of the firing arm where sighting was integrated with the suit cameras via the computer. An infrared aiming point was
projected from the gun's barrel and picked up by the cam-

eras. The gun also drew power from the suit because unlike guns that came before, it did not use gunpowder to fire the projectiles but rather an electromagnetic rail system built into the length of the tube.

The cylindrical magazine held eight rounds, which were the key to defeating the Valkyrie armor. Each round was just under two inches in diameter so it could slide down the barrel without having metal-to-metal contact, kept in the exact center and accelerated by the electromagnetic field produced by the barrel on each firing. It took about a second for the barrel to recharge so the rate of the fire of the gun was thus limited.

Each round was a pointed sabot, a casing that held the secondary round that would do the actual armor penetration. The sabot would impact the suit armor and come to a complete halt, stopped by the reactive nanotechnology. A millisecond after being halted, the sabot would split open, revealing the secondary round, which was an inch in diameter. It was a flat-nosed slug that contained a thermal charge that the scientists had discovered could momentarily burn a hole in the armor. The opening was very brief, less than half a second before the nanotechnology repaired it, but it was enough, for behind the thermal charge was the part of the round that killed whatever was inside the Valkyrie suit: a shell that exploded right after the thermal charge, sending a cluster of flechettes through the hole. It was a very complicated system that had taken years to perfect and had yet to be proven in combat.

Chamberlain and his soldiers lined up fifty meters from the base of a long ridge. Engineers had placed targets, both stationery and moving, along the base, and the battalion spent a day firing.

Chamberlain had never gotten totally used to firing the

M-6 after being initially trained on conventional firearms. The silent operation as the round was accelerated down the tube and exited it was strange to him. The only sounds came when the round hit a target and the thermal charge went off followed closely by the flechettes charge, a strange double-pop that was slightly preceded by the flash of the thermal charge as it ignited, then the sound wave reached the firer.

As the brutal sun went down, Chamberlain finally called a halt. They were ready. Now it was a question of when they would get the opportunity that decades of training and development had prepared them for.

11

Dane watched as they lowered the dolphin that was to be his link into the larger tank. It looked none too pleased at being encased in the black suit and rolled a baleful eye at Dane as the derrick put it in the tube filled with thick green liquid. A woman in a wetsuit was on the edge of the tube, holding the large black helmet that would cover the creature's head.

"What's the green stuff?" Dane asked, which he figured was a reasonable question given that he would soon be in it.

"We call it embryonic fluid," Talbot said. "The tanks are important because we use them to reduce to almost zero the physical sensation coming into your brain, allowing you to focus on the mental task at hand."

Dane watched as the woman slid a tube into the dolphin's mouth. The creature did not seem to like what she was doing, thrashing back and forth, occasionally hitting the surrounding glass with a solid thud.

"What's going on?" Dane asked.

"She's putting the breathing tube in," Talbot said. He paused, glanced at Dane, then continued. "That's not the worst part. Watch."

The tube appeared to be in and the woman gave a thumbs up to the scientist manning the console between the two tubes. He hit a button. The dolphin thrashed even more wildly for almost a minute before becoming still.

"What the hell was that?" Dane demanded. He was beginning to have second thoughts about his plan of action. "That doesn't look like oxygen."

Talbot led him forward to a bulky machine that had clear lines coiled around the outside. A pump was moving, pumping a reddish liquid into the breathing tube that led up to the dolphin.

"It's a cooled, liquid oxygen mixture that is pumped directly into the lungs," Talbot said. "We—the navy—perfected it for deep-sea divers so they could handle the pressures at extreme depths. The machine is doing the lung's jobs because once we go into operative mode the autonomic nervous system doesn't function properly anymore, and we can't count on either occupant of the tube to be able to breathe on his or her own."

"I'm going to be breathing a liquid?" Dane asked, knowing the question was stupid as the answer was right in front of his eyes.

"It's not too bad," Talbot said, sounding completely

unconvincing and belying his earlier statement about the worst being yet to come. "Come with me. Let's get you geared up and explain what you're going to experience."

"Great," Dane muttered as Talbot led him along a short corridor to another room filled with equipment and consoles. A cluster of scientists waited, eyeing Dane as Talbot went to a table and picked up a black helmet, the human version of what had been placed on the dolphin. He turned it so Dane could see the interior. There was a thick padded liner.

"This is the thermocouple and cryoprobe liner," Talbot said. "Our goal is to allow you to focus your brain more clearly than you ever have before in your life. More than even the best trained monk. More than any human has ever been able to achieve.

"I was faxed a top secret report from your boss, Mister Foreman," Talbot continued. "In it he described some of the unique aspects of your brain. Your capabilities. We can help you with that. We know about the speech center on the right side and we tap into it with this"—he held up the helmet—"It is indeed the center for a residual tele-pathic capability, which apparently isn't so residual for you and those like you."

Talbot paused and his eyes got a distant look. "If only we had known about you and your kind. We could have—"

"Ditto," Dane cut him off. "If I had known this technology existed, we might have been able to do a better job against the Shadow. But let's stop the what-ifs and get on with it. What are you going to do to me?"

"All right. First we're going to focus on your parasym-pathetic nervous system. This helps the body relax. Your pupils will constrict, heart rate slow, the digestive system shuts down, and—most important—your muscles all relax. We do this by lowering your body temperature."

"How low?"

"Low enough," Talbot said. "Then we give you some juice—electricity. Not much. And only in targeted areas. Thus we can increase brain activity in those areas we want to. And in those areas we don't want to be active we insert a cryoprobe that lowers the temperature in the brain target areas to around ninety-three degrees. The neurons in those areas stop firing."

"What parts of the brain do you shut down?" Dane asked.

"Those connected with the parasympathetic nervous system since those bodily functions are taken care of by the isolation tank," Talbot said. "Every milliamp of power we can save is critical."

"What exactly is the microprobe?" Dane asked.

"A microscopic wire that is inserted directly into the targeted areas of the brain." Picking up Dane's unease, Talbot hurried to continue. "The wire is so small that you won't even feel it go in and when it's removed there is no bleeding. The wire is less than point zero zero eight millimeters in diameter."

Dane sat down in a chair. He felt old and tired. He heard Talbot's next words but didn't really care. Explanation wasn't that important anymore.

"The thermocouple does the opposite of the cryoprobe," Talbot said. "We direct thermal probes into those areas we want to emphasize. The wires we use are so thin you won't even feel them go in."

That did little to reassure Dane.

"After you're in the tank and hooked up," Talbot continued, "we then establish a link between you and the dolphin." Talbot shrugged. "My RVers use the link to draw power. I'm not sure exactly what you're going to do."

Neither am I, thought Dane.

"Are you ready?" Talbot asked.

"Yes."

• • •

Dane stared at the dolphin in the other tank as he was lowered into his own tank. It was a bizarre sight, floating in the water completely still, its head covered with the black helmet and the body with the skin-tight suit.

Dane was surprised that the fluid was warm, given that Talbot had said it would be used to lower his body temperature. He was lowered to neck level, then one of the scientists in a wetsuit climbed to the edge of the tank holding the black helmet and a flexible tube.

Dane reluctantly nodded. The scientist slipped the end of the tube into Dane's mouth. He gagged as it passed into his throat, his body automatically trying to reject the foreign object. He could see Earhart and Ahana watching, and he sensed Earhart's attempts to send him calming thoughts and emotional support.

"Easy," the scientist whispered as she placed a hand on the back of his head, holding him still. His throat was still spasming when the woman nodded. Dane could see the red fluid coming in the tube and it took all his strength to remain still and not rip the tube out of his mouth. He felt a ripple in the tube.

Dane's chest heaved as liquid poured into his lungs.

"Take it easy," the scientist advised. "Try to relax."

That was impossible. Dane was drowning, his lungs filling. His diaphragm heaved as he tried to expel the fluid in a basic survival instinct. To no avail as more was pumped in.

Although Dane knew the liquid contained oxygen and was sustaining him, his body couldn't accept it for several minutes. Finally, however, his body stopped fighting the invasion and became still. Dane suddenly realized that the solution around his body was cold, very cold. They must have been lowering the temperature even as they poured the solution into his lungs.

He couldn't move. He watched with wide eyes as the helmet was slipped on and then his world went dark. He was lowered farther down, until he was completely immersed. He had little sensation other than an overwhelming feeling of cold.

"I know you can hear me," Talbot's voice sounded loud in his head. "The cold feeling will go away very quickly. You're doing all right."

Dane felt a buzzing inside his head and a light flickered in his eyes. He knew he couldn't actually see anything so he had to assume the image was being fed into his brain via the various probes.

"Watch the dot," Talbot said.

Dane focused on the small white spot. He realized it was changing colors, going from white to blue.

"It should be changing colors," Talbot said.

Dane realized he could feel nothing. No sensation at all from his body. It was as if he were asleep yet awake at the same time.

"All right," Talbot's voice now had a distant echo. "Your peripheral nervous system is shut down. We've got control of your breathing and your heart beat. Everything is working fine." Talbot's voice was growing fainter, as if he were moving away. "We're going to—" and then the

voice was gone and there was total silence. There was
only the dot, now bright red.

Then an explosion of pain that blanked out the dot for
several seconds and brought only complete and utter darkness. It felt as if someone were tearing the top of his head
off. Dane wanted to scream, but he couldn't feel his lungs
or throat or mouth to even make the effort. The feeling of
helplessness was overwhelming.

Then the dot was back and the pain began to fade.

And there was noise. A very faint noise. Clicking.
Something Dane had heard before. Where? When?

It was a dolphin. Rachel had made the same noise.

The ocean. Dane was in the ocean, swimming. Not
using arms and legs, but his entire body. The water was
gliding by on his skin, so smooth. He'd never felt so powerful. So free. He could see sunlight glinting above and
darkness below, but he was in a warm band of cobalt blue.
And he wasn't alone. To his right was a dolphin, keeping
pace with him.

It was all so natural that it took Dane a little while to
realize he had the same form as his companion. He was a
dolphin, swimming with thrusts of his flippers. He realized this was the avatar that Talbot had talked about. He
was being projected into the psychometric plane in the
form most suitable to do what was needed.

Dane had no idea how long he swam alongside the dolphin before he remembered why he was here. He turned
toward the dolphin and focused his thoughts. The Ones
Before.

The dolphin halted and floated still, staring at him.

The Ones Before.

The ocean was gone and Dane realized he was in a
tank. Trapped. Darkness. But there was a sound. A steady

throbbing sound. He felt pressure all around. He was moving, he knew that, but how?

Then the pressure was gone, although the sound remained. Dane realized he was not only floating in water but the tank was floating inside whatever enclosure it was in. He realized he was in space, in zero gravity.

Then the sound was gone. There was light, but artificial, not sunlight. All around, from all directions. Dane was moving but he was still in a tube. A long one. The water was pushing him forward.

Then he was in open water, but still under a strange bright light. And there were other dolphins. A half dozen. All around him. Staring at him with their dark eyes.

The Ones Before.

Then Dane understood. As if the information were a bucket of water that was poured into his brain and absorbed by the cells with instant awareness.

The Ones Before.

The Shadow.

And, most important, what he had to do.

12

General Lee was surprised and for once he did little to hide it. "You say the main bulk of the Federal Army is north of the Potomac?"

The spy was covered in mud from a hard night's ride. His face was haggard from both exhaustion and stress. He had just traversed many miles of enemy territory. It was a hard journey on the nerves because he knew that if he were caught he would be hanged immediately. He nodded at Lee's question. "Yes, General. I saw two corps at least." The spy went to the map on the field table and pointed. "Stretched from here to here."

Lee looked at Longstreet. His senior corps commander was the only person in whom he would confide, and he did not need to speak out loud his shock that the Union forces had moved so quickly as he saw it reflected in Longstreet's face.

"And they got a new commander, general," the spy continued. "Hooker got sacked by Lincoln. Meade is in command."

That was one piece of information Lee had already received, although it was not common knowledge throughout the Army of Northern Virginia.

Several of the junior officers gathered in the tent laughed at the mention of Meade's name, and one who had served in the prewar army pointed out that Meade was about as mediocre as Hooker. Lee shook his head, silencing the derision. "I, too, served with Meade. He is not audacious but he will commit no blunder on my front. And if I make one, he will make haste to take advantage of it."

"Then we best make no mistakes," Longstreet said, but Lee was focused back on the spy. "Did you see anything of Stuart? Of my cavalry?"

"No, sir."

It was a question Lee had started asking almost hourly, of anyone who wandered too close to him. Lee switched his attention to the map. As near as he could tell, the terrain between him and the place where the spy indicated the Federals were, was relatively flat with some hills and ridge but no piece jumped out at him as the place to choose for battle. The streams mostly ran to the Potomac, and while there were many, none seemed particularly outstanding from a military point of view as an obstacle. There were numerous roads crisscrossing the area and an army could move relatively quickly if unopposed.

"What direction were the Federals moving?" Lee asked.

"North."

Lee frowned. "A blocking force to keep us from Baltimore?"

No one answered the question as none could know.

"You say two corps," Lee said to the scout. "What about the rest of the Army of the Potomac?" The larger Union Army had seven corps, which meant Lee still didn't know where the bulk of Meade's force was.

The spy shrugged. "I saw only those, but they were moving. The rest might be following or they might be in Washington or they might still be in Virginia for all I know, sir."

Longstreet was now looking at the map. "There are hills to our west."

"I know there are hills to our west," Lee snapped, a little more irritably than he intended. He knew Longstreet wanted to find a nice hill and dig in and wait for the Federals. "The problem is we might sit for a very long time waiting for the Federals to come to us. And our supply line is long and could easily be cut. Meade could sit all summer between us and Washington and Baltimore with interior lines. If only I knew his intentions."

The atmosphere in the command tent was one Longstreet had never experienced before in two years of war. There was an air of uncertainty as Lee stood staring at the map and musing options out loud. Longstreet had never seen the Old Man so indecisive, but he also understood the lack of intelligence due to Stuart's disappearance was weighing heavily on his commander. They were blundering around in enemy territory.

"All the better reason for us to sit tight for a few days," Longstreet said. "Stuart will come back."

"We have the initiative," Lee disagreed. "We must keep it." He reached down with his right hand, fore and middle finger extended. They touched the map on two towns. "Cashtown and Gettysburg. Ewell is already in the area. We will move the rest of the army in that direction. Via Middletown."

"Which town is the primary objective?" Longstreet asked.

Lee kept his fingers on the map. "I'll decide when I reach Middletown." He looked up and tried a smile. "I hear there are shoes in Gettysburg."

One of the division commanders heard this. "If there is no objection, General Lee, I will take my division in the morning and go to Gettysburg and get those shoes."

• • •

Colonel John Buford had an objection to any Rebels coming to Gettysburg. He was a Kentuckian who had served in the Regular Army before the war. He'd fought Indians on the frontier and was already an experienced combat leader when the Civil War broke out. Since the beginning of hostilities, he had seen more than his share of combat. He commanded two brigades of battle-tested Union cavalry. His reputation was as a hard and energetic leader who pushed himself as hard as he pushed his men. He pushed himself so hard, that less than six months after the battle that was approaching he would be dead. The coroner's report would state simply that he had died of exposure and exhaustion.

At the moment, he was very much alive, just west of Gettysburg, looking through his binoculars down the Chambersburg Pike. There were fields on either side of the pike, and his military mind saw an axis of advance that was wide and open, other than for a number of easily removed rail fences splitting the fields. He was standing in the cupola of the Lutheran Seminary that held a commanding view of the terrain all around. He turned and looked back toward Gettysburg.

"This is good terrain," Buford said. His two brigade commanders were next to him in the cupola, waiting for orders. He waved an arm, indicating the road and fields. "Good fields of fire and we have the high ground. I'm sick and tired of charging the Rebels. Let them come to us."

"There is no report of Confederates in the area," one of the brigade commanders noted. "Some of the townspeople said some passed through a few days ago, but then withdrew. If anything, all we'll most likely see is a patrol in the morning. We should be able to hold that off with no trouble."

Buford shook his head. "They're going to come, and they'll be coming in force. Skirmishers across those fields, three deep. We'll have to fight like the devil tomorrow. I can feel it." He shook his head. "Strange thing is we'll be coming from the South and the Rebels will be coming from the North."

He called out for a rider. "Go find General Reynolds. Tell him to come fast at first light. Things are going to get hot in the morning."

Then he spoke to his two brigade commanders. "We will hold here, gentlemen, until Reynolds comes forward. I want a line from there"—he pointed toward a streambed on the right—"up to this ridge, and along the ridge four hundred yards past the pike. Have your men start digging in."

· · ·

President Lincoln was also looking at a map, almost a duplicate of what was on Lee's field table. Reports from

Meade were sketchy at best, but at least the Army of the Potomac was on the move and mostly north of the river after which it was named. The private door opened and Mary came in. She walked to his side without a word.

Lincoln's large hands moved over the paper, taking in the states, from Maine to Florida then westward, all the way to the territories and the Pacific Ocean.

"There is so much potential," Lincoln whispered, "from such a vast land. The world has never seen such a great land, one united in democracy. Who knows what such could do?"

Sometimes Lincoln felt the issue of slavery obscured other, as-important issues. For him, the Union was the most critical thing. He had never allowed recognition of the Confederacy as an independent nation. He wanted them to remain to all in the North, and to the rest of the world, as criminal states in illegal rebellion.

He felt it went beyond just the Union though. The United States was a young country, a grand experiment the likes of which had never been seen on the face of the planet. It was a symbol of hope to those around the world who believed in democracy, in an age where kings and despots ruled almost everywhere else. Lincoln saw the war as a test whether those who ruled via election could also suppress a rebellion.

Lincoln had only those three months of militia time in his youth and thus had little military experience. But as the war dragged on, he began to realize that common sense mattered as much as a West Point education. The first large battle of the war had taken place in July 1861, when the first commander of the Army of the Potomac that Lincoln had appointed, McDowell, suffered defeat at the first Bull Run.

That was when people began to realize that ninety days wasn't going to bring about the end of the war. Two years later, the war still raged.

"It's coming very soon," Mary finally said.

"Are you sure?" Lincoln asked her.

"Yes." She looked at the map and placed a finger on a small dot. "Gettysburg. The storm is gathering."

EARTH TIMELINE—XIV
Southern Africa, January 1879

After four days of road improvement, Chelmsford decided it was time to move forward a bit farther. He sent out a patrol of mounted troops who found no sign of Zulus. It was as if the land had been scoured clean not only of people but of animal life as well. Some of the more observant men noticed there weren't even any birds in the sky, a most ominous token. It was as if the animals and birds knew something they didn't. There was also a feel about the land that none could quite describe but that left an uneasy feeling among many of the men.

Chelmsford had the army move forward to Isipezi Hill, where he set up an intermediate camp. He had the wagons off-loaded so they could be sent back to Rorke's Drift for more supplies. He decided this would be his jump-off point to the next significant piece of terrain, a large bluff called Isandlwana about four miles farther on. While Chelmsford could see Isandlwana, there was much he could not see, as the terrain was full of wide ditches, known as dongas, which criss-crossed the land.

Farther to the north was a large escarpment—the Nqutu Plateau—beyond which one could not see. Several officers expressed concern that a patrol should be sent to the escarpment, but Chelmsford decided against it. If the Zulus came, he felt they would see them in plenty of time to be prepared.

Nor did Chelmsford follow through on standing orders to fortify any camp site. The ground was rocky, making digging difficult, and the supplies that had been off-loaded from the wagons needed to be sorted, something that he felt was a higher priority at the moment.

* * *

At Rorke's Drift a single company of infantry was charged with holding the small outpost and keeping the ford across the river open. Their commander, Lieutenant Bromhead of the Twenty-fourth Infantry, unlike Chelmsford, believed in rules. From the moment they entered the small compound, he'd had his men building walls and fortifying the position.

Rorke's Drift was a Swedish mission station consisting of two single-story thatched buildings. One was the missionary's house, which had been converted into a hospital. The other was a church, which Bromhead had also appropriated and made into a storehouse for the supplies that were to be forwarded to the column when the wagons came back.

When the wagons did arrive, they were accompanied by an engineer officer, Lieutenant Chard, with orders to improve the ford on the nearby Buffalo River. Chard and Bromhead were rather old for their rather junior rank and both had undistinguished military careers that so far appeared to be heading nowhere.

That was going to change shortly.

EARTH TIMELINE—III
Antarctica, July 2078

Chamberlain came awake to Captain Eddings looming over him. "What is it?"

"There is a message from the Oracles."

"A message?" Chamberlain got to his feet. "What is it?"

" 'Be ready.' "

13

Coming back to reality was as painful as leaving it had been, Dane decided. The first sensation was one of intense cold starting from his chest and then spreading throughout his body.

Then came Talbot's voice: "—about two minutes to get the fluid out of your lungs and clear them for air. It will take about two minutes to get the fluid out of your lungs and clear them for air. You should be able to hear me now. Hang in there. You'll be warm and breathing air in just a couple of minutes."

It felt as if his lungs were being ripped out of his chest as the flow on the pump was reversed, and the special breathing mixture was pulled out of them. The pain was

so intense he almost passed out, sliding back into the co-
coon of unconsciousness, but he held on.

Light blinded him as the helmet was lifted off. The
woman who had taken the helmet off, grabbed the tube
and with one smooth movement, pulled it out of his lungs,
throat, and mouth. Dane gasped for air. He felt straps
tighten around his shoulders as he was lifted. The embryonic fluid let go of him reluctantly and with a sucking
noise he was dangling in the air. He was swung over and
lowered.

His knees buckled as his feet hit the ground. Earhart
was there, throwing a blanket over his shoulders and putting an arm around him to steady him. Ahana was on his
other side, also assisting.

"What happened?" Earhart asked as Dane slowly
straightened and got his feet under him.

"I saw them," Dane said. "The Ones Before. They have
a plan that they've been working toward for a very long
time, using several timelines."

"Who are they?" Ahana asked.

Surprisingly Dane laughed. "It's been there in front of
us all the time." He pointed to the other tank where Rachel
still floated. "Dolphins. From the Shadow's timeline. The
first timeline."

"What?" Earhart echoed the confusion they all felt on
hearing this.

"Let's go to the conference room," Dane suggested.
"And we need to link with Foreman so he can hear this.
Because we've got things to do."

• • •

It took fifteen minutes to set up a satellite link with Foreman who was still on board the FLIP. Gathered round the

conference room table were Dane, Earhart, Ahana, and
Commander Talbot. Foreman had suggested doing two
more links to the Pentagon's War Room and the White
House, but Dane had vetoed the idea, saying that they
could accomplish what was needed and bringing in others
would only slow everything down.

"Slow what down?" Foreman demanded, once everyone was ready. His voice echoed out of the small speaker
set on the table and Dane was glad the CIA man was over
a thousand miles away. He could not deny that Foreman
hated the Shadow, but he had also found him to be du-
plicitous, unable to shake decades of operating in the
covert world in his battle against a threat no one had taken
seriously.

"All right," Dane said. "Let me tell you what I saw as
best I can. First, the Shadow. As we feared, it is a human
timeline, not aliens or some strange malevolent force. You
might call them Earth Timeline I. The oldest—well, not
the oldest, but the first if that makes sense, given that the
portals can cut across time.

"Also, as we suspected, it's a timeline that is severely
damaged. They raid other timelines for raw materials,
power, and people for spare parts—as we saw in the
Valkyrie cave in the Space Between." Dane pressed a
hand against his head, trying to sort it all out in his own
mind so he could tell them. While he had been imparted
with a great deal of information in one fell swoop, his
brain could process it only bit by bit, trying to put together
the big picture of a very complex puzzle that they had
been fighting.

"In Timeline I, Atlantis never got destroyed. That's
why the first thing they—the Shadow—did when they
were able to use portals, was destroy all the other At-

lantises in every timeline they attacked. They destroyed ours. Because they believed—believe—only a timeline as technically advanced as theirs can mount a threat to them."

Dan tapped the side of his head. "Those of us with the Sight, who can hear the voices, we are descendants of survivors from Atlantis. Because all Atlanteans had this ability. They were able, the original Atlanteans, to develop equally in both the physical and mental fields. They learned to harness the power of the mind, which led them to harness the power of the planet itself. Which also brought them to disaster."

Dane paused and was greeted with silence. Earhart, Talbot, and Ahana were just staring at him, waiting for him to continue. Even Foreman was silent.

"They tapped into the core of the planet itself for power. But they did it before they were ready to harness it one hundred percent. They made mistakes. They damaged their ecosystem terribly. So badly that they need to constantly replenish their water, air, and other basic elements."

The first question finally came. Foreman's voice came out of the speaker. "Why don't they just go to another timeline? Ask for help?"

"Because, initially, there were no other timelines," Dane said. "Only a handful of humans survived this disaster in Timeline I. They had access to tremendous power and had a much deeper understanding of physics than we do. Someone, one of their best scientists, realized the possibility of parallel worlds." Dane shrugged. "Remember. I got all this from the Ones Before. Even they don't completely understand what the Shadow did. Which came first—the chicken or the egg? In trying to access parallel earths, did the Shadow in essence give birth to the other timelines? Or were the timelines there already and they were able to reach across to them? The Ones Before don't think the Shadow even knows what happened when they pushed the power they had into the Space Between and beyond.

"But they were able to reach other timelines via the portals and connecting gates. Timelines that, if left alone, might not make the mistakes the Shadow had made. Despite their advances, the Shadow were human. They were scared. Afraid that they would be denied what they needed. Afraid of a timeline more powerful than theirs. So they acted like scared humans.

"They attacked first. And they've been doing it ever since."

"The Ones Before?" Earhart asked.

Dane smiled. He looked at Talbot. "This program. The Atlanteans of Timeline I did it too. One man. One true human. Maybe it was you. Another you. They went beyond the International Space Station. They established a base on the moon. They sent dolphins there. For instant communication back to Earth via what you do here.

"When the disaster struck—apparently, something similar to what they almost did here when they tried to tap the core of our planet via the Nazca Plain. They unleashed too much power, power they couldn't control." Dane closed his eyes for a few seconds. "South America was gone. Which then spread to the Ring of Fire. The entire Pacific Rim was gone. All coastal areas were hit with massive tsunamis. Then the Mid-Atlantic Ridge gave way. Iceland, Greenland, gone. The climate changed." He opened his eyes. "They totally screwed their planet up.

But they had an unbelievable amount of power. And with it they developed the ability to travel to other timelines.

"But the moon was cut off. The dolphins did it. With the help of the few humans there. They closed themselves off, totally against what the Shadow began to do. And they've tried to help the other timelines."

"The Ones Before are dolphins?" Foreman didn't sound as if he believed it.

"Yes," Dane said. "They send the messages to other timelines through small portals, ones too small for the Shadow to use. And on a mental wavelength that the Shadow can't intercept or block. And the messages go to other dolphins in those timelines who resend them to humans. Humans like me, the descendants of the original Atlanteans."

"So in a way," Earhart said, "you really are fighting yourself."

"Yes."

Foreman's voice cut into the short silence that followed this. "Okay. So how do we go to Timeline I and defeat them?"

"We don't," Dane said. "That's for others. We have to help them get there."

"Who?" Foreman demanded. "What others?"

"There's a force in another timeline. A dying timeline that the Shadow has cut off from all the portals and abandoned. They fought the Shadow and lost. But they learned a lot fighting them. They've got a unit that can fight the Valkyries."

"But if they don't have portals—" Ahana left the rest of the statement unsaid.

"That's where we come in," Dane said. "And others." He held up a single finger. "First. The Ones Before don't know exactly where on Timeline I Earth the Shadow is holed up. They think there are only a few thousand of them left. So—"

"A few thousand?" Foreman cursed. "They're destroying entire timelines? Killing billions to keep just a few thousand alive?"

Dane knew Foreman had lost his brother in a gate. He himself had lost his Special Forces team in Cambodia through the Angkor Kol Ker Gate more than thirty years ago. Millions more had died since then in the war against the Shadow in this timeline alone. He sympathized with Foreman but he knew they had to accept the reality of the situation.

"The Ones Before have helped Atlanteans in our timeline in their battle against the Shadow. I've seen how the minds of special people, people like me, can redirect power, although the cost is high, resulting in transformation into a pure crystalline skull.

"Our timeline Atlanteans fought a war that spread around the globe until the very existence of life was threatened. And in the climactic battle, the Atlantean priestesses and warriors with the aid of the Ones Before stopped the Shadow, but the price was high. Their home of Atlantis was destroyed. The resulting tsunamis touched every shore on the planet with such devastation that the legend of the Great Flood was written both in the Tibetan Book of the Dead and in the scriptures of the Jewish people on the other side of the world.

"There were survivors in a handful of ships, who scattered and planted the seeds for future civilizations to arise thousands years later. What we call the modern world. The Atlanteans stopped the Shadow but lost their civilization and their home in the process.

"We know that since the destruction of Atlantis, the Shadow has kept a presence on our planet via the gates. Sometimes these gates expand, such as when the capital city of the Khmer Empire in Cambodia was swallowed up by such a gate—the one at Kol Ker which you"—he glanced at Foreman—"sent me into. Sometimes the gates grew larger."

Dane turned to Ahana. "You said something once about the multiverse?"

Ahana nodded. "There are scientists who theorize that there are an infinite number of parallel universes, existing side by side, so to speak. What is called the multiverse. The problem with trying to understand the universe is that we don't really know how it started. If you view time as a line, and we are currently at the right-hand end of it, the universe began at the left hand end and that formation may rely on cosmological evolution that is outside the scope of even the deepest theory we can come up with."

"We have to recon the Shadow timeline," Dane said, "and pinpoint where their base is. Second, we need to power up the sphere. Which means powering up the crystal skulls. Third, we need to get the sphere to the timeline where this force is. Fourth, we then need to get the sphere to the Shadow's world. And, five, at the same time, we need to cut the current power source that the Shadow is tapping."

"Is that it?" Earhart asked. "Just five things?"

Dane had to laugh at the tone of her voice. "Yeah. And even those aren't straightforward. The Shadow guards the portal to their world very closely. So we have to get there in a way they won't expect. That's the bad news. The good news is we've got help out there"—Dane gestured vaguely—"in other timelines."

Dane pointed at Earhart: "You're in charge of getting the skulls powered up." At Ahana: "You're in charge of the power flowing to the Shadow's world." Then at himself: "I'm going to do the recon."

"And how are you going to do that?" Earhart asked.

"I'm going to the Shadow world the same way I went to the Ones Before. Via Dream Land."

"And how am I going to charge the skulls?" Earhart pressed.

"At a place called Gettysburg," Dane said.

14

The Confederates came up Chambersburg Pike and the surrounding fields just as General Buford had predicted: at first light and in force. The first shot of the battle that would be named after the town was fired from a Sharp breechloading rifle by a Union horse soldier. The incoming Confederate division deployed, sending a line of skirmishers in, while one brigade wheeled to the left and one to the right of the pike.

Outnumbered, Buford's men fought fiercely for over an hour, holding their ground, until finally the sheer weight of the oncoming Confederates forced them to withdraw back toward the town. At the same time, General Reynolds, the commander of the Union corps came up and immediately saw what Buford had realized the previous day—this was a good place to defend. And, like Buford, he sent word back for all units to come as quickly as possible.

On the other side, the unexpected stiff defense by the Union cavalry turned a raiding party looking for shoes into a full-fledged attack, and caused the Confederate division commander to send a request for more troops to his own rear.

As Napoleon had said earlier in the century, armies should march to the sound of the guns and as the sun rose on the morning of July 1, every division from both sides within hearing distance of Gettysburg turned toward the town.

Neither side was able to coordinate the events that transpired throughout the morning, as reinforcements rushed in from both North and South and were thrown pell-mell into the battle. The Union suffered the first setbacks as General Reynolds was shot out of the saddle, and the Confederates were able to drive the temporarily disorganized Federal troops out of the town to the heights to the south and east.

Union forces counterattacked and smashed the Confederates back, only to be attacked in turn by fresh Southern divisions. Through midday the battle swung back and forth.

Then Lee arrived at 2:30 P.M. With Ewell's corps already embroiled in the first, Lee rolled the dice and immediately threw then next corps in line, A. P. Hill's into the fight. The Union forces fell back to Seminary Ridge in disarray.

The Union's Iron Brigade from Wisconsin saved the day from becoming a rout by holding their positions, but with an appalling casualty rate of almost 70 percent. Despite their efforts, the Union forces were thrown off of Seminary Ridge, back through the town once more, onto Cemetery Ridge. Here, luck and good leadership played into Union hands as a division had been left on the Ridge since early morning to act as a reserve. The commander had put his men to work building breastworks, although the men, who saw the battle being waged to the north and west, complained.

Those breastworks came in handy, as fleeing Union troops hid behind them and slowly reconsolidated.

From his position on Seminary Ridge, Lee could see the Union position on Cemetery Ridge, and his forces in between. He had been in this sort of position before, with Union forces on the retreat to his front, and he knew what was needed. He sent orders to A. P. Hill to press the assault just as Longstreet came riding up at the head of his corps. He ended the short note with the polite words "if practicable."

"How goes it, General?" Longstreet inquired as he surveyed the terrain ahead through his binoculars.

Lee told Longstreet of the orders he had sent to Hill.

They were still discussing the situation when a rider came galloping back from Hill's headquarters with the corps commander's response to Lee's order. Lee read the note and handed it to Longstreet without comment.

"He's been in the fight all day," Longstreet said, trying to explain Hill's response that his men were exhausted and about out of ammunition, and he would not be able to press the assault as ordered—with greatest regrets.

Lee was already scribbling on another piece of paper which he gave to a rider—the same order, with the same polite ending, this time to Ewell. "We must take that height," he said to Longstreet, indicating Cemetery Ridge and the hasty stone wall that snaked across its crest.

"Sir."

Lee slowly turned to his Third Corps commander. "Yes?"

"They have always come to us," Longstreet said. "Now you've just twice ordered us to go to them."

"Your recommendation?" Lee asked brusquely.

"My corps is ready to keep marching out on the roads west of town," Longstreet said. He knelt in the dirt at Lee's feet and sketched his plan as he spoke. "Let me march hard south and then east. Swing around the Union army. Take up a position between them and Washington. I'll find good terrain for the defense. Meade will have to come to us. This will give you time to disengage Ewell and Hill and bring them around to hit the Union on the flank."

Lee was watching the battle, barely bothering to glance down at Longstreet's dirt drawing. "We still do not know how much of the Union we have engaged here," Lee said. "If Meade is coming at us piecemeal, as I believe he is, we should take the fight to him now. Here. Before he can gather his forces."

Longstreet got to his feet. He glanced up at the sun. "It's late."

"Ewell can take that ridge," Lee whispered fiercely.

• • •

On Cemetery Ridge, General Hancock was slowly sorting out the confused Union situation, repositioning the forces that had been routed from Seminary Ridge and thrown back through Gettysburg in headlong retreat.

"Sir."

One of his division commanders had just ridden up, blood dripping from a wound on his scalp.

"Yes?" Hancock asked, scribbling one order after another and handing them to couriers, all basically saying the same thing. *Hold. At all costs.*

"There's two Confederate corps down there in the town and around it. And my flankers tell me that Longstreet's corps is to the west. We have to pull back."

Hancock had been at the base of Marye's Heights in Fredericksburg. He'd spent a night with a corpse covering his body from the Confederate snipers who shot anything that moved. He reached up and physically pulled the division commander off the horse and dragged him stumbling forward to the stone wall.

"Do you see that? Do you see the field of fire we have here? Those Rebels are going to have to come to us across that." Hancock gave an evil grin. "They'll learn what it feels like before this is over. They'll learn it hard. Get back to your division and hold. I don't care if you lose every man. You'll hold with your dead bodies, damn it. Move."

• • •

The sun was lower and Lee could no longer wait. He finally got on his horse and rode to Ewell's headquarters. He was shocked to find Ewell standing with his staff, no orders for an advance given, no preparation made.

"General." Lee bit the word off. "Did you receive my order?" Lee knew that Ewell was new to corps command. Always before it had been Stonewall who he had sent his orders to. Stonewall Jackson would already be pressing home the assault Lee knew.

"Yes, sir I did," Ewell said. "But I sent a courier to Hill

and he said he could not support my attack. And your order said assault only if it were practicable. And sir, my men have been hard tasked today."

"So have the Federal's," Lee snapped. He pulled up his field glasses and peered up at Cemetery Ridge in the dying light. He could see new unit flags there. Two more Union corps at least.

Lee put a hand on Ewell's shoulder. "The day is about done any way. Take defensive positions for the night. I'll send you orders later for the morning. We'll take it up again tomorrow."

Lee went to his horse and mounted. He paused in the saddle, looking up at the Ridge one last time and the ground in between. His stomach lurched. At first he thought it was the soldier's curse again, but then he knew the truth. The moment—that one moment that comes in every battle and had to be seized—had been lost. The initiative that he had told Longstreet was so important was now gone.

• • •

Lincoln threw the newspaper down on the desk. "They dare call me a dictator."

Early in the war, Lincoln had suspended the rite of habeus corpus, the constitutional guarantee by which a person could not be imprisoned indefinitely without being charged with a specific crime. He'd done it so he could silence many of the most vocal opponents to his policies.

"You do what is necessary," Mary said.

The ever-present map was underneath the newspaper. Even with the war going on, the country was expanding. Kansas, Nevada, and West Virginia were now states. Hundreds of thousands were migrating west. There were real plans now for a transcontinental railroad.

There was a knock on the door, and a courier from the War Department walked in and handed Lincoln a telegram, leaving as quietly and as quickly as he'd entered. Lincoln opened it.

"The battle has been joined."

EARTH TIMELINE—XIV
Southern Africa, 20 January 1879

The center column once more took up the march, moving all of ten miles forward to Isandlwana. The road back to Rorke's Drift was just to the south of the outcrop, passing over a rise between it and Stony Hill. To the north, Isandlwana was attached to the Nqutu Plateau by a narrow spur. To the east was a wide open plain, cut by a donga beyond which there was a conical hill.

Chelmsford deployed his column on the front slope of Isandlwana. He was very pleased with the position as he had excellent observation and fields of fire to the east, the direction from which any Zulu attack might reasonably be expected to come from Ulundi, Cetewayo's capital.

However, once more he did not order the column to take the rudimentary defensive preparations. The wagons were not circled up, breastworks were not built, and no pickets were placed on the top of Isandlwana. Cavalry pickets were sent out by the militia commander, but one of Chelmsford's staff officers recalled them, saying that they were too far away and of no use up there.

The night of the 20th was an uneasy one for the more

experienced men in the camp but it passed without incident.

Already having split his force into three columns, Chelmsford compounded things early on the morning of January 21 by splitting up the center column. He sent mounted troops and sixteen companies of militia under Major Darnell of the Natal Mounted Police to scout to the southeast, searching for the Zulu. His orders were to return before darkness.

Chelmsford himself stayed in camp, spending most of the day in his tent. In the afternoon, he rode out north, to the Nqutu escarpment, where he saw Zulu for the first time—a half dozen warriors who immediately fled. As he rode back to camp, Chelmsford was met by a messenger from Darnell who reported encountering a large force of Zulus, somewhere between five hundred and a thousand warriors, about ten miles from camp.

Most disturbing to Chelmsford was the addendum to the report in which Darnell stated that he was bivouacking for the night in place and requesting reinforcements. Irritated that Darnell had failed to comply to the letter of his orders, Chelmsford denied the request for reinforcements.

That night's sleep was not as restful for the commander of British Forces. He was awoken at 0130 in the morning by another messenger from Darnell. The messenger, who had left Darnell while it was still light out, had had difficulty finding his way back to the main encampment, thus the late arrival.

The message reported that the Zulu force in front of Darnell had been reinforced and now numbered well over two thousand warriors and once more requested reinforcements.

Chelmsford was now in a bit of dilemma. Darnell's

contingent was too small to engage the Zulu force, yet it was large enough to be an attractive target for the Zulus to attack. Chelmsford also had his doubts about the militia element supporting Darnell and their ability to fight. On the other hand, he figured that if Darnell was in serious trouble, he would have withdrawn by now, many hours after the original message had been written.

Tired and irritated, Chelmsford made a fateful decision in the darkness. He decided to send a relief column to Darnell. And he decided to lead it himself. So for the third time, Chelmsford was dividing his column. He split the Twenty-fourth Regiment, ordering half to come with him in the relief and half to remain at Isandlwana on the defensive. He also sent an order for more troops to come up from Rorke's Drift to aid in the defense at Isandlwana.

As the orders were issued, the camp at Isandlwana came to life in the middle of the night. Cursing soldiers geared up, wondering why their sleep had been interrupted. They fell in line, and Chelmsford led them out of the camp toward Darnell.

⬤   ⬤   ⬤

From the Nqutu escarpment, Shakan and Cetewayo could see the activity in the British camp. Cetewayo was confused by the actions of his enemy as they seemed to make little sense. Why had the British general sent a reconnaissance into the open ground to the east when the most dangerous terrain lay exactly where Cetewayo was, to the north? Did the general have a secret plan?

"He is being foolish," Shakan said, as if reading his thoughts.

"No one is that stupid," Cetewayo argued. He had been

told that the British were fierce warriors, with an empire that stretched far and wide.

"You can see it with your own eyes," Shakan said.

Cetewayo knew of Darnell's patrol. It had run into the left horn of his formation. Since the days of Shaka, the Zulu had adopted the bull as the format for their attack. Two horns that attack on either flank and a massive center on which the enemy would be broken. There were variations to the actual tactics—sometimes the center would be weak and pretend to break, drawing the enemy foolishly forward to be swallowed by the horns; sometimes the center would be the only force that attacked while the horns kept the enemy fixed in place for eventual destruction. Cetewayo had not yet determined exactly how he would assault the British, because the enemy general was acting in such an erratic and uncertain manner that Cetewayo could not predict the possible next movements.

"You must wait another night," Shakan said.

"Why?"

"The voice has told me when it should happen."

Cetewayo grimaced. His men were deployed. The left horn had already been discovered by the enemy. His right horn was to the west, on the Nqutu escarpment. And the center, the bulk of his forces, over twenty thousand warriors strong, was just to the north, hidden in a valley. Keeping many warriors in place for another twenty-four hours was going to be difficult even given the Zulu's excellent discipline. Plus, he was not sure what the British had planned.

"I will give you one day," Cetewayo reluctantly agreed, "but only because you have been correct so far in your visions."

He walked away in the darkness to rejoin his warriors.

Alone on the escarpment Shakan pulled her cloak tighter around her body. The voice had told her the day it was to happen. And it had told her that someone was to come to her. Someone she was to help. But who? And where were they?

And what was going to happen on top of Isandlwana? Even this far away from the hill she felt the foreboding evil growing there.

• • •

Down to just one company of infantry, Lieutenants Bromhead and Chard were not happy with things at Rorke's Drift. They'd built up the compound's defenses as best they could, using bags of millet to form walls connecting the two buildings.

Now they waited completely unaware of what was beginning to develop less than ten miles away.

EARTH TIMELINE—III
Antarctica, July 2078

"We have a second message," Eddings informed Chamberlain.

They were in his office, set high in the wall of the large chamber two hundred feet below the surface of Antarctica. From the windows along one wall he could look out into the chamber that housed the bulk of his Battalion. At the current level of alert status every man and woman was present, minus those in the infirmary.

Eddings turned to the map tacked to the other wall. It displayed the current world's surface, a much different view from one a hundred years ago. She tapped a spot on the North American coast.

"We're to move here."

Chamberlain walked over. He knew the spot. New York. Where one of the gates had been during the Shadow War.

"Has a gate opened?"

"Not yet," Eddings said. "But the Oracles assume that if we got a message for you to move your troops there, that one will."

15

Dane had said quick farewells to both Earhart and Ahana as they departed onboard military transport to fly back to the Devil's Sea Gate. Then he had gone back into the Dream Land compound to prepare for his second trip into the psychometric plane.

As the tank was being readied, Dane pulled Talbot aside. "I've got some questions for you."

"What?"

"Where exactly am I when I go over to the psychometric plane?"

Talbot frowned. "What do you mean?"

Dane pointed at the tube. "My body is there. And my mind. But my thoughts, obviously, are elsewhere. But are those thoughts being generated inside my mind, or is some part of me, some essence, actually traveling?"

Talbot nodded, understanding what Dane was trying to ask.

"To be honest with you, we don't really know. Going over to the psychometric plane via Dream Land is transcending to a level that we don't know much about. To be frank, the closest experiences recorded that are similar to it are from people who have near death experiences."

"The long tunnel leading to the light?" Dane asked.

"Sort of. Floating above one's body, looking down on it. No one really knows what those are either. If you think we don't know much about physics, we know even less about how our mind works, which is a bizarre paradox if you think about it. We're trying to understand something that we have to use in order to understand it.

"We've had some RVers panic. Even with the screening we do beforehand. A couple of people have gone over and then become afraid they were never coming back to their bodies. We had to pull them out right away as their bodies began to respond negatively, despite all our attempts at control via the tubes."

"I don't think it takes place all in my head," Dane said. "First, I meet the dolphin."

"Trina, this time," Talbot said. "Rachel's sister."

"Okay. First I meet Trina. Second, I go places I've never been. So either I'm going or someone or something is transmitting those images into my brain."

Talbot waited as Dane struggled with what he was trying to get to. "I'm getting ready to try to recon the Shadow's timeline," Dane said. "So I have to go there. Since the Ones Before don't even know where their base is. So wouldn't that prove that in some manner, I—my essence—is traveling out of my body."

Talbot shrugged. "I suppose."

"My point," Dane said, "is what happens if something goes wrong with that essence? Do I die?"

"Your body will still be here and alive," Talbot said. "The structure of the brain will still be intact, so there's no reason to believe you'd be really harmed if something happens when you are on the other side."

Dane didn't buy it. "There's got to be something that makes us conscious. That makes us human. A core to our selves. The soul you might call it. And that's what's going out there. And if it doesn't come back, I don't care if you have my body in that tube, I don't think there's going to be anybody home."

· · ·

Going under was as difficult, if not worse, the second time around. Part of the problem was he knew what to expect this time, especially in regard to the breathing tube and solution. Dane had always found that anticipating bad things did not lessen their effect for him.

He bore up through the process and soon was once more in the ocean, swimming with the dolphin, whose name he had learned was Trina, Rachel's sister. This part of the experience, at least, was pleasurable as he felt the warm water sliding against his skin as they coursed through the water. He could also pick up a strong sense of intelligence from Trina and a sense of inquisitiveness. He realized that while she had helped him go to the Ones Before, she did not know what he had learned there.

Dane turned to Trina and focused his thoughts.

The Shadow.

With a flick of her tail. Trina backed up several feet, opening the gap between them.

The Shadow.

Trina turned and was moving away rapidly.

Dane gave chase, at the same time projecting the images the Ones Before had given him. Trina finally slowed and Dane went past her and then turned blocking her.

The Shadow.

The fear coming off the dolphin was overwhelming. Dane noticed that the sun was no longer shining above and the water had grown cold—even just the mention of the Shadow was changing the environment their minds had constructed for the worse.

Danger.

The single emotion resonated from Trina through Dane's head.

Danger.

In response he projected reassurance as best he could but it was futile effort. Finally he gave up on that, realizing that if he were on the other side of this, in Trina's position, he wouldn't be buying the reassurance angle either. He wasn't too keen to try to go to the Shadow's timeline either.

He projected the images he had of the Ones Before and that finally seemed to have a slightly calming effect on Trina. Dane had no idea how much time was passing or if any time at all was passing.

The Shadow.

Dane's world suddenly went dark and he lost all sensation. It was different from what he had experienced initially in the isolation tube though, because he felt like his essence was being squeezed down into a tiny space. And moved. He began to get a sensation of movement.

Then he was in a tube, but without form. Just a dot, being moved along. Not in water. But in space. A golden tube that twisted and turned as he was borne along by some strange power through it.

The tube actually felt familiar, and it took Dane a little while to come to the shocking realization that he was inside one of the strands of the sphere map. No. That wasn't right, he knew as soon as he had the thought. He was actually inside a portal line, the real thing.

And then he was slowing, the golden walls not flashing by as quickly. A bad feeling began to overwhelm him. He came to a halt in the tube. The wall opposite him was flickering, with blue mixed in with gold. Whatever the wall was made of was actually pulsing.

Dane remained still for a while, not sure if he was supposed to do something or if the force that had been propelling him would take another action. He knew that force was Trina, as he could feel a strong connection with the dolphin even though she was nowhere in sight.

Nothing. Except Dane realizing the bad feeling was rising and falling in rhythm with the pulsing of the wall in front of him.

He had thought the small golden sphere just a map, but he was beginning to realize that perhaps it was a literal representation on a small scale of what the portals actually were. And he now knew what was on the other side of the wall in front of him—another portal strand, but one that led to the Shadow world.

This was the way in. Slipping from one portal strand to another, avoiding going through the Space Between. And it could only be done by him. Here. Now.

Dane moved forward. When his essence touched the wall, he recoiled from the sheer evilness that hit him.

There was no doubt he was next to the Shadow portal. It was the same feeling he'd experienced before when entering a gate the Shadow used, except magnified. This had to lead to their timeline. And he was beyond whatever blocks they'd put in to keep invaders out.

Dane pressed forward. The wall of the portal he was in seemed to wrap around him, smothering. He had to force himself to accept that his body was back at Dream Land and this was just a thought he was experiencing. It worked. Partially. He was completely wrapped in flickering gold.

Then he was through, into another portal. A wide one, so large he could barely see the other side. As he floated there a large black sphere rushed by—one of the Shadow's crafts. Coming or going? Dane wondered.

Coming, he knew in an instant simply by turning in the direction of the stronger evil sensation. Dane rushed after the sphere. Without form he had no clue how he was moving, he just was.

And the link to Trina was gone. Dane missed her as he moved forward. He'd been a loner all his life and the connection with her, even though she was another species, was stronger than most of the bonds he'd had in his life. There had been his Special Forces team; his dog, Chelsea; and Sin Fen.

Concentrate, Dane reminded himself.

There was something red ahead, silhouetting the massive black sphere. Dane paused as the image was disturbed, as if the sphere were the pupil of a large evil eye. Then the sphere was gone, and all he saw was a large red circle.

Dane came out of the portal through a gate into Timeline I.

The Space Between

"Are you ready?" Earhart asked Ahana. They were in the Space Between having traveled there from the FLIP via submersible. Now they were on top of the submersible, looking at the two Valkyrie suits they'd brought with them to use. The suits were split wide open, an invitation for them to enter, but neither felt particularly anxious to do so. Rachel splashed water with her tail, soaking both women.

"Take it easy," Earhart muttered.

"How do we know—" Ahana began, but Earhart cut her off.

"We follow Rachel," Earhart said. "This is so far beyond us." She shook her head. "We're pieces on the board being moved. We just have to do our part."

"I'm not really sure what my part is," Ahana said.

"You'll figure it out." Earhart lifted a large plastic case in which the nine depleted crystal skulls were set.

Ahana had her own plastic case, which she had packed on board the FLIP. It contained an array of sensors along with her laptop, since she wasn't sure exactly how she was supposed to find the back door or even what timeline she would be going to or time.

"At least you know when you're going to," Ahana said.

"Right in the middle of a battle," Earhart said. "The largest battle ever fought on American soil." She'd brushed up on her knowledge of the climactic battle of Gettysburg on the flight to the FLIP. "You've got to be going somewhere better than that."

16

"It is like a great fishhook," Meade said as he looked at the map of the terrain his senior engineer had just finished sketching.

Meade had arrived at Gettysburg in the dark, around 3:30 A.M., and had immediately been briefed by the senior generals who had fought the previous day's battle. He had already decided on the trip up to hold in place, regardless of terrain. At the very least he was between Lee and Washington, and he planned on keeping it that way. He'd issued orders from the saddle, directing every unit under his command to converge on Gettysburg with all possible haste.

Then, as it began to grow light, he'd ridden the length of the Union line with his generals and senior engineer,

getting a feel for the land. At the very south, beyond the
Union left flank were a pair of hills, Little and Big
Round Top. Both were currently unoccupied by either
Union or Rebel troops. They would be the eye of the
large fishhook. Then Cemetery Ridge extended for two
miles north, the shank, Cemetery Hill was the curve in
the hook and Culp's Hill on the Union right was the
barb. The actual town of Gettysburg lay just to the north
and west and was currently occupied by the Confederates.

Meade felt a thrill of excitement from the morning
ride. It was a good place to defend. He had the high
ground with good fields of fire toward the Rebels. He
also had short lines of communication given that his
flanks curved back. That meant he could resupply his
army with relative ease and also move reinforcements
quickly.

Meade took the pencil from his engineer as soon as the
man was done. The commanding general quickly delineated corps responsibilities on the paper along with specific orders. "Copies to each corps commander," he told
his adjutant.

Throughout the morning Meade had never even considered attacking. Lincoln's admonition still stayed with him,
and he thought the commander-in-chief's advice to be
quite sound. Meade would let Lee come to him.

• • •

Lee was also looking at the terrain and issuing orders
from his position on Seminary Ridge. He also saw what
Meade in his excitement had not paid enough attention
to—that the Union line extended south only to the end of

Cemetery Ridge, but did not encompass the two Round Tops.

"General Longstreet," Lee called out.

His senior corps commander was drinking some coffee from a battered tin cup. He came over, large hands cradled around the warm metal. "Sir."

"Wait a moment," Lee said as a junior officer he'd sent off at first light to conduct a reconnaissance appeared.

The officer rode up and saluted. "General."

"Your report, captain?"

"The two hills are unoccupied, sir. The nearest Union forces are about a half mile away and digging in, showing no indication of moving."

"Very good." As the captain left, Lee turned to Longstreet. "Take your divisions south and then attack northeast and seize those hills. Once you have them, I will coordinate for Hill's corps to attack on the Union center while you force his flank. Ewell will hold our left; and then once the enemy begins to break, I will send him against Culp's Hill."

"Yes, sir."

Lee put a hand on Longstreet's arm. "You must make your preparations and movement undetected. I do not want the Union to know your objective."

Longstreet frowned as he looked to the south. "It's pretty open land there. I'd have to swing wide, behind this ridge. That will take some time."

"Take the time," Lee said. "The Federals have interior lines. If they know your objective, they can get there first."

"Sir."

Lee looked tired in the early morning light, his face tight and drawn. "Yes?"

"Let me go straight for the hills," Longstreet suggested. "By the time the Federals react, I'll have them. With two divisions, I could hold them against three Union corps."

"Please do as I've ordered, general," Lee said.

Longstreet realized the discussion was over. He saluted and headed for his horse.

• • •

The corps that Meade had given the left flank to was General Sickles's. He, unlike the other generals, was not impressed with Cemetery Ridge, especially as the southern end was the lowest. He felt the slight incline was vulnerable and looking to his front saw an elevation on which there was a peach orchard, which he felt would provide his corps with a better defensive position.

Seizing the initiative, Sickles ordered his corps forward to occupy the peach orchard before the Confederates could take what he now considered very important terrain. So the Union left flank began to march to a position a half mile in front of the rest of their forces.

The next corps commander up the line was shocked to see his own flank becoming exposed as Sickles's men moved forward. He sent a messenger to Meade to inform him of this potentially disastrous turn of events. By the time Meade rode down to straighten things out, literally, it was too late. Sickles's corps was already occupying the peach orchard and was in contact with the Confederates.

Meade demanded of Sickles why he had moved forward, beyond the positions which Meade had personally drawn on the map that morning.

Sickles's response was straightforward. "Sir, this is favorable high ground."

Meade had slept less than an hour in the past several days and had little patience. "General, this is indeed higher than the ground you were on. But"—Meade pointed to the west—"there is higher ground yet in front of you and if you keep advancing you will find constantly higher ground all the way to the mountains!"

Meade could feel the excitement he'd experienced earlier in the morning as he'd reviewed his positions start to slip away as the sound of firing began to rise from the peach orchard. Sickles's foolish move had apparently cast away the advantage.

* * *

In reality, Sickles's foolish move turned out, in the freakish way of combat, to save the day for the Union forces as Longstreet's corps ran right into a Union force in the peach orchard where they had expected nothing but a clear road on their circuitous route to assault the Round Tops.

Like Meade, Longstreet cursed as he heard the firing at the front of his columns. To follow Lee's orders, he'd been forced to turn his corps around and march back up the Chambersburg Pike to the northwest to get out of sight of the Federals. Then he'd turned his troops south. This had taken him the better part of the day and it was now afternoon as his men ran into the unexpected Union presence.

His lead division commander, General Hood, realized the situation immediately. He saw the undefended gap between the Union forces in the peach orchard and the main line and the two Round Tops still unoccupied. He sent a runner back to Longstreet, requesting that he be allowed to change directions and attack through the gap, straight for the hills, even as his forces become more and more embroiled with Sickles's corps.

The answer was no.

Hood sent a second runner.

The answer was no. Longstreet was determined to follow Lee's orders to the letter.

Hood sent a third runner with a note, officially protesting the order, something he had never done in two years of heavy combat.

The answer again was no.

Hood decided to ignore his orders and do what his military common sense told him, but he had already lost valuable hours requesting permission.

. . .

Amelia Earhart came out of the eight-foot-high black circle, floating less than six inches above the ground. She was in a forest. Alone. She unsealed the Valkyrie suit and carefully stepped out onto the ground. Behind her, the gate that had opened slowly shrunk to a small dot and disappeared. She had to hope that the Ones Before would open it back up again when she needed to leave.

She cocked her head. There was thunder in the distance.

She looked about as she removed the plastic case from the Valkyrie's pack. She needed a place to hide the suit. She decided the easiest thing to do would be to put it where people didn't ordinarily look—up. First she hid the plastic case with the skulls between some boulders, piling leaves on top of it.

Then, climbing a tree, she pulled the suit up on a short

tether and secured it high in a tree, pretty much out of sight from the ground. She paused high in the branches, remembering how as a child she used to climb trees all the time in her first attempts at getting up in the sky. She'd always enjoyed being above the ground. She was close to the summit of the hill and through the adjoining trees she could see some of the land around her. She was just below the crest of the hill, on the southern side. To the south was another hill, slightly higher. Earhart cocked her head. The thunder was persistent and she finally realized it wasn't thunder. It was cannon fire.

Then she knew exactly where she was. Little Round Top.

* * *

Jeb Stuart was finally back. There was firing all along the front as Stuart arrived, exhausted from five straight nights of marching. Lee's staff fell silent as the dust-covered cavalry commander rode up. The stare with which Lee greeted Stuart was as cold as any had ever seen their commander give.

"General Stuart. Where have you been?" He didn't give Stuart a chance to immediately respond. "I have not heard a word from you in days, and you are the eyes and ears of my army."

Stuart stiffened. "I have brought you one hundred and twenty-five wagons and their teams, General."

"Yes, General, but they are an impediment to me now."

Stuart's head dropped and all in earshot turned away, pretending not to hear. As if sensing the profound effect his harshness had had, and that the battle was far from over, Lee stepped forward and put a tender hand on his cavalry commander's shoulder. "Let me ask your help

now. We will not discuss this any further. Help me defeat
these people."

• • •

The lead units in Hood's division were two regiments
from Alabama. They made a beeline for Big Round Top,
and except for a handful of Union snipers that they
quickly ran off, found the hill undefended. They charged
up the hill and took it in a few minutes.

The commander of the Fifteenth Alabama looked over
to the next hill, Little Round Top, and saw no activity on
it. His men were tired from charging up the hill, so he
gave the order for a short period of rest before they would
resume the attack and seize Little Round Top.

• • •

There were some Union soldiers on Little Round top, not
far from where Amelia Earhart was hiding her Valkyrie
suit. Meade had not completely ignored his left flank and
sent his chief engineer, General Warren, there to ascertain
the terrain and the possibilities for defense.

Warren was astounded to find only a handful of signalmen on the hill, and these were preparing to leave hastily
as they had seen the gray wave sweep up Big Round Top
and knew they were next. Warren ordered the signalmen
to stay in position and sent runners off, one to Meade and
the other to Sickles, recommending that troops be sent immediately to hold Little Round Top.

Once more luck and good leadership played a role as
one of the runners passed by Colonel Vincent's Third
Brigade. Vincent had the runner show him the message he
carried and recognized the importance. Disregarding the
orders he had received earlier, Vincent ordered his thirteen

hundred men toward Little Round Top, at double time, with Colonel Joshua Chamberlain's Twentieth Maine in the lead.

. . .

From her vantage point, Earhart saw it all unfold and with what she had studied on the flight from San Diego to the Devil's Sea Gate, she knew the history of what she was witnessing.

A wave of blue came rushing in from the east and raced up the hill and then partly down the western and southern sides, halting in a thin defensive line. Directly below Earhart was the Twentieth Maine, now the southern-most end of the Union line, facing to the south in a curving line.

Fewer than five minutes after Chamberlain's troops arrived in position, the Confederates from Big Round Top arrived at the base of the hill and began charging up the steep incline, weaving their way through the trees, undergrowth, and boulders.

The men from Alabama ran right into the men of Maine. At stake was the entire fate of the Union Army, because if the Confederates could turn the Twentieth Maine, they would turn the flank of the Union Army and accomplish what Lee had set out in the morning to do.

Earhart watched as the Confederates charged, to be met with close-range volley fire from the Union lines. The effect of the 50-caliber minié balls fired from the muzzle-loading rifles was devastating. Even a hit on an appendage caused so much trauma that many men died from such wounds. The screams of the wounded and dying mixed in with the rattle of musketry. Earhart felt as if she were in some strange, dream world as the air around her filled with gunpowder smoke, forming a man-made cloud that cut visibility down to less than a hundred yards.

Again and again the Confederates charged, and again and again they were thrown back by Chamberlain's regiment. Each time, though, like the incoming tide, the Rebels got closer and closer to the Union lines. The ground was littered with casualties, in some places so many that the charging men had to run across the bodies of their comrades.

Earhart could not believe that men could stand such carnage, yet the men in blue stood tall, firing steadily, and the men in gray kept coming. Another Confederate regiment joined the assault. The toll on the Union line began to show as the left flank slowly began to give ground, step by bloody step, back up the hill.

Soon the Twentieth Maine's line was so bent that it represented a V, with Earhart's tree exactly at the point juncture and Chamberlain almost directly below her, issuing orders. Among the shouted orders, and screams of the wounded, a new yell began to be heard—Union soldiers calling for ammunition. Over twenty thousand rounds had been fired and bandoliers were growing empty. Earhart saw men stripping the dead of their ammunition, even darting forward and taking weapons from the Confederate bodies in front of their line.

The situation was reaching a critical point as the Rebel tide fell back once more, readying itself for another charge, the lines less than thirty yards apart. Earhart was watching Chamberlain, knowing what was to come, something that if she had not read it, would not have believed possible given the dire circumstances of the Union forces.

Chamberlain gathered his company commanders

around him and gave his orders quickly, trying to take advantage of the brief lull before they were attacked again. The shocked looks on the company commanders reflected the audacity of Chamberlain's plan. Despite their surprise and misgivings, the officers went back to their men and relayed the orders.

Sunlight glinted off steel and the Maine fixed bayonets. With a yell, and Chamberlain in the lead, the left branch of the V, began to charge downhill. In less than ten seconds they were into the startled Confederates who were hiding behind trees and rocks, gathering their strength and courage for the next charge.

Men finally broke. The Confederates had charged uphill, again and again, over the bodies of their comrades, into a withering fire, and they could take no more. The Rebel line broke and ran, the Twentieth Maine sweeping down among them.

Earhart watched as a Confederate officer offered his sword to Chamberlain in surrender even as he pointed a pistol at the Union officer's head and pulled the trigger. The gun was empty and Chamberlain knocked it from his hand, sending him back with the detail that was gathering the prisoners.

Little Round Top was clear of Confederates and the Union left flank was secure.

Earhart stayed hidden in her tree and hoped that when nightfall came she could climb down and reclaim the skulls. This brutal fighting had to have charged them, of that she had little doubt.

She wanted no more of this fighting.

· · ·

The news coming from Pennsylvania was spotty at best. Lincoln sorted through telegrams, but could not get a feel for what was happening as many of them were contradictory. The South was attacking in some. The North in others. Meade was retreating. No, Lee was retreating. Stuart was reported riding on Washington.

"Tomorrow," Mary said.

"More death?"

"Yes," Mary confirmed. "But also hope."

EARTH TIMELINE—XIV
Southern Africa, 21 January 1879

Wrong. Ahana remembered Amelia Earhart's last words to her before they parted; that she had to be going to a better place than Gettysburg. And she now knew those words were dead wrong.

Ahana came out of the gate into night, but there was enough moonlight to see that she was surrounded by thousands of Zulu warriors. Cries of alarm were sounded at the sudden apparition of the white creature coming out of the black circle, floating a few inches above the ground.

Within seconds she was encircled by a ring of warriors brandishing short, wide bladed spears. One jabbed it forward, the point bouncing off the Valkyrie suit armor. The blow slowly spun Ahana about and as she turned she could see that she was in a valley and the ground was literally covered with warriors, thousand and thousands of them.

She brought the suit under control and raised her arms in the universal signal of surrender, but that didn't stop a half dozen warriors from trying to skewer her. Their efforts were to no avail as the blades didn't even scratch the hard white shell she was encased in.

After several minutes the warriors moved back, leaving a ten-foot-wide empty circle around her. Ahana wasn't certain what to do. The strange stalemate continued for thirty minutes before the circle parted and two people stepped forward. One was an old man, obviously someone of great importance given the deference the warriors showed him; the other was an old woman, wearing a long cloak and with a crystal amulet around her neck.

The two had a rapid discussion with much waving of arms, before the old man barked out some orders. The circle around Ahana widened to fifty feet as the warriors pulled back, the old man going with them. The old woman remained and she mimicked Ahana's gesture, raising her empty hands above her shoulders.

With no other option, Ahana unsealed her suit and exited.

If she was surprised to see a woman, an Asian woman at that, come out of the suit, the old woman showed no surprise. She smiled and pointed at herself.

"Shakan."

Ahana imitated the gesture. "Ahana."

The woman indicated she should follow. Ahana tethered her suit and the case attached to its back. She followed Shakan out of the valley, the warriors parting in front of them with many curious glances.

Ahana had no idea where she was, although between the warriors and the terrain she suspected somewhere in southern Africa. Given the weaponry the warriors had, she also guessed she was sometime in the past.

They came up out of the valley and Ahana could see

they were now on a large east–west escarpment. There
was a rocky hill to the right, several miles away on which
she could see the glow of campfires. There also seemed to
be some activity there, as torches ran to and fro. Shakan
led her to the left, toward a conical hill.

As they moved across the plain toward the hill, Ahana
noticed that the eastern sky was beginning to lighten,
bringing a new day.

                    •   •   •

With Chelmsford gone, the camp at Isandlwana was under
the command of Lieutenant Colonel Pulleine. If things
had been bad under Chelmsford, they were worse now as
Pulleine had never seen combat. He also had the problem
of guarding a camp that was much larger than the force
that remained in it, as he still had the tents for the men
who had marched off with Chelmsford.

The camp sprawled over nine hundred yards long,
along the front face of Isandlwana. Besides the tents,
Pulleine was also saddled with over one hundred wagons
and the animals that pulled them. He had five companies
of the Twenty-fourth Infantry and nine companies of the
Native Natal Contingent along with assorted other elements left to him.

Pulleine wasn't completely incompetent. He put out a
screen of mounted troops to the north and east, along with
a closer line of infantry pickets. As the sun rose, he spread
his remaining troops along the line he had to hold. One of
his company commanders pointed out that the line was
spread too thin to offer an effective defense using volley
fire—the forte of the British Army—but Pulleine pointed
out that he had no other choice, short of leaving part of the
camp uncovered.

Shortly before 8:00 A.M., one of the mounted soldiers rode in from the northeast reporting a large Zulu force moving across the Nqutu Plateau. Pulleine immediately sent a runner after Chelmsford and pulled in his infantry pickets, leaving the mounted men still out. He ordered stand to.

Then came confusion as Colonel Durnsford finally arrived from Rorke's Drift with his column. Given that Durnsford outranked Pulleine, there was some issue over who was in command. Worse, while Chelmsford had ordered Pulleine to hold his position, Durnsford did not feel those orders applied to him. Given that Durnsford not only outranked him but was a more experienced officer, Pulleine was more than willing to hand over command to Durnsford. Durnsford dogged the issue by telling Pulleine that he and his command would not be staying in the camp. All could see small scattered parties of Zulu on the plains to the east, and Durnsford was determined to ride out and clear the ground of the enemy.

A more experienced and aggressive officer would have pointed out to Durnsford that he had been ordered forward to Isandlwana by Chelmsford, and the orders from the commander for the force at Isandlwana was to hold the defensive, but Pulleine said nothing. The two sat down for lunch, indicating that they did not take any threat very seriously at the moment.

Even when a patrol came in with two Zulus they had captured, and the two said that the entire Zulu army was close by the camp and preparing to attack, the two British officers were not alarmed. Pulleine sent another messenger after Chelmsford while Durnsford got his command ready to move. He asked Pulleine for two companies of infantry for support. Already stretched thin, Pulleine initially demurred but finally gave in, further depleting his force. However, Pulleine's adjutant protested so forcefully that Pulleine reversed his decision just before Durnsford left.

At noon, Durnsford rode off to pursue the Zulus on the plain even though he had just been told by the prisoners that the Zulus were coming to the British.

Pulleine ordered his mounted pickets to be more vigilant and move farther out. Thus putting in action a series of events trying to protect his command that would lead to its destruction.

• • •

Standing on the top of the conical hill, Ahana could see the movement of every player in the game except the massive army she had left in the darkness, which was still hidden in the valley to the north.

Using hand signals, Shakan indicated to Ahana that battle would not be joined until the sun had set and risen once more—the next day, which did little to calm Ahana. She could see parties of Zulus moving here and there, along with various British columns. She had a good idea of when and where she was, although she did not know if this were her own timeline or another one. She had vague recollections that a major battle had been fought by the British against the Zulu nation but she could not recall the outcome. Shakan was little help as they did not speak a common tongue and the Zulu woman could not predict the future, although she did know a great battle was coming.

Ahana wasn't certain what all this had to do with finding a back door into the Shadow's timeline. While Shakan watched, she opened the pack of equipment she had brought and began trying to determine if there was any-thing out of the norm in the area that she could pick up with her sensors, particularly focusing on scanning for muons, the telltale of a gate and Shadow activity.

She immediately picked up muonic trace activity to the west in the vicinity of Isandlwana. Not enough to in-dicate a gate, but enough to indicate the Shadow was ei-ther coming or had left. Ahana had no doubt it was the former.

. . .

Cetewayo had agreed with Shakan that the attack be on the following day, but it did not sit well with his impatient warriors. Keeping twenty thousand men crammed into the narrow valley was proving to be a chore. He was forced to send small foraging parties out to gather water and food for the main force. One of those parties, driving some cat-tle before them, were spotted by a mounted patrol from Isandlwana, which gave chase.

Cetewayo was almost grateful when the mounted pa-trol came chasing the foraging party over the edge of the ravine and saw the valley crammed with Zulu warriors. It was hard to say who was more surprised.

Cetewayo did not hesitate though as he gave the order to attack. He knew he had lost the element of surprise and waiting would only allow the various British columns to consolidate.

Twenty thousand Zulu warriors surged out of the ravine toward the south. As they moved, the force sepa-rated into three columns, the two horns taking form on the flanks and the massive center moving straight toward Isandlwana five miles away. As they moved, they were engaged by the mounted patrols to their front, which were forced to pull back against the overwhelming force bearing down on them. The front of the center force of the Zulu army was over a mile wide as it advanced toward Isandlwana.

. . .

Pulleine did not greet the reports of the incoming Zulu army with particular alarm although he was concerned. He felt confident that his British regulars would bear up well against force from the savages that came against it. The Twenty-fourth Infantry were veteran soldiers, tough and well-disciplined. They came from rough backgrounds and made a home in the army. They were part of an army that was world renowned for being able to stand fast on the battlefield and fire precise, controlled volleys into enemy lines, blowing huge gaps in them. They were armed with breechloading Martini-Henry rifles, which gave them a fivefold increase in rate of fire over their predecessors who'd had muzzle loaders.

Even as he prepared his defense, a rider came from Chelmsford with an order for him to strike camp and follow after the commander. Seconds later a breathless rider came in from the north, stammering about a horde of Zulus coming. The man's descriptions of the size and numbers of the force he claimed to have seen made no sense to Pulleine who could not conceptualize such a large force.

On the plain, Durnsford was the first British commander to actually see the Zulu army coming. The left horn was cresting a ridge directly in front of his column and he estimated its number to be roughly five thousand warriors. He immediately ordered his column to reverse direction and head back toward Isandlwana.

. . .

The conical hill that Ahana and Shakan were on was like an island amid a storm, as the left horn of the Zulu army swarmed around, splitting at the base and passing by on either side.

Ahana turned to Shakan with a questioning glance. The Zulu had said the battle would not be until the following day. Ahana's instruments were spread out on the ground and so far had picked up nothing other than the muonic trace activity. She hurriedly began to gather them up but Shakan put on hand on her arm and indicated for her to wait.

Dark clouds were moving in overhead, indicating a storm was coming.

. . .

Pulleine could now hear heavy firing to the north where his mounted troops were, but still could not see anything in that direction. To the east he could clearly see Durnsford's column retreating under pressure from a large body of Zulus. This put Pulleine in another dilemma as he was torn between positioning his force to face what sounded like a large threat to the north and supporting Durnsford's retreat to keep it from becoming a rout.

Pulleine hedged. He ordered one of his company of regulars to swing to the east and stretch their line toward Durnsford. Then he had the companies facing north extend their lines even farther to cover the new gap.

There were two major problems with his new alignment though. One was that his line was stretched to a point where volley fire would not be as effective as it normally was. The second was that his lines were now almost a thousand yards away from their ammunition wagons.

As the main Zulu army came onto the plain, even the veterans among Pulleine's troops were shocked. The front was now several miles wide and twelve men deep. It came toward Isandlwana like an unstoppable tidal wave.

Pulleine's artillery began engaging the Zulu center at maximum range. Many warriors fell to the shot, but it did not slow the advance.

Durnsford's column reached the company that Pulleine had extended. The British front now extended from just below the crest of Isandlwana, arcing right in a quarter circle to the east. Against the twelve-deep front coming toward them, the British companies were formed two deep, with the front rank kneeling. Also there were large gaps between the companies.

Still, when the Zulu center came within rifle range, the British volleys were devastating to the front ranks. Hundreds of Zulus went down. The advance wavered, halted, then resumed. The volleys of lead poured into the Zulu line and the attackers wavered once more, then dove to the ground en masse, less than three hundred yards from the British lines. The British gave no mercy, firing at the prone figures, killing many more.

At the very rear of the Zulu lines, some of the warriors even began to change direction, but this movement was checked immediately by Zulu commanders who had the first to turn slain in their tracks. The few Zulus armed with rifles returned the British fire, but their aim was poor and most rounds passed harmlessly overhead.

On the right flank, Durnsford's men managed to halt the left horn, also with well-disciplined fire. Of the right horn, there was no sign and in the heat of battle none of the British could spare the time to be concerned about the missing part of the Zulu army.

It looked as if the day would be won for the British as they continued to pour hot lead into the halted Zulu army prostrate before them.

Except for the slight problem of ammunition.

Runners were sent back from the line companies, scampering back to the wagons where the quartermasters had the rest of the regiment's bullets. But a quartermaster is a man trained to be responsible for the supplies he has signed for. In the long run back to where the wagons were and in the confusion of battle, runners didn't have time to seek out their specific unit's quartermasters. Too far away from the front line to realize the pending danger, the majority of the quartermasters refused to issue bullets to men not from their own unit, who could not rightfully sign for such.

Instead of the usual nails, screws had been used on this particular lot of ammunition cases and there was a distinct lack of screwdrivers among the wagon train. Also, the bullets were stored in heavy wooden containers designed to sustain damage, thus making them difficult to break open. So even when desperate troopers shoved aside the furious quartermasters, they had a difficult time getting the cases open.

* * *

Ahana and Shakan could see the halted Zulu line like a thick black snake frozen to the ground. And they could hear the volleys being fired every few seconds and see the gunpowder smoke floating over the thin red line of British troops.

How long could the Zulu army just lie there and allow themselves to be slaughtered? Ahana wondered.

. . .

The change was ever so slight, but to those being shot at, very noticeable. The volleys were not as swift and there were less firers. Something was wrong in the British lines.

Zulu war leaders sprang to their feet and urged their warriors forward. As the Zulu center rose to their feet, the right horn appeared to the British rear, having run all the way around Isandlwana and cut the road leading to Rorke's Drift and then turning toward the British camp.

The battle, which the British had appeared to have under control just a minute earlier, immediately changed character.

With Zulus to his rear, and out of ammunition because none of the Twenty-fourth Infantry quartermasters would issue bullets to his men, Durnsford's command fell apart. His officers were running about the camp desperately searching for ammunition while the men gave up their positions, reasoning that if they were not able to fire, they might as well flee.

Sensing his line unraveling, Pulleine told his bugler to signal retire, hoping to reform his lines closer to the camp and the wagon train. It was a decision made a minute too late. As the British lines tried to disengage the front ranks, the Zulu center struck. Brutal hand-to-hand fighting broke out.

The British regulars tried to fight with bayonets in their squares. And they took their toll on the attacking Zulus, but one by one, the small islands of red were swarmed over.

Finally, seeing the inevitable, Pulleine ordered the adjutant to carry the regimentals to safety. The adjutant rode off with another lieutenant who was wounded. They were both run down by Zulus and killed as they attempted to get to the Buffalo River and safety.

. . .

There were no more figures in red standing. That was clear from as far away as the conical hill on which Shakan and Ahana stood.

With shaking hands, Ahana checked her instruments.

The muonic indicator was beginning to show an increase in activity.

At her side, Shakan stood perfectly still. Eyes looking beyond the battlefield, head cocked as if she were listening. There was a loud peel of thunder. Shakan grabbed Ahana's shoulder and pointed.

At the very top of Isandlwana there was an unnatural dark cloud that seemed to have lightning inside of it.

Ahana glanced at her instruments. The muonic reading was off the chart.

. . .

Chelmsford did not believe the reports that came to him. The camp overrun? Everyone dead? Zulus pillaging among the dead?

Impossible. He'd left almost two thousand men in the camp.

Chelmsford finally turned his column toward Isandlwana. He came close to the bulk of Isandlwana just before and halted his column just short of it. He forbid his men to enter and led a contingent of officers forward to ascertain what had happened. The silence foretold bad news, but what their eyes beheld under the moon and star light shocked them.

Most of the bodies were stripped naked. Their bellies were sliced open, which was actually a sign of respect by the Zulu as they believed it allowed the spirit to escape and go to the afterlife. At one place in their camp a circle had been made of a dozen men's heads, all peering at each other with lifeless eyes. Every living thing, including oxen, horses, even an officer's dog, had been slain.

Where were the Zulus?

Looking up he could see the strange dark cloud atop the peak.

Chelmsford ordered his men back away from the mountain.

· · ·

Shakan tapped Ahana on the shoulder and pointed to the southwest.

"What?" Ahana asked, even as she uttered the word knowing the other woman couldn't understand. She was still focused on the top of Isandlwana.

Shakan pointed once more to the southwest. "Rorke's Drift," Shakan said, words that meant nothing to Ahana.

The Japanese scientist did notice though, that a small red light was flickering on one of her monitors. There was just the slightest trace of more muonic activity somewhere not too far away from Isandlwana. Ahana picked up the detector and slowly swung it back and forth until she had the direction from which the signal was coming—the southwest.

Shakan nodded. "Rorke's Drift."

· · ·

The diamond lattice field deep underneath Isandlwana was now one hundred percent connected. The power of desperation from the last stand of the British force on the slopes of the hill flowed into the planet, much deeper than their blood had. It gave the necessary power for the field to become a self-sustaining crystal, one that now generated its own power.

Power that flowed upward to the gate on the top of the mountain, that directed the power into a portal that led directly to Timeline I.

EARTH TIMELINE—III
New York City, July 2078

Colonel Chamberlain IV remembered traveling down to New York City while he was attending West Point for many fun-filled weekends. Now he was circling above what remained of what had once been the greatest city on earth.

He could see the top one hundred feet of the towers for the George Washington Bridge—which had once linked New York and New Jersey—poking above the waves as his MK-90 swung down low along the course of what had been the Hudson River but was now part of the Atlantic Ocean.

To his right, some of the towers of Manhattan that were tall enough to reach above the water dotted the skyline. To his left, the top of the Palisades, the cliffs that had once lined the Hudson on the Jersey side, were still above water. There was no sign of Manhattan south of what had once been the Central Park area—no skyscrapers poking above the water. Chamberlain remembered watching im-

ages of what happened to the southern tip of New York
City during the end of the Shadow War. A large sphere had
floated above the city and pulverized the tip of Manhattan
repeatedly, blasting a hole into the ground that afterward
was measured to be almost six miles deep. It had immediately filled with water and historians and scientists had
speculated to no avail why the Shadow had done this
strange version of overkill.

The plane banked toward the Palisades as the wings rotated up, to provide lift as it decelerated. They touched
down and Chamberlain walked off the back ramp as his
visor snapped down into place.

Why here? He wondered.

17

EARTH TIMELINE—I

Dane's essence floated in the swirling red mist that represented the atmosphere in Timeline I. Whatever they'd done to their planet, Dane thought, it had been extreme. Even the light was wrong, he realized after a few moments. The large black portal that he'd come out of was directly behind him, floating above a sluggish, gray ocean.

Dane froze.

Evil all around.

The human essence corrupted. Warped and twisted.

The immediate source was obvious. There were hundreds of Valkyries, spears in hand, floating in the air all around the portal. Also several large platforms hung in the air, with no visible means of support. There were large devices on board each, manned by a half dozen Valkyries, which Dane had no doubt were very powerful weapons of some sort. Oriented at the portal.

This was not the way to come, Dane thought.

And they didn't see him or sense his essence in any way, he realized. But he was powerless. So he did not matter. He was no threat.

Where was he?

The ocean was completely flat, no waves, no swell. The water looked—the word that came to Dane was *heavy*. Not normal. And it went as far as he could see in all directions.

Dane looked down. There had to be a reason the portal was here.

Dane descended. He paused just above the turgid water. One more terrible thing to endure among all the other things he'd had to so far.

Dane got angry. Who were these people who made up the Shadow to do these things they had done? To destroy entire timelines to keep this worthless existence alive? Living in a world that was bereft of beauty? Of purpose other than to exist?

Dane plunged down into the oily, thick water.

What light there had been quickly disappeared but Dane continued downward. He had no sensation of swimming now, just movement. He had no idea how long he descended, but soon a light appeared ahead, growing brighter as he got closer.

Dane came to a halt.

There was a city below, enclosed in a huge clear shield. A magnificent city with a golden palace in the very center, with a main tower that had to reach almost a mile upward, ending just short of the very center top of the shield. From Dane's perspective above, he could see that there were numerous other golden buildings surrounding the palace, then a ring of water—fresh water he assumed. Then a ring of land on which there were white, smaller buildings, apparently homes. Another ring of water enclosing that. To the right was something that appeared out of place, an add-on—a large black building, like a warehouse, and a tube that extended out of the clear shield to a gigantic latticework of black, in which nested at least a dozen of the large black spheres that the Shadow used to traverse the portals.

Dane continued down, passing through the clear shield, which was not clear when seen from the other direction. He paused, slowly taking in the panoramic view of bright blue sky with a few lofty clouds visible and the sun shining. On the edge, where the shield met the ground, there was a surrounding ocean. Not the dirty diseased one that surrounded the city completely, but a clean one with waves running across its surface.

This was how Atlantis must have looked in its heyday Dane realized. It might have been swallowed by the ocean because of their mistakes, but the Atlanteans of Timeline I had used their technology to at least visually re-create what they had once known.

But where were they?

There was no movement in the city that he could discern.

Dane headed toward the center tower. Despite the horrid atmosphere of corruption and evil that he was picking up, he had to admit that it was spectacular. He estimated it was almost a mile high and the surface glittered in the false sun that was projected onto the inner surface of the shield.

Dane passed inside near the very top, speculating that

if it was occupied, someone would be near the top. After all, why build such a thing if not to be above it all?

He was in a spiral corridor that was wrapped against the outer wall of the tower and went up a slight incline. The corridor was about fifteen feet wide and Dane could only assume it went all the way to the base below and to the tip just above. On the outer wall, the view was clear— obviously the Shadow had perfected a means to make a material that was opaque on one side and clear on the other.

Dane halted, looking out over the city. It was most impressive and it was false. He thought it summarized what the Shadow had developed into quite well.

Dane followed the spiral corridor upward. As the tower narrowed, so did the corridor, and the turn tightened. The corridor ended abruptly and he floated into the base of the top of the needle. It was an open space, a hundred meters wide at the floor, narrowing to a point more than four hundred meters above his head.

Filling the chamber was a latticework of gold spheres, each about three feet in diameter, attached to each other by thin tendrils of gold. It was mesmerizing and Dane stared at it for quite a while. He estimated that there were several thousand gold spheres, all linked together.

His first guess was that perhaps this was some elaborate work of art or some sort of religious symbolism to the Shadow. Who knows how they had developed from the other timelines since the time of Atlantis?

Dane had been guarding himself against the bad feelings given off by his environment ever since coming into the Shadow portal. But now he lowered this mental barrier a little to get a feel for this strange place. It was a barrier he had perfected as a child to keep the emotions of others at arm's distance from him. He'd learned early in his life that he was different from others, able to sense things normal humans weren't.

He snapped the protection back in place immediately as he realized, with a power that knocked his projected essence backward, what exactly he was looking at: those golden spheres were the Shadow. Each one contained an original Atlantean, his or her mind, in a timeless existence.

And now they knew he was here.

18

Darkness fell but the fighting did not abate. Lee had grudgingly accepted that Longstreet's flanking attempt had failed to the right. He had watched thick smoke from furious fighting float off of both the Round Tops throughout the afternoon, but just before dusk it was a Union flag that still flew at the very top of Big Round Top.

Still, there was some success there as Sickles's exposed corps, badly battered, was thrown back out of the peach orchard and sent tumbling back to the main Union line. By this time, Ewell and A. P. Hill's corps had managed to bring themselves on line in the center and north, preparing to coordinate with the flanking maneuver of Longstreet. Despite the latter's failure, Lee did not want to give up the initiative and allow the Union troops the chance to counterattack.

At Lee's command, Ewell's artillery opened fire from Seminary Ridge toward Cemetery Ridge. The response from the more numerous Northern guns was instant and furious. Within twenty minutes, Ewell was forced to silence his guns and pull them back behind the cover of the ridge to keep his men from being destroyed by the counter-battery fire.

On the Union right flank, the Union corps occupying Culp's Hill had had the better part of the day to prepare their positions as had the troops along the length of Cemetery Ridge. Still, Lee issued orders for an attack. By the time the orders were disseminated down, night was falling across the land. The focus of Lee's thrust was the Union right, from his own left, at the juncture of Cemetery Ridge with Culp's Hill.

Initially, the attack did not go well as the terrain was difficult to move across in the dark. Then Union batteries began firing, inflicting heavy casualties on the advancing Confederates. Still, the Southern forces came forward and then found a reprieve as they reached the base of the ridge and hill as the Union guns on top could not depress their angle of fire to hit them any more.

The ebullient Rebels, glad to be out of the artillery fire charged uphill, striking the Union lines. They were soon in among the artillery itself and hand-to-hand fighting broke out. Meade counterattacked immediately with his reserves, and the exhausted Confederates, having already charged forward over a mile under heavy fire and engaged in heavy combat, fell back before the fresh Federal troops.

The situation began to get confusing in the darkness as neither senior commander could tell exactly where his forces were. In some places, Union units fired on fellow Union units in the confusion.

Gradually, the men of both sides simply decided the day was done. Units pulled back to their original lines and despite the horrific casualties of the day, neither side could claim victory.

At Lee's headquarters, Lee was grudgingly accepting the pause of night. He had launched night attacks before, but this situation was simply too confused and his units too scattered to do so now. He felt he still had the initiative though, and considered his plan for the next day.

Despite Lee's optimistic thoughts, the reality of the situation was far different. The Army of the Potomac was massed inside the fishhook, new units arriving all day, until over eighty thousand Federal troops were crowded into a defensive position less than three miles long. Lee's forces, numbering fewer than fifty thousand, was stretched around the fishhook in a line almost five miles long. Meade also had three hundred and fifty artillery pieces to Lee's two hundred seventy-two. Dividing men and gun totals by mileage of front, Meade had an overwhelming force advantage.

There was another problem, one that the last attack on the left had clearly shown—his troops might be able to breach the Union lines, but to gain victory he would have to be able to sustain the assault. In fact, Lee's victory over Sickles's exposed corps on the right had shown the problem also.

Lee stared at his map in the flickering light of a lantern. The headquarters was bustling as couriers came and went, but around Lee there was a reverent circle of silence as his staff waited for him to do what he always had before— come up with a brilliant plan that would defeat the Federals.

The circle was broken as Longstreet walked up. Old

Pete was the last person Lee wanted to see right now. He felt his subordinate commander had not pressed the attack sufficiently during the day on the Round Tops or at the Union left. Lee sensed that Longstreet was almost sulking after having been rebuffed in his tactical suggestions repeatedly. What Lee did not know was that Longstreet was indeed upset, not only from having his suggestions rebuffed but also from having spent the day doing the same—as per Lee's strict orders—to his own subordinate's pleas for the ability to maneuver farther to the south around the Union flank. His lead divisions had thus thrown themselves into futile frontal attacks that had been smashed with high casualty rates.

Elements of Longstreet's corps had seen their most brutal of the war in places like Little Round Top, the peach orchard, the wheat field, and Devil's Den. Most of his divisions had been chewed up badly, to the point where they were almost combat ineffective. Some had taken almost 50 percent casualties. Longstreet was proud of the fighting his men had done but not happy with the results as the line had little changed other than throwing Sickles back.

As exhausted soldiers on both sides collapsed to the ground to catch much needed sleep, the two army staffs waited for orders from their commanders. Longstreet came to Lee's headquarters to see what devilment the next day would bring and, for one more time, to make his own case.

"How is your corps?" Lee finally looked up from the map and acknowledged Longstreet's presence.

"They fought well," Longstreet said. "My adjutant has the initial casualty figures and gave them to your adjutant." He paused, but Lee did not ask, so he continued. "We lost many good men today."

"So did the Federals," Lee said.

Longstreet felt what little energy he had left drain out of his body. He sat down heavily on a camp stool, not even interested in looking at the map. He knew the terrain now by memory.

"You have an intact division," Lee said. "One that has not yet entered the fray."

Longstreet nodded. "Pickett came up just before dark. I held him back as it was too late for him to join the fight."

"Good," Lee said.

"Do you remember what we did last year at Gaines' Mill?"

Longstreet blinked, not quite believing what he was hearing. "Right up the center?"

"The Union lines are solid," Lee acknowledged. "They're packed along that damn ridge tight. *But*"—Lee emphasized the word—"last year they had the same type of position at Gaines' Mill on Turkey Hill. Hood smashed right into them and once he broke the line, their collapse was complete."

"Hood's wounded," Longstreet said. "The surgeon thinks he'll live, but he's out of the fight."

Lee looked to the east, as if he could see Cemetery Ridge in the dark. "We break them there, we can run over their entire army. They're packed in there so tight, they won't be able to retreat.

Longstreet found Lee's logic strange, looking only at a possibility instead of the initial reality of what it meant for the Union forces to be so tightly formed.

"I also have two divisions from Ewell that saw little action today," Lee said. "Pickett will make the initial assault and breakthrough. Then Ewell's men will finish the Union men."

Lee smiled. "And Stuart's cavalry is on the way. Two of his brigades will be here tomorrow. We'll be able to chase the Federals all the way to Washington in disarray."

"Sir," Longstreet finally said, "the only advantage to the position we hold now is that we can abandon it with relative ease in the morning."

Lee's head snapped around toward Longstreet as if he had been struck a blow. "Retreat?"

"Disengage, and then flank Meade," Longstreet argued with little conviction, knowing the decision had already been made.

"Pickett will do it," Lee said. He stood. "I am going to get some sleep."

Longstreet watched his old friend walk to his tent and disappear inside. It was only then that Longstreet realized Lee had issued him no orders nor sent any out.

. . .

Across the way, Meade was meeting with his corps commander, contemplating doing exactly what Longstreet was suggesting—pulling back. He'd even had his chief of staff draw up orders for a withdrawal earlier in the evening. All that was needed was to hand them out.

The day had been bloody and long. While Meade had initially felt very confident about his position and army, having repulsed the Southern attacks all across his front, as darkness grew, so did his doubts. Lee was over there and who knew what the Virginian planned for the morning?

They met in the small parlor of a house the army had commandeered. Twelve generals crowded into a room less than ten feet by twelve to discuss the future of the Army of the Potomac. There was a card table in the center on which a map was placed, lit by two sputtering candles.

Meade began the meeting in a way Lee would have never considered, saying he would follow the course of action the majority of those in the room agreed on. He posed three questions to his generals, which they would vote on:

1. Should the army remain in position or retire to a position closer to their lines of supplies?

2. If they remained in place, should they attack or await Lee's attack?

3. If they decided to stay on the defensive in the current position, how long should they wait?

It was a strange meeting, one that West Point had certainly not taught as the proper way for an army commander to operate. But Meade was shaken by the casualty lists that were coming in to his headquarters and he felt it best to give some responsibility for the decision on the army's course of action to the men who had seen the combat firsthand that day and whose men were the names on those lists.

The vote went quickly. On question 1 it was unanimous that the army stay in place and not withdraw, indicating the confidence all of the generals felt in their positions. The vote on question 2 was also unanimous, that they should remain on the defensive and await Lee's attack rather than leave their positions and attack Lee. Only on question 3 was there some disagreement, and Meade realized those who favored staying longer had seen less combat whereas those who wanted a shorter wait had seen more that day.

Meade ended the meeting by telling his generals that

they would remain in place. He dismissed them all but General Gibbon, who held the center of Cemetery Ridge.

"If Lee attacks tomorrow, it will be on your front," Meade told Gibbon.

Gibbon was surprised. "Why do you think that?"

"Because he has made attacks on both our flanks and failed," Meade explained. "If he decides to attack again, it will be in the center, which he has not seriously tested."

Gibbon smiled grimly. "I hope he does come. Because if he does, we will defeat him."

. . .

Amelia Earhart waited until long after darkness fell to leave her tree. The Union lines had moved forward, leaving her in the company of the dead from the battle earlier in the day. Occasionally distant shots rang out, but other than that there was an eerie silence, given that so many men were gathered within a half dozen miles of her location.

She reached the ground, pulling her Valkyrie suit with her on its tether, and moved toward where she had hidden the crystal skull case. She stumbled over a corpse, the man's arms extended upward in some last plea, and locked in place like that. She found the boulders and dug through the leaves, pulling out the case. With trembling hands she lifted the lid.

There was a faint blue glow deep inside each of the nine skulls. Very faint.

If today had not been enough, what more was needed?

Earhart immediately knew the answer to that because she knew what the next day would bring and she knew where she had to be with the skulls. She closed the lid on the case and began carefully making her way down the hill to the north, pulling the Valkyrie suit behind her. She considered putting it on, but thought she was better off presenting herself as human rather than a strange white creature if she ran into anyone. When she passed a cluster of bodies, she forced herself to go over them. Strapped to one of the corpse's back was a spade. She removed it and took it with her.

As she cleared Little Round Top, she walked onto a long field with knee- to waist-high grass. To her left were the Confederate lines, hidden in a treeline. To her right, on the high ground, were the Union forces. Campfires clearly delineated both lines but there was little sound.

Earhart made her way about a mile and a half north, then stopped. She put the plastic case on the ground. She looked right, toward the stone wall of the Union lines, then left to the treeline. She was about equidistant between the two.

There was a small farmhouse, its roof ripped off by artillery fire and the walls smashed and mostly knocked down. On the eastern side she found a small storm cellar for storing goods, accessible through an opening covered with a thick wooden plank. As quietly as possible, she pulled the plank up and peered in. She slid the shovel inside, then followed it. It was not large enough for her to fit with the case and suit.

Earhart began to dig.

●　●　●

"They are fighting in earnest," Lincoln said as he shifted through the mound of telegrams on his desk. As the day had changed into night, the situation had become a little clearer. "All around Gettysburg is as you said it would be," he added, glancing up at his wife.

Mary Todd Lincoln was in the middle of the room, seated on a couch. Her head was back and her eyes were closed. She was in the midst of one of her migraines and although Lincoln had insisted she take to bed, she had refused.

"As near as I can tell, reading general-speak," Lincoln continued, "today was a stand-off with heavy casualties on both sides. The latest cable from Meade says he will hold his ground. Now if General Lee would oblige and attack him, tomorrow—this day, actually—might bring some conclusive result."

"What happens here," Mary said, "what happens now, is not as important as the larger war, the larger battle."

"It matters to the men who will fight the battle," Lincoln said. "Those who will die or be maimed for life."

Mary opened her eyes. "I know. But, not only will there be a greater goal achieved but this will change the tide of the war. Our war."

"Will it end it?"

Mary Todd Lincoln closed her eyes once more. "No."

The emotion behind that single word hit Lincoln in the chest and remained there, a heavy weight. For the last two years the cry had been to have peace by Christmas. By his wife's tone he knew now there would be no peace by this Christmas. The tide may change today but it would be a long time going out.

EARTH TIMELINE—XIV
Southern Africa, 21 January 1879

Ahana packed her gear up while Shakan waited. There were campfires on the plain below Isandlwana, whether

British or Zulu, she neither knew nor cared. Against the dark sky, there was a blackness on the top of Isandlwana.

Ahana threw the backpack over her shoulder and nodded. Shakan led the way off the conical hill and toward the pass to the south of Isandlwana.

As they reached the plain, a small war party of Zulus suddenly appeared out of a donga, brandishing their spears, the metal covered with dried blood. One of them ran toward Ahana, ready to strike.

Shakan stepped between them and raised her hand. Surprisingly, the warrior came to a complete halt.

"You will let us pass," Shakan ordered.

The warrior backed up, but one of his fellows did not. The second warrior cocked his arm back to throw his spear, when the leader of the party cut him down before he could let loose.

The leader waved his spear, indicating they could go by.

· · ·

Having the bulk of Isandlwana between their location and where the battle had taken place meant that the small group of soldiers manning the missionary outpost had not heard any of the battle that had just been fought. Bromhead kept his men at work, improving the defensive position and also preparing some of the supplies to be loaded on the oxen wagons that were supposed to come from the main camp.

Chard had gone over to the camp at Isandlwana in the morning to get further orders and returned about noon. He'd then gone back to work with a platoon of Bromhead's infantry, improving the ford.

At a quarter past three in the afternoon, they received

the first indication that something was wrong as two riders appeared, pushing their mounts hard. Chard hurried back to the station, arriving just as the riders did.

Chard and Bromhead stood shoulder to shoulder just outside the mealie bag wall the men had built as the two riders pulled up. They were from the Natal National Police, locals, and both looked as wide-eyed as their mounts.

"They're gone," one cried out.

Chard glanced over his shoulder, noting that some of the men were edging closer to the wall, trying to hear what was happening.

"Easy, man," Chard said, as he stepped forward and took the man's reins. "Who's gone?"

"All of them. Isandlwana. Every one of them. Dead."

"Chelmsford?" Bromhead asked, confused about who exactly the man was referring to.

"No," the man gasped as he tried to catch his breath. "Chelmsford took off with a column. Those he left behind. All of them. The Zulus wiped them out. There's thousands dead."

"Lower your voice," Bromhead hissed, knowing it was already too late, that the word was spreading through their camp.

"Where are the Zulus now?" Chard asked.

The man gave a hysterical laugh. "Coming here. Right this way. Thousands and thousands of them. We saw them." The man gestured vaguely to the northeast. "On the march. Coming fast."

"All right," Chard said. "Take your mounts into the station—"

"To hell with you," the man jerked his reins, pulling the bridle out of the Chard's hand. Before another word could be said both men were galloping away.

"That was helpful," Bromhead said.

Chard turned and looked back the way the men had come. There was no sign of the Zulu, but as an engineer he knew this terrain could hide an entire army until it was just about on top of them.

"We have quite a few sick and wounded," Bromhead said.

"And?" Chard asked as he used his binoculars to take a closer look, searching for a dust cloud, any sign.

"We have some wagons," Bromhead said. "We could evacuate to Helpmakaar across the border."

"We didn't respect the border," Chard noted, "what makes you think the Zulu will respect it?"

"There will be more men at Helpmakaar to help defend."

"We'd never make it," Chard said. "We're better off here, with some walls, then out on the track. Let's finish the defensive preparations."

There were a couple of things they had not done yet, since it would require damaging the buildings, but Chard saw no option now. Rifle loopholes were knocked in the walls of the buildings. He also directed the mealie bags and ration boxes that had been stacked to load onto wagons that apparently were never going to come, to instead be used to build up a final wall, a last outpost in front of the storehouse where they could retreat to if the outer wall was breached.

It was clear that word of what the rider had said had already spread throughout the camp. Men worked with a high degree of earnest, while many a worried eye was cast to the northeast. Chard sent out scouts to the nearby hills to give them some warning.

Even as the scouts moved out, everyone noted a cloud

of dust approaching rapidly along the track that led to Isandlwana. Bromhead ordered the men to stand-to, and they exchanged mealie bags for weapons.

They were not needed as the incoming forces were recognized as cavalry as they got closer. Approximately one hundred men, militia, came galloping up, not even slowing as they raced by the camp, despite Chard's attempts to get them to. Obviously, they knew what was coming and had no desire to hang around.

"It's your damn country!" Chard yelled at one of the officers as he tried to intercept him.

"It's your damn war," the man yelled back as he lashed his horse.

As quickly as they had approached, the cavalry was gone.

"This is getting a bit awkward," Bromhead observed. Chard silently agreed. The native contingent in the camp was restless, muttering among themselves. Muttering turned to panic when one of the outposts came running down hill toward the station, crying out a warning.

"Here they come! Black as hell and thick as grass!"

That was all it took for the native contingent to bolt after the other who had already fled. Several of the British regulars, outraged, fired at the fleeing militia, killing a few.

Chard saw no reason to make an issue of this fratricide. His command had just been more than halved in the space of a few minutes. As he shouted orders, realigning the defense to close the gaps just created, he sensed first, rather than heard, something in the distance. So, apparently, did everyone else, as the station came to a standstill.

There was the slightest vibration in the ground. Then there was a noise. The nearest Chard could describe it was like a locomotive engine in the distance—a rhythmic pounding. It took him several moments before he realized what he was feeling and hearing: the Zulu army on the march, coming this way.

The right horn of the Zulu army came over the high ground to the northeast, more than four thousand strong. Their spears had not tasted blood at Isandlwana due to the roundabout march, and they were eager for the battle. Technically, Rorke's Drift was not a target in Cetewayo's plan, but the commander of the right horn felt he had enough flexibility in orders to swing this far out of the advance. The station was simply too tempting a target, obviously lightly defended. Also, it represented the missionaries who had corrupted many of the people.

The Zulu force did not halt on the high ground but came straight on, deploying from column to wide front for the attack while on the move, an example of their superb training.

There was no time for a plan, Chard knew as he watched the Zulu come on, nor was one needed. They had to hold in place. As soon as the front of the Zulu line was in range he gave the order to fire.

The massed volleys did their job, smashing into the ranks of Zulu warriors, killing and wounding many. But the ranks behind leapt over their fallen comrades and kept coming.

The odds were not good for the small outpost. There were slightly over one hundred defenders while there were thousands of attackers. And some of the Zulu also had rifles, scavenged from the edges of the Isandlwana battlefield as they had passed by. As the main force charged, a cluster of Zulu riflemen fired down into the camp from a nearby hill. Their fire was terribly inaccurate, yet they did hit an unfortunate few British regulars.

Volley after volley rang out from the British walls, yet the Zulu kept coming, useless shields held in front of their bodies, their shoulders hunched, in the way all men advanced against fire, as if moving into a fierce wind.

"Independent fire," Chard called out as the Zulu got within one hundred yards of the wall, allowing each man to fire at his own pace. He pulled his pistol out and checked the rounds, then cocked it. He drew his saber with his other hand and waited for the inevitable.

. . .

Shakan and Ahana reached past the track that crested between Isandlwana and the next hill to the south. Ahana had her Valkyrie suit tied off to her waist now, pulling it along as she moved. They had been hearing the fire for a while and now they could see the cause. The missionary station was a small island of red surrounded by a surging black sea. As they watched, the sea hit the island.

. . .

The defenders of Rorke's Drift had two advantages that their comrades at Isandlwana had not had. First, they had tighter lines, allowing better volley fire. And second, they were behind a wall. As each Zulu reached the wall, he had to lower his shield to try to climb over. As he did so, he left himself vulnerable to British steel. Bayonets glinted in the setting sun as British soldiers spitted Zulu warriors on their bayonets as they tried to climb into the compound.

Still, numbers counted. Here and there, the outer wall was breached and Zulus poured into the compound. They were met with more volley fire as Bromhead rushed to and fro with a platoon that he would form up wherever there was breach. And when the volley fire wasn't enough, the platoon would charge, shoulder to shoulder, bayonets in front, to push those Zulu still alive out of the breach and reseal the perimeter.

The battle raged for what seemed like hours, days, to the participants, but in reality was little more than a half hour, before the Zulu finally managed to breach the outer wall in so many places that Bromhead's platoon could not seal them all. Darkness was falling, but the battle was well lit by the burning hospital roof.

Most of the patients had already been evacuated from the hospital to the storarge building by that time. But some men were still in there as the roof burned and Zulus began to surround the building. Chard realized the outer wall was lost and ordered a withdrawal to the final outpost near the storage building, unfortunately abandoning the hospital in the process and the men trapped inside.

The situation was further exacerbated by the fact that the rooms of the hospital did not have inner connections, only opening to outside doors. As the Zulus broke into the end room, the British inside were forced to use a pickax to cut through the internal walls to create an opening to the next room in order to retreat, dragging their wounded with them.

Those who fought the rear guard action in this room-by-room retreat were overwhelmed and hacked to death as Zulu swarmed over them. A handful of men managed to make it to the other end of the building in this manner and then dashed across the open ground to the final outpost.

. . .

Shakan and Ahana were making their way closer to the besieged station. In Ahana's hands was her muonic detector and as they closed the distance, the reading got stronger.

Shakan put out a hand and halted Ahana. The Zulu woman pointed. About three miles from the station, a column of British soldiers was approaching. Even as they watched, though, the column came to halt, seeing the glow of the fire ahead and hearing the firing.

Ahana noticed that the amulet that Shakan wore around her neck was beginning to emit a faint glow. Shakan noticed it too and wrapped her hand tight around the crystal.

. . .

On the roof of the storehouse, Chard also saw the column. He'd climbed up there in a brief lull in the battle, as the Zulu pulled back to prepare another assault. Thankfully he was the only one who could see the column, because as he watched, it turned and headed back the way it had come, obviously assuming either everyone at the station was dead, or that they could do little to help.

Chard watched the last of the soldiers disappear in the moonlight with a heavy heart. The Zulu had smashed the entire outer wall and were just on the other side, preparing another attack.

He had no doubt they would come again and again until they wiped out every living soul.

. . .

Ahana and Shakan reached the rear of the Zulu force assaulting Rorke's Drift. Lifting her crystal amulet high,

Shakan cried out for the warriors to let them pass. As they made their way forward the glow from the crystal grew brighter and the muonic reading on Ahana's instrument was beginning to spike.

Ahana's instruments gave her some idea of the amount of power that was flowing through the Isandlwana Gate. She knew this was the latest tap by the Shadow to draw power to itself.

She just didn't see how she could do anything about it. If anything, this battle at Rorke's Drift was adding more power.

EARTH TIMELINE—III
New York City, July 2078

Colonel Chamberlain had the MH-90s deployed along the Palisades, using the craft as temporary lodging for his battalion. He'd sent out patrols, both on the ground and in the air. Not that he expected trouble, but one thing that had always concerned him was that the Final Assault didn't necessarily mean it would be his forces attacking the Shadow—it could also mean the Shadow attacking this timeline for the last time and completely wiping it out.

Shortly after the patrols had gone out, he received an alert that an aircraft was inbound. Chamberlain suited up and went outside to await its arrival. It was a cargo plane and it landed along the remains of a highway that had once run along the top of the Palisades. Chamberlain remembered driving on the same road while a cadet at West Point, heading south, away from the academy on leave, happy to be free for a short while, and later driving north back to school, usually on dark Sunday evenings, anticipating another week. At the time, his major concern had been passing his classes and making it to graduation.

So much had been lost.

The cargo plane landed and came to a halt. The back ramp came down and Chamberlain was surprised to see the Oracles on board. The High Priestess walked off, black robe tight around her body and a black veil covering her face. Captain Eddings, in full combat gear, was at her side.

Chamberlain switched to tactical frequency to talk to Eddings so the Oracles wouldn't hear. "What the hell are they doing? Those robes aren't exactly the best shields and they're breathing unfiltered air."

"I told the High Priestess that," Eddings said.

Chamberlain dropped to one knee as the High Priestess halted in front of him. To his shock, the old woman pulled back her veil, exposing her face and eyes to the sun's rays.

"It is good to feel the sun after so many years hiding from it," the High Priestess said.

"Ma'am." Chamberlain got to his feet. "I highly recommend that—"

"That I go back to hiding?" the High Priestess cut him off. "I know the effect the sun is having on me. And the air. But it doesn't matter now. Because the end, what I have lived for all my life, is coming now. Beyond that does not matter. All that counts is that we Oracles do our duty."

She turned from Chamberlain and looked out toward what had once been New York City. "They are coming."

"Who?" Chamberlain asked. "The Shadow?"

"No. The orcas. They come."

19

EARTH TIMELINE—I

They knew he was here because he was what they were, Dane realized. The Shadow had no bodies, only their consciousness, their essence, just as that was all he had here. They could sense each other and they could sense the intrusion into their lair of one like them, even though he was not visible on the real plane.

He didn't have much more time to ponder this.

A dozen Valkyries floated into view, coming from the ramp he had just followed here. They had their long spears in their hands and two of them also had some sort of green tablet about a foot long by six inches wide in their off-weapon hand. Dane wondered what that was and then got the answer right away as the two lifted the tablets up in front of their faces and peered through them. All twelve Valkyries immediately vectored in on his location.

The tablets allowed them to see into the psychometric plane in some manner Dane realized. And he had no doubt that if they could see into the plane he was on, they could do him damage in some way on the plane also. He descended, passing down through the tower as the Valkyries gave chase.

He almost ran straight into the ambush that had been set up. He hit a wide open level of the tower where approximately a hundred Valkyries, every sixth one with a tablet, waited. A spear thrust cut the air, nearly hitting him. As it passed by, he saw that the blade of the spear was glowing very slightly as he felt a disturbance, as if the very fabric of space near him had been upset. He knew instinctively that if that blade had touched him, he would be destroyed.

He switched course and went out of the tower's wall to the air outside. Where more Valkyries floated, waiting. For Dane it was a surreal chase as he dodged spears and Valkyries. He was so caught up in it that it took him a couple of moments to realize that they were herding him in a direction—toward the tunnel that led to the external sphere docking area. He had no doubt that they had some sort of ambush ready for him if he tried that way. So he went where they couldn't follow or be waiting—straight down into the ground, into the planet itself.

Passing through solid rock was disorienting as the only way he could tell direction was to try to keep going the way he had gone. How long though? Dane wondered. And would he know in which direction to turn and how far to go to get out of the planet itself? He remembered how in Special Forces training, during land navigation, the instructors had demonstrated that blindfolded men tended to be unable to maintain a straight line, most going off to the right, some going off to the left. And that was in a two-dimensional plane.

Dane fought his sense of panic, surrounded by rock as he came to a halt realizing he had no idea which way to go or which direction he had come from. And even if he got back to the surface of the planet, he had no doubt that the Valkyries would be guarding the gate to the portal—and using the green tablets now.

Relaxing was difficult as all the physical techniques he'd used to do that weren't available to him—no slowing his breathing, untensing muscles, etc. There was just his mind and the overwhelming feeling of disorientation and fear. Dane pictured Sin Fen's face as she lay on top of the Atlantean pyramid near the Bermuda Triangle Gate. The calmness in her features as she gave her life to channel the power to stop the Shadow's assault. He had to have that in him also. He was the warrior-priest, the latest in a long line of what had been just priestesses.

As his own negative feelings dropped away, Dane became more aware of his surroundings. While his physical surroundings were the planet itself, mostly rock, there was more to the space than that. He picked up a sense of power. Immense power flowing.

Dane moved toward the power.

It was as if he moved from darkness into a supernova as he hit the power stream flowing through the tunnel. The tunnel was over a half mile wide and a beam of pure white light poured through it from left to right. It felt as if the power stream were bathing him, stripping him clean.

Dane realized he could channel this power, use it, but only if he had his body. Not with just his essence.

Is that what the Shadow had learned too late? Dane

wondered. Is that why they needed that latticework of spheres? To be able to use the power?

He turned against the flow and moved upstream. He had to see where this was coming from, the source, even though he had a very strong suspicion based on what the Shadow had done to his timeline.

He moved swiftly through the power stream until he came out of the tunnel into a larger tunnel. In the very center of the cavern the power stream made a ninety-degree turn, going from horizontal to vertical, heading down into the planet. A gigantic crystal was the device that turned the stream, absorbing it as it came up and turning it.

Dane went forward.

The stream came straight up out of the floor of the cavern. Dane paused before going down. He checked out the cavern. The walls were black and smoothly cut, much like the Space Between.

Rather than curving up to meet in the top center, though, the roof of the cavern was perfectly flat. Dane moved up to get closer to it. Black beams criss-crossed gray stone. It appeared that the cavern was beneath a solid slab of granite.

Dane reversed course and descended, moving into the power stream, and heading into the planet. The walls of the tunnel began to change. First solid rock, then he moved through layers of rock mixed with lava. While there was no apparent lining to the tunnel, he sensed that the power itself kept the path open.

Then Dane came out into the core of the planet. A vast open space, the far edge beyond his ability to pick it up. And in the very center of the earth was a massive crystal, over five miles wide, that emitted the power beam.

And to his right was a beam of power coming into the power crystal. Dane knew this was the Shadow's new source, from some other timeline it was in the process of draining.

Another piece of the puzzle.

20

EARTH TIMELINE—VIII
Pennsylvania, 3 July 1863

It was going to be a hot day. That was apparent to all on both sides of the lines as they woke with the rising sun. Cooking fires filled the air with their aroma but few had the desire to eat. If the previous day had been any indicator, many of those who greeted the morning sun had seen their last sunrise.

For the Federals, there was little movement to be made as the plan that had been decided was simple—hold in place.

On the Southern side, things were more complicated. Lee had not held a meeting with his subordinate commanders the previous night, nor had he had his staff issue any written orders. So, despite having decided on a course of action, Lee now had to implement it.

Lee started the morning by riding to Longstreet's headquarters. On his way to his right flank corps, he scanned
the length of the Union position as he rode along Seminary Ridge with a few of his staff officers. Just south of
Cemetery Hill he saw something that he liked. There was
a six-hundred-fifty-yard-wide stretch of almost bare
ridgeline crowned by a copse of trees. From the Confederate skirmish line to the Union line was about thirteen
hundred yards of pretty much open field. There were a
few farm buildings and fences, but overall it was good terrain.

Lee continued south and found his senior corps commander with his staff, discussing a possible flanking
movement. Lee was both stunned and angered.

"General, I wish to speak with you in private," he told
Longstreet.

The corps staff scattered out of earshot, before Lee
continued. "You were with me, last night. You know my
desires."

Longstreet shook his head. "Sir, we had a discussion of
possible courses of actions but you issued no orders last
night, nor have I received any today. I have been over the
terrain since first light and my scouts have also reported
in. The Union holds both Round Tops but beyond that
they have practically nothing. We can flank them still, and
put ourselves both astride their supply and retreat line and
between Meade and Washington."

"We have had this discussion before," Lee said. "I have
not changed my mind."

"Neither have I," Longstreet shot back, the most visible sign of discontent he had ever shown the commander
whom he revered.

"You will bring up General Pickett's division," Lee ordered. "I have already issued orders for artillery to mass opposite where I want him to attack. We will fire a prolonged artillery preparation before Pickett attacks."

Lee turned on his heel and walked away. Longstreet stared after him as his adjutant came up. "He thinks the Army of Northern Virginia can do anything," Longstreet muttered. He gave in to the inevitable and began issuing orders.

As Lee rode off he realized it would take hours for Pickett's division to be brought forward and move into assault position. Rather than let the Union forces sit still for the day, and to draw off reinforcements from the center, he engaged the part of his army most ready to attack immediately, his left flank.

Waves of Confederate troops attacked Culp's Hill. Uncharacteristically as the morning progressed, the Southern forces seemed unwilling to press forward with their usual vigor. Not only was the terrain not favorable for the assault, being steep and rocky, there was little artillery support for them as Lee was massing his guns in the center. It was as if the Confederate troops involved were attacking simply because they had been told to, but not with any true determination.

This did not mean that men were not dying in droves. For each Southern attack, there was a corresponding Union counterattack and the same terrain saw bodies from both sides drop on it, soaking the ground with their blood. But overall, there was a strong sense of anticipation in the air as if a powerful thunderstorm were coming and all were awaiting its arrival to see what it would bring.

• • •

Inside the storage cellar she had dug out the previous evening, Amelia Earhart felt the sweat begin to come to the surface of her skin. She had the plank covering lifted about an inch, held in place with the haft of the shovel, so she could peer out. The Union line was silhouetted against the rising sun. She sat on the plastic case that held the skulls. She couldn't tell if it was from the small amount of power the skulls had gained from the battle on Little Round Top or from the summer heat, but the case felt warm.

She drank from a canteen she had scavenged from a body the previous evening. She spit out the contents as it seared into her throat. Some terrible rot-gut from a camp still. Earhart considered sneaking out to try to find water, but she knew her position was too exposed to the Union lines. She would be spotted.

All she could do now was wait.

• • •

Meade rode his lines one more time, making small adjustments here and there, but overall he was very satisfied with the way his men were positioned. He decided to join General Gibbon and his staff for lunch on Cemetery Ridge.

• • •

Lee intended to keep his word to Longstreet. He had spent most of the morning gathering his artillery together along a thirteen-hundred-yard front facing the copse of trees on Cemetery Ridge which he had determined to be the focal point of the attack as it was very noticeable.

Most of the guns were massed in two great batteries. One consisted of seventy pieces lined up hub-to hub on the southern part of Seminary Ridge. The other was a set of thirty-five and another of twenty-six guns on the northern part of the ridge.

. . .

Meade was informed by his own chief of artillery of the Rebels moving their guns into position as he ate some of the fried chicken Gibbon's staff had cooked up.

"Where are they aimed?" Meade asked, wiping his hands on his breeches.

"Here," the artillery officer said.

"Will their fire be effective?" Meade asked.

"Somewhat. But many of the guns are at maximum range given their lateral displacement. Also, they will have to elevate to fire. Either they will be dead on and hit the front side of this ridge or else their shells will go overhead harmlessly."

"And how many do you think will be dead on?" Meade asked.

"At the range they're firing, not many."

"Good."

"Should I initiate counterartillery fire?"

"No," Meade ordered. "Conserve your ammunition. I think you will soon have more targets that you could have dreamed for."

. . .

Pickett had had a hard time getting his troops forward, moving through the rest of Longstreet's corp that was in front of it. Also they had to ride against the steady flow of ambulances moving to the rear, overloaded with moaning and crying wounded, not the most motivational scene. Still, morale was high among the Virginians of his divi-

sion because the word had spread that Robert E. himself
had chosen them to carry the day and the battle.

Pickett had no idea what the battlefield ahead looked
like. He drew his forces up according to the orders he had
received, on the western slope of Seminary Ridge, out of
sight—and artillery fire—of the Union lines. He deployed his division in two waves, each about eight hundred yards wide. Each wave consisted of two ranks with
file closers behind. In front was a thin line of skirmishers
who would lead the way. Some had been sent out in the
early dawn, crawling forward into the field before the
Union lines to pull down fences and other obstacles. Now
they lay still in the high grass, waiting.

By noon it was in the eighties, and troops lay in position, waiting, as all men in the military spent most of their
time doing. A couple of the brigade commanders who
would lead the assault gathered together for a liquid lunch
of some liberated whiskey. It was a common, if not widely
reported, practice for soldiers on both sides before the attack. It was somewhat easier to charge into hot lead with
some hot liquor in one's belly. It might becloud the mind,
but it emboldened the spirit and held fear a little further at
bay.

Throughout the morning there had been little firing
along this part of the front, although heavy fire had been
heard to the north in the vicinity of Culp's Hill. Snipers
occasionally put out a round here and there. A few artillery rounds were fired, but these were for ranging pur-
poses, to lay the guns.

As noon came a strange silence descended. Even the
battling at Culp's Hill died off. There was no breeze, and
the stillness was heavy over both sides. Yet, both sides
also brimmed with confidence about what was to come.

Save for Longstreet. Remarkably, he even sent a courier with a message to the Confederate commander of artillery. The message directed him to tell Pickett to call off the attack if the barrage did not have the anticipated effect on the Union lines. This was a bizarre message given that Longstreet commanded Pickett's division, but it was the only thing Longstreet could think of to try to forestall the attack short of disobeying Lee's orders.

The artillery commander sent a message back to Longstreet, bouncing the ball of responsibility back. The message said that if there were any doubt about the wisdom of this attack, it should be called off *before* the barrage began as it would use most of the remaining artillery ammunition. Longstreet realized that his first message had been inappropriate and dropped the issue.

At 1:00 P.M. the Confederate batteries opened fire.

· · ·

Earhart's morning had not been uneventful. Confederate skirmishers had crawled forward, several not far from where she hid. Around eleven, a half dozen Rebel snipers actually took cover in the house and opened fire on the Union positions, bringing fire back at them. Earhart was forced to shut the cover to her hole.

She heard firing for almost a half hour, then shouts as the Confederates were forced to relinquish their position as a strong Union patrol charged forward. Earhart thought she was safe when she heard the Union soldiers retreat back to their lines. She pushed up the plank and was greeted by the strong smell of wood smoke. Twisting her head she could see that the remnants of the farmhouse had been set on fire by the Union troops to destroy it as a refuge for snipers. She shut the top and hunkered down, praying that the plank would not catch fire.

After an hour or so she carefully pushed up the top. The farmhouse was smoldering remains. Then a roll of thunder roared over the battlefield, and she saw the Union lines explode with the incoming artillery.

* * *

The infantrymen did as infantry had done since the invention of the cannon and when receiving incoming fire. They sought cover. Given no orders to return fire, the Union artillerymen quickly did the same.

General Gibbon jumped up from his lunch with Meade and yelled for his horse. As an orderly brought it, a piece of shrapnel from an exploding shell tore through the man's chest killing him instantly. The horse fled. Gibbon ignored this and strode off for the nearby front line on foot.

Men were torn apart, animals killed, and occasionally an ammunition wagon would explode, causing a distant roar of applause from the unscathed Confederate lines. Meade headed to his headquarters, behind Cemetery Ridge, which actually was a more dangerous position than the front lines as most Confederate shells were high and landed on the reverse slope. Meade arrived to find that his chief of staff had been wounded.

Along the Union front, the massed Confederate firing was having an effect, although not as great as Lee had hoped for. The Union artillery commander was almost playing games in response. He allowed some of his batteries to fire back for short periods of time, more to bolster morale among the beleaguered infantrymen than to counter what was coming in. He also had some guns deliberately not fire among those batteries, to make the Confederates think they had knocked out many of his pieces.

Casualties among the infantry were actually relatively light as they had the advantage of hiding behind the stone wall and most of the rounds sailed harmlessly overhead. Officers had the highest rate of dead and wounded as they strolled along the line, shouting encouragement to the men. In a strange way, the fact that so many of the shells were high discouraged any who might have thought about running as it was actually safer to be behind the wall. Also, the lack of trees, except for the copse, along the place receiving the most fire, was advantageous as it reduced the possibility of wood splinters from exploding shells.

The one effect the bombardment did have, though, on the Union troops, was to convince them an attack was coming.

General Gibbon, who would later admit that he had been terrified throughout the day, found another horse, mounted it, and then sat on it, perfectly still, in plain view of his men, throughout the rest of the bombardment. Such was the role of officers.

General Warren, the engineer who had helped save the day at Little Round Top, was still there, watching to the north. He realized that the Union counterfire was very ineffective and sent word to Meade. The Union commander sent orders to all his batteries directing them to cease fire and conserve ammunition for the expected infantry assault.

His orders reached the various batteries that had been firing at different times, meaning they fell silent gradually, giving the impression to the Confederates that they were stopping because they were running short of ammunition. This, combined with the selective withholding of pieces by the Union artillery commander, led the Confederate artillery commander to decide his fire had been extremely effective in silencing the Union guns. Thus, even if he had agreed with the message Longstreet had sent him earlier in the day, he would not have acted on it.

The Confederate artillery commander then hastily penned a note for Pickett: "For God's sake come quick."

With his own guns just about out of ammunition, he gave the order to save fire, then looked over his shoulder, anxiously awaiting the attack.

The courier found Pickett in conversation with Longstreet. Pickett read the note, then handed it without comment to his corps commander. Longstreet read it without comment.

"General, shall I advance?" the excited Pickett asked.

Longstreet could not speak. He bowed his head.

Pickett saluted. "I shall lead my division forward, sir." He pulled a note out of his tunic and gave it to Longstreet. "For my fiancée." Then he bound onto his horse and galloped off, without seeing the tears that were streaming down Old Pete's face.

Longstreet wiped the tears from his cheeks and rode forward. He was dismayed to find that the battery of guns he had ordered held in reserve to support Pickett during the advance were nowhere to be seen. He learned they had retired to the rear and that it would take an hour for them to be brought back forward. This delay would extend the time between the end of the barrage and the assault too long.

Longstreet shifted uncomfortably in the saddle as he saw that Pickett's men were moving. It was now three in the afternoon.

· · ·

General Warren on Little Round Top saw the advance from his vantage point and had signalmen with flags relay the message north. Along Cemetery Ridge the infantry slowly peeked over the stone wall. Wounded were carried off, ammunition was brought forward, and artillery pieces were lined up and zeroed in.

"Here they come!"

The cry echoed along the Union line as the first of the Confederate troops appeared cresting Seminary Ridge. It was magnificent spectacle as Pickett's division appeared on line, flags flying, in perfect order.

A Union artillery officer, wounded in the stomach, used one hand to hold his intestines from spilling out, resited his guns. Men made sure their rifles were loaded. Solid shot was loaded into artillery pieces.

The Union artillery opened fire.

· · ·

Pickett already had a problem. He had formed his lines on the outward curved reverse slope of Seminary Ridge. Which meant there were gaps, and some of the units' orientations were not on line with the objective.

Federal troops were shocked and impressed as the Confederate lines in places actually wheeled and aligned, slowing their advance, under the rain of shells coming into them. As the long line of gray formed, there was no doubt in the mind of anyone in the Union lines that this was the final assault.

EARTH TIMELINE—XIV
Southern Africa, 21 January 1879

The commander of the right horn, Dabulamanzi, was not happy to see Shakan and the strange woman and the strange white being she pulled with her. He had lost many warriors to get to this point, and he knew he was going to lose more in the final assault to take down the last outpost that the British had been forced into. The redcoats had fought bravely. Still it was just a matter of more force and a little more time and he knew he would be victorious.

A small band of his men had captured the two women coming down the track from Isandlwana and brought them to him. He was just outside the outer wall of the mission that his men had already breached, issuing orders for another assault.

"I have the protection of Cetewayo," Shakan said, standing tall between the two warriors holding her arms.

"Cetewayo is my brother," Dabulamanzi said. "I was there when you first came to him. You may have bewitched him, but you will not do the same to me."

"I do not bewitch," Shakan said.

"Who is that?" Dabulamanzi pointed at Ahana. He reached out and touched her eyes. "I have never seen the like."

"She is one like me," Shakan said. "From a place far from here."

"And why is she here? Why are you here?"

"To serve the greater good."

A warrior called out that all was ready. Dabulamanzi turned from the two women and issued his orders. With a great surge, a thousand warriors leapt up from the cover of the outer wall and charged the final outpost.

• • •

"Steady," Chard called out, his voice cracking from both dryness and fear. He knew what Dabulamanzi knew. It was just a matter of time and numbers.

"Fire," Chard ordered as the next assault wave appeared in the firelight. Huge gaps were torn in the Zulu line as they vaulted the wall and came forward. "Independent fire," Chard quickly yelled. He had abandoned his pistol for a rifle and he joined his men on the mealie bag rampart, firing as quickly as he could load.

The distance between the two walls was short and the ground was filled with Zulu bodies, so much so that the other warriors had literally to run on top of the bodies to get to the British lines. Such a dash in the face of the rifle fire resulted in frightening apparitions, covered with the blood of their comrades, reaching the mealie bag wall. Bayonets went against *iKlwa*. Black against white, united only in the redness of the blood that came from their veins and mixed together, soaking the bags and ground.

A handful of Zulu warriors made it into the final outpost, but they were quickly cut down and the wave receded. Left behind, the British were lower in numbers, close to the critical point where all the walls could be effectively manned.

• • •

"What do you want?" Dabulamanzi demanded as he watched his warriors come back, their numbers greatly depleted.

"A great victory has already been won," Shakan said. "Cetewayo defeated the camp on the slopes of Isandlwana." She did not add what had appeared on the top of

Isandlwana. It was something she sensed was beyond words.

"And I will defeat them here," Dabulamanzi said.

"There is no point to it," Shakan said.

"Do you want me to just walk away?" Dabulamanzi laughed. "We have paid in blood and we will take what we have earned in their blood."

"I do not want you to just walk away," Shakan said. "I want you to help me. Help her and her people"—Shakan indicated Ahana—"And many more people in many places and times."

"You speak foolishness," Dabulamanzi said.

Shakan indicated for Ahana to take out the muonic detector. Ahana pulled the device out of the pack. Dabulamanzi stared at the LED display and the blinking lights, but did not seem overly impressed.

"This," Shakan indicated the detector, "says something great can happen here. We can make something good happen out of this terrible day and night."

"And how do I do that?" Dabulamanzi asked, even as his warriors formed for another assault.

"The British are brave, are they not?" Shakan asked.

Dabulamanzi had to grant that. "Yes. They fight well."

"And the Zulu, we fight with great bravery also."

"Of course."

"Then do something different," Shakan begged.

"And that is?" Dabulamanzi asked.

"Combine the Zulu bravery with the British bravery to change the course of things."

EARTH TIMELINE—III
New York City, July 2078

Chamberlain flew over what had once been Manhattan. The wings rotated up and the specially modified MH-90 came to a hover. That particular Nighthawk had a cargo bay full of sensors and imaging equipment. Both walls were crammed full of displays with seats in front of them manned by scientists.

Waiting was fine, but Chamberlain figured he'd been brought to this location for a reason, so he wanted to get an idea of the lay of the land, even if most of it was buried under hundreds of feet of water. He had a feeling the extreme Shadow reaction during the war to the tip of Manhattan had to have been for a reason. He wanted to know what that was. Oracles and prophecies were fine, but facts helped.

"What do you have?" Chamberlain asked the lead scientist.

The man looked up in surprise. "We're getting low level muonic activity. We haven't seen this since the end of the war."

"Is it the Shadow?" Chamberlain asked.

The scientist shrugged. "It's just low level activity right now. Traces." He pointed down. "Directly below us." The scientist turned to the man on his left and checked his screen. "Sonar indicates we've got an opening in the earth itself. Geez, whatever the Shadow did to blast this place, sure went through. We're reading a narrow tunnel all the way to the center of the planet."

21

EARTH TIMELINE—I

This was what Ahana and Nagoya had speculated might be the case, Dane realized as he took in the immensity of both the diamond crystal and the power it was receiving, transforming, and then emitting. Even before the two Japanese scientists, the Russians had speculated that such a thing existed at the very center of the planet.

The Russians had labeled the places where the gates were occasionally active as Vile Vortices. They claimed these spots were external manifestations of power surges from inside the planet, part of a matrix of cosmic energy that had been built into the planet at the time of its formation.

Ahana had told him that if it existed, this crystal held its power from the birth of the planet, hard as it was for Dane to believe. Its initial power began when the loose collection of rocks that was pre-earth, was bombarded by asteroids and meteors for millions of years. The energy released from these impacts melted everything, and the planet slowly began to cool from the outside in. The immense temperatures, gravitational pressure, and sheer weight of what was on top formed this crystal, allowing it to absorb all that power being directed inward. Only one material could sustain such forces and that was diamond. And that was what the crystal was made of.

Dane realized he was looking at the inner core of the planet, something scientists in his day had only been able to speculate about. While man had traveled to the moon, he had barely scratched the surface of his own planet. Apparently the Atlanteans had done considerably more than scratch.

Dane became aware of something else as some time went by. The planet was moving, revolving, but not the crystal. Dane tried to recall what Ahana had said about that, knowing it was important. He knew that the Shadow had demonstrated an ability to tap into the power coming out of the splits between the tectonic plates. He wondered why this tap was where it was, wherever that was.

Realizing the location of the tap and tunnel would be important, Dane reversed course and raced up the tunnel. When he reached the chamber underneath the granite slab, he continued on the same vector. Passing into the stone was disconcerting and he concentrated on trying to stay in a straight line.

He came out into pitch black water, the only difference from the stone, being the element that surrounding him.

Where was he? What had this place been before the deluge?

Dane moved up, toward the surface. He burst up out of

the water and halted, searching in all directions. There was something above the water to one side and he headed over there.

Land. Above the waves. He saw a rock wall rising barely thirty feet above the water but the place sparked some memory. He moved closer. The top of the rocks were scoured clean of life. And the land to west of them sloped down into the water again.

Where had he seen similar rock? He knew the context was all wrong, given the water level. He added a few hundred feet to the rock, envisioning cliffs.

Dane knew where he was. The rocks were the very top of the Palisades. And the core tunnel had been dug underneath what was New York City in his timeline. If the tunnel existed here, it might exist in other timelines, the key issue being when the Atlanteans had dug it.

Dane stayed in place, trying to think this through. He was here for a reason. He had to trust the Ones Before. He, a man who had never trusted anyone other than the men he'd gone into combat with in Vietnam. He realized that he'd gone into combat with the Ones Before many times in the past year.

Why was he here?

There was power below. More power than any of the other timelines had ever tapped. It was what had both destroyed the Shadow and kept it going.

Did he need his body?

The thought was startling to Dane. He'd thought earlier that he could not redirect power without his body, but was that true? Sin Fen had told him he was the step beyond what she was. He was the warrior-priest.

It was time to go back, Dane knew. Time for all the pieces to come together.

22

Over twelve thousand men on a front slightly more than one mile wide.

It was an artilleryman's dream target. The officers who commanded the Union batteries were well schooled in their deadly science. Since the Confederates had over a mile of open ground to cover, it worked out that it would take them, if they kept a steady advance, approximately sixteen point nine minutes to reach the Union lines. In that time, a typical gun battery of six twelve-pound Napoleon guns could fire two hundred and twenty-eight rounds.

There was also a science to the order in which different types of ammunition were fired. As the Confederate lines first appeared, the Union guns were loaded with solid shot. This was a solid ball of cast iron, designed for long distance firing. The round would fly to maximum range, and then hit the ground, bouncing several times, often cutting swathes through packed formations.

Stacked near the guns were other types of ammunition, readied for use as the enemy closed. Once the incoming troops came within a thousand yards, shrapnel rounds would be used. And then, at the very end, inside of four hundred yards, there was canister.

The Union guns fired round after round of solid shot at the massed lines coming toward them. This made the maneuvering of the Confederate lines to get in position even more amazing as it took up valuable minutes and got them no closer to their enemy.

Even more devastating, Union batteries that had been moved up by General Warren onto Little Round Top now opened fire, parallel to the Confederate lines. Some of the solid shot from these batteries would hit the end of a line of men and plow through them, taking out dozens at a time.

The Union infantry, their guns primed, waited and watched. Veterans of Union assaults such as those at Fredericksburg and Antietam were happy to be behind their stone wall and not out in that field, having experienced what their enemy was now facing. They were torn between empathy for fellow human beings and a base desire for revenge.

· · ·

General Pickett was having difficulty keeping the various units in order and trying to gain contact with Trimble's division on his left. It took almost fifteen minutes of maneuvering for his left to meet Trimble's right. At this point their front ranks were about eight hundred yards from the Union lines.

Pickett's heart soared as he saw the solid line of gray troops moving forward. He grabbed a courier and sent him dashing back to Longstreet with a request for reinforcements to support what he considered the inevitable breakthrough of the Union lines which he believed would happen very quickly. Nothing could defeat such a display of Southern manhood.

"On men!" Pickett cried as he stood up in his stirrups, waving his sword. "On for Virginia."

For the men in the front ranks, things weren't looking so positive. As the two divisions connected, the troops crowded into each other. Even under these terrible conditions, Southern politeness held sway as a young officer from Virginia cried out to the regiment of Tennesseans his unit was mingling with: "Move on, cousins. You are drawing the fire our way."

. . .

A solid shot hit the pine board over her hole and ripped it away. Earhart decided enough was enough. She managed to unseal the Valkyrie suit and crawl inside. Then she shut it. She scrunched down as tight as possible in the bottom of the hole, wishing she could become an earthworm and crawl even deeper into the dark soil.

The sound of battle, the screams of wounded and dying filled the air. She could hear Confederate officers exhorting their men forward. Then there was another sound, which at first she couldn't make out. Something being shouted from the Union lines, a chant. It took her a few moments before she realized what it was:

"Fredericksburg. Fredericksburg. Fredericksburg."

• • •

The colonel in charge of the Eighth Ohio regiment didn't wait for the Confederates to come to him. In fact, his best estimate watching the oncoming wave of gray convinced him that the attack was directed to his right and that his unit would be spared any frontal assault. His men had been deployed on a wide front as skirmishers, about five hundred yards in front of the Union line but it appeared the attack would pass them by.

So he attacked. He formed his men into a line a hundred yards wide and charged forward into the right flank of Pickett's division. It was an audacious move, even more unorthodox than Chamberlain's charge the day before as there was no desperate need for it.

But like Chamberlain's it worked because the Confederate troops they charged into were already dispirited from being under constant artillery barrage for over half an hour and having taken considerable casualties without even having fired a single shot in retaliation.

Pickett's right flank began to crumble as men threw down their weapons and headed for the rear.

The lead elements of the attack now reached the critical four-hundred-yard range from Union lines.

Shot was replaced by canister in the Union guns. These were basically large-bore shotgun shells, each canister containing scores of oversize musket balls. Four hundred yards was also rifle range.

The first volley of rifle fire from the massed Union lines hidden behind their protective walls brought the Confederate advance to a momentary halt, as if every man had absorbed the incoming rounds, not just those hit. Canister tore gaping holes, scattering the ground with men screaming in pain from grievous wounds.

It got worse the closer they got. At two hundred and fifty yards, the Union cannons were filled with double loads of canister. Every Union soldier with a rifle was firing now.

Many among the Rebel ranks knew it was now or never.

A Confederate lieutenant waved his sword, rallying his men. "Home, boys, home. Remember, home is over beyond those hills!"

A colonel exhorted his cowering men to advance. "Go on, it will not last five minutes longer." It didn't for him as he immediately fell, shot through the thigh.

The Confederate advance began to break apart.

One Confederate brigade commander, still on his horse, disappeared in a cloud of red as a round of canister hit both man and horse directly. Given that the Confederates were now taking fire from three sides—the center of the Union line, which they were approaching, and flanking fire from artillery on Little Round Top and from Culp's Hill—the ranks that weren't running began to cluster toward the center.

Directly opposite the center was the Angle—a place in the Union line where there was a ninety-degree angle formed by a bend in the stone wall behind which the Union troops had positioned themselves. General Armistead, one of Pickett's brigade commanders, led the final assault toward the Angle.

The bloodied line of gray finally reached the stone wall. Armistead put his hat on a sword and stood on top of the stone wall, urging the rest of the Confederate survivors forward. He fell mortally wounded—and with this,

the high water mark of the attack had been reached as
Union reinforcements raced up and pushed the Confederates back, capturing many of them.

●   ●   ●

Earhart heard a strange sound, something she couldn't
recognize at first. It took several moments for her to realize what it was: men sobbing. She carefully lifted her head
and saw small clusters of Confederate soldiers falling
back by her position, most carrying wounded comrades,
and many crying, tears staining their dirty faces.

It was the most heart-rending thing she'd ever seen.

She could not believe that less than an hour earlier
these dirty, bloodied, dispirited men had been part of the
magnificent display of shoulder-to-shoulder soldiers with
flags flapping.

She'd almost forgotten about the skulls in the horror
that had surrounded her. Almost, but the pull of duty came
through. Even through the armor of the Valkyrie suit she
could feel the heat coming off the case. She unlatched the
lid and lifted it. She was almost blinded by the glow coming out of the crystal skulls.

She shut the lid. It was slightly after four in the afternoon. Darkness would not come for a while. When it
came, she hoped her way out of here would come. She had
what she came for.

EARTH TIMELINE—XIV
Southern Africa, 21 January 1879

The second and third assaults were also beaten back. The
piles of Zulu dead were deeper in between the outer and

the inner walls. Dabulamanzi was not fazed. He had passed through the line of sanity, and in a way Shakan could understand how it happened.

The roar of the British rifles, the war cries of the Zulu, the screams of the wounded, the dead all around, everything eerily lit by the burning building, all combined to make the normal world seem very far away. Dabulamanzi was berating his subordinate commanders, urging them into another assault. Shakan could tell even these hardened warriors were growing weary of battle.

Ahana was seated on the dirt, her head bowed, her hands covering her face, her Valkyrie suit floating in the air behind her. They were where they needed to be, but neither woman had an idea what was to come next. The muonic levels were still rising, but with Dabulamanzi unwilling to listen, they were growing short of hope.

Then Cetewayo arrived with his personal guards. The Zulu leader had passed through the stage Dabulamanzi was in and come out the other side. Shakan knew that as soon as he walked up, his shoulders slumped with weariness.

Dabulamanzi greeted his brother by going to one knee. "We are preparing to attack once more."

Cetewayo looked at the carpet of bodies between where they were and the wall of bags beyond which the strange white helmets of British troops could be seen. Cetewayo waved for Dabulamanzi to stand.

"How many?" he asked.

Dabulamanzi was uncertain what his brother was asking. "There are but a few of the enemy left and—"

"How many warriors have you lost?" Cetewayo cut him off.

Dabulamanzi blinked. "We—there have been—"

Cetewayo put a hand on his brother's shoulder. "We have won the day, but I fear we have lost more than we have won."

They all staggered as the ground shook.

"What was that?" Cetewayo demanded.

"The evil spirit has gone into the land," Shakan said. "It grows stronger as it eats into the soil."

The land was all important, every Zulu knew that. He turned to Shakan. "What do we do now?"

EARTH TIMELINE—III
New York City, July 2078

Captain Eddings grabbed Chamberlain's arm and pointed. "Look."

In the water below the MH-90 were a dozen dark figures, slicing through the water. Killer whales.

"What are they doing here?" Chamberlain asked, remembering the High Priestess' prediction that they were on their way.

"They are part of this too," Eddings said.

"How deep can they dive?" Chamberlain was thinking of the tunnel that plunged into the planet. That had to be the reason they were here.

"Not as deep as you need," Eddings said, knowing why he had asked.

"Nothing can go as deep as we might have to," Chamberlain said, "if the data on that tunnel are correct."

Eddings looked at him. "Don't you have faith?"

" 'Faith'? I'm a soldier."

"You're the commander of the First Earth Battalion,"

Eddings said. "You volunteered for this unit many years ago. If you don't have faith, why did you do that?"

"It has nothing to do with faith," Chamberlain said. "It's about vengeance."

Eddings shook her head. "That won't work. This is not about defeating the Shadow or paying them back for what they did to us. It's for the future." She looked down at the orca. "Even they know that and they were born to kill."

23

EARTH TIMELINE—I

As soon as Dane went back down in the water that covered Manhattan Island, he knew he was not alone. There
were other presences in the water. Real presences. Pure
evil. As evil as the Shadow, but different. Mindless creatures that existed for only one reason—to kill.

He'd seen them before.

Kraken.

And he knew what they were now. Bio-engineered
creatures, designed by the Shadow to kill dolphins. Given
the betrayal of the dolphins the Shadow had placed on the
moon, there was nothing, no creature, the Shadow hated
more.

Dane knew this hatred sprang from the subconscious,
that the Shadow on a very deep level understood that the
Ones Before were better than they were. More human.

The kraken were altered deep ocean giant squids. A species that had eluded scientists and oceanographers in Dane's timeline, and remained a myth, just like Atlantis. In the Shadow's timeline, they had captured the creatures who inhabited the dark depths of the ocean. Over seventy feet long to start with and natural carnivores, they were the perfect creature to adjust to fight dolphins. Their only natural enemy were sperm whales. And vice versa.

Kraken had a massive head, but Dane didn't sense much intelligence, just malevolence. Stretching back from the head were eight sucker-bearing arms and two contractile tentacles with spatulate tips. The latter had rows of suckers encircled by rows of hard, horn hooks. The Shadow had transformed those into mouths with razor sharp teeth, that could not eat, only kill.

They were waiting.

Let them wait, Dane thought.

He focused his self, his core.

He did something that only the Shadow from this time-line had ever done. He made his own gate.

24

Longstreet had been watching the assault through his fieldglass while perched atop a split rail fence. As the gray line closed on the Union lines, a British officer, Colonel Freemantle, sent to America to observe this new type of warfare, came riding up, almost out of breath.

"General Longstreet, General Lee sent me here and said you would place me in a position to see this magnificent charge."

Longstreet lowered his binoculars and stared at Freemantle at a loss for words at both the timing and the comment. The British colonel looked to the east and was astonished at what he saw. "I wouldn't have missed this for anything!"

Longstreet laughed, a most strange sound amid what

was happening. "The devil you wouldn't. I would like to have missed it very much. We've attacked and been repulsed. Look there."

Freemantle lifted his own fieldglasses, but all he could see among the smoke drifting over the field were men fighting desperately. Longstreet however, seemed resigned to defeat. "The charge is over." He turned to a courier. "Ride to General Pickett and tell him what you heard me say to Colonel Freemantle." It was a most curious way to issue a retreat order, but the entire day had been most strange for Longstreet.

The senior corps commander was interested in only two things now, which is why he kept his binoculars trained on the field. How many men would be coming back, and when would Meade counterattack?

• • •

The feelings of shame and disgrace the surviving Confederate soldiers felt as they fell back from the Union lines turned to shock and dismay as they saw the field they had charged across and the number of bodies that littered it. They'd made the charge and known it had been bad, but only by re-traversing it did the full spectrum of how terrible it had been hit home. Men saw friends, brothers, fathers, sons, with their bodies torn to pieces, staring blank-eyed up at the sky. Many of those retreating walked backward, preferring not to be shot in the back, sometimes stumbling over bodies they couldn't see.

Less than half the men who had gone east returned west across the battlefield. More than seventy-five hundred men had been killed, wounded, or captured. They had gained nothing but glory and lost the cream of the Army of Virginia in less than one hour.

So many prisoners had been taken, that as Meade belatedly galloped to the vicinity of the Angle, he saw a mass of gray coming down off Cemetery Ridge and thought for several anxious seconds that the Rebels had broken through his lines. Only when he saw that the Confederates had no arms and were under guard did his heart rate go back to something close to normal. The men of the Army of the Potomac had never seen Confederates look so utterly beaten and tired. The jubilation of just minutes earlier, when the vengeful Fredericksburg chant had echoed across the field gave way to empathy, some Union soldiers even doffing their caps to their defeated foes.

Meade galloped up to the ridge and inquired how things were going. When informed the attack had been repulsed, he could scarce believe his ears. His eyes, however, looking out over the bloody field and the fleeing men in gray, confirmed this report.

On the other side, Longstreet was riding along Seminary Ridge, trying to prepare the defense. If he were Meade, he knew what he would do—attack.

Lee, on the other hand, had watched Pickett's charge from the ridge and now rode down among the men flowing back. He spoke words of encouragement, knowing these men needed to hold on to Seminary Ridge in case the Federals attacked. Such was his presence that the majority of the men who even just saw him halted, and began to reform.

In the midst of this, General Pickett came riding back, a dazed look on his face, his customary swagger gone. Lee moved up to him and ordered him to move his division to the rear of the hill to be a reserve.

"General Lee, I have no division now," Pickett replied with tears streaming down his face. He began to run down

the losses, starting with all three of his brigade commanders.

"Come, General Pickett," Lee broke in. "This has been
my fight, and upon my shoulders rests the blame. The men
and officers of your command have written the name of
Virginia as high today as it has ever been written before.
Your men have done all that men can do. The fault is entirely my own."

Pickett was not the only one Lee said this to as he rode
about the field. Many men heard him as he repeated the
last line over and over.

"The fault is entirely my own."

    •   •   •

Earhart realized that the field was finally clear of men
other than the dead and the wounded who had been left
behind. She could hear men crying out in pain, many calling for their mothers or other loved ones. She dared to rise
up higher in her hole and she could see the field of dead
and dying all around in the waning daylight. She looked
up to the Union lines where there had been much cheering
and laughter, but now it was quiet and there was no sign
of any counterattack.

Earhart grabbed the plastic case. It felt heavier.

It was time. She knew it, as if Dane were at her side
and had whispered it in her ear.

She stood up tall, not caring if any on either side saw
her in the little light that was left to this most bloody day.
A small black dot appeared in front of her, elongating,
until it was eight feet high and three wide. Carefully holding the case, Earhart stepped through the gate.

    •   •   •

Longstreet could not believe what he had just seen. It appeared as if an angel had come out of the ground itself in the middle of the field near a burned-down farmhouse. The vision had floated in the air, then a black hole had appeared in front of it, which it had gone into and then disappeared.

Longstreet was not the only one who had seen the white figure. On top of Cemetery Ridge, Meade had been scanning the terrain between his lines and the Confederates as staff officers urged him to the attack.

"Did you see that?" he asked in surprise.

None of the others had been looking in the direction he had been and all replied negatively.

For Meade it was a clear sign. The battle was done. There'd been enough killing. It was time to turn to man's better nature, if just for part of a day. He gave orders for his troops to stand down.

• • •

"It is done," Mary Todd Lincoln told her husband.

The president was standing behind his desk, his back to the room, peering out the window. It was dark outside and all he could see were the lights of Washington. He slowly turned around. His desk was covered with telegrams, forwarded from the War Department. The last one, several hours old, indicated that Meade expected Lee to make an assault today.

"The result?" Lincoln asked.

"What was needed was received and taken from the battlefield," Mary said strangely.

"And what exactly was that?" Lincoln asked his wife as he sat down at his desk.

"The strength to win a war."

There was a knock at the door and a courier from the War Department bustled in, excitement in his face. He handed a bound folder to Lincoln.

"What is it?" the President demanded as he opened the folder.

"Lee's been thrown back with heavy losses. Our men hold the ground at Gettysburg."

The first telegram on top of the packet, whether placed there by design or chance, was a preliminary casualty roll. Lincoln's hands shook as he scanned the numbers. If these losses did not bring the war to a close, he wondered, what would it take?

EARTH TIMELINE—XIV
Southern Africa, 21 January 1879

Lieutenant Chard slid a round into the chamber of the rifle and peered over the mealie bag he was leaning against. He was very tired and wanted nothing more than to lay his head down and sleep. Even the specter of another wave of Zulu warriors charging at him could no longer bring a jolt of adrenaline to his system. He dared not put his head down, though, because he knew he would not be able to wake. He issued orders, making sure none of the men tried to nap, because he knew they too would not be able to rise once more.

Dawn was still a couple of hours off and he did not see the sun coming up as bringing a respite. He wondered where Chelmsford and the rest of the British army were. As the minutes stretched on, he began to wonder where the next Zulu assault was.

"I wish they would get it over with," Bromhead said to him.

A single Zulu appeared on the outer stone wall, standing tall, with neither spear nor shield.

"What is this?" Bromhead asked.

"Your guess is as good as mine," Chard replied as he ordered his men not to fire. The Zulu warrior raised his hands to the sky. Then he began to chant.

"Bloody hell," Chard muttered.

The Zulus on the other side of the wall picked up the chant.

"What the—" Bromhead said, pointing.

A figure in white was now floating over the stone wall, slowly coming to a position in between the Zulu and British lines. It had some kind of pack on its back, but the face was featureless except for two large red bulges that might have been eyes.

"Either an angel or a demon," Chard whispered. He turned. "Sergeant Major."

"Sir?"

"I believe we should reply."

"Yes, sir."

Within seconds, the British troops were roused out of their lethargy and their voices were raised in song.

. . .

Inside the Valkyrie suit, Ahana felt goosebumps on her arms. The two sides were singing in different languages, but somehow there was a harmony to their songs. She glanced at the muonic indicator. The level of activity was rising. She turned to the northeast and headed for Isandlwana.

EARTH TIMELINE—III
New York City, July 2078

"Stand to," Chamberlain ordered over the battalion frequency. He was in full armor and his weapons were loaded with live ammunition.

Glancing out the portal on the right side of his MH-90 he could see the circle of Oracles. They had not moved for over thirty hours, and the skin on the High Priestess's face was red and blistered from exposure to the sun. Her eyes were staring vacantly, having been blinded beyond repair already.

Captain Eddings had just come from the circle and had relayed the High Priestess's report that something was going to happen very shortly.

"Report," Chamberlain ordered.

"Alpha company, ready."

"Bravo company, ready."

"Charlie company, ready."

"Headquarters, ready."

Chamberlain turned to the crew chief. "Seal us up."

The back ramp slowly came up and locked in place.

Chamberlain walked over and sat down. They were ready.

"Take off," Chamberlain ordered the pilots. The first MH-90 rose up into the sky.

25

The Space Between

Earhart came out the other end of the portal into the Space Between to be greeted by a splash of water from Rachel's tail. The dolphin immediately took off and Earhart followed, moving in the Valkyrie suit after her. She saw right away where Rachel was headed—the massive Shadow sphere floated in the water directly ahead, half submerged. With the skull case firmly in hand, Earhart reached the sphere. Rachel splashed her tail once more in approval and then raced off on some other task.

Earhart knew the way now. She floated up to the top and entered the split where the petals of metal were slightly parted. Then she descended through the open top half where the Shadow had captured ships and planes during forays into her timeline. A sphere like this, maybe even this one, had captured her and her plane during her attempt to fly around the world.

She went down a tunnel to the power room. The mummified bodies of the crew of the *Nautilus* were grim reminders of the cost of this war as they occupied their niches around the circumference of the room. Remaining in the suit for protection, Earhart opened the case.

The skulls were still glowing as brightly as they had on the battlefield. She took them, one by one, in the claws that extended from the Valkyrie suit hands to the niches at the same level as the central power globe. As she placed the ninth in place, the glow from the skulls increased, filling the chamber. Lines of power shot from one skull to the other, then all nine linked with the power globe.

The sphere was ready.

Earhart headed for the command center.

As she enclosed herself in the pilot pod, she felt a strong presence close by.

"Dane?"

I'm here.

The voice was inside her head but Earhart automatically scanned the controls and panel on the inside of the pilot pod. There was no one else on board the sphere. "Where are you?"

I'm here. I'm still on the psychometric plane. I opened the gate for you.

"What now?" Earhart asked. She felt slightly foolish to be speaking to empty air but given all that had happened it was pretty much par for the course.

We have the power. Now we get the force.

EARTH TIMELINE—III
New York City, July 2078

Chamberlain was almost thrown across the cargo bay of
the MH-90 as it banked hard right. He heard the excited
voices of the pilots, but couldn't make out what they were
saying. Stabilizing himself, he made his way to the cockpit.

It wasn't hard to miss what had caused both the maneuver and the excitement as a large black column, over a
mile wide, had appeared over what had once been the
southern tip of Manhattan.

"Arm weapons," Chamberlain ordered the pilots and then
the order was relayed to all the other planes. The forty-
millimeter cannon underneath the nose of the plane was
aimed at the gate and missiles under each wings were armed.

Something was coming out of the portal. It took a few
seconds and then Chamberlain recognized it—a Shadow
sphere. He had seen imagery of them taken during the
Shadow War. It was his worst fears coming true—the
Final Assault was the Shadow coming to this timeline, not
them going to the Shadow.

"All elements, we will attack in echelon," Chamberlain
ordered. "I want Alpha and Bravo companies to hold in
case the sphere opens, and then try to get inside and deploy. Charlie company will attack at—"

Easy.

Chamberlain checked his commo status. No one
should be talking on the command frequency while he
was giving orders.

"Charlie company will—"

Easy, Colonel.

"Who is that?" Chamberlain demanded.

"Who is what?" Eddings was next to him.

"Didn't you hear that?" The voice had to be coming over the command net, Chamberlain knew, because he was sealed from the outside world inside his suit.

We're here to transport you. We're in the sphere. We're not the Shadow. We're from another timeline the Shadow has attacked. Bring your craft on board.

"Who are you?"

Eddings turned toward Chamberlain but he signaled for her to be quiet.

My name isn't important.

Looking through the cockpit window, Chamberlain could see that the entire sphere had emerged from the gate and was floating motionless. The gate snapped out of existence. Then the top of the sphere began to open, splitting like a bulb opening to become a flower.

Ask your Oracles.

. . .

Dane could understand the colonel's reticence about trusting a voice that just appeared in his head, especially in connection with the arrival of a Shadow sphere. Then he sensed something below. Dane shifted his attention to the water below. He saw a half dozen large black fins sticking out of the water.

. . .

"The High Priestess says do as the voice says," Eddings told Chamberlain.

As Chamberlain prepared to change his orders, the sphere began to move—downward. The top was still open and now he could see the large open floor bisecting the interior. An excellent landing field. He directed his craft to enter the sphere and land.

The MH-90s flitted forward, settling down on the black metal one by one, a dangerous maneuver as the sphere itself was now moving. As a commander should, Chamberlain took the last position in the line of Nighthawks heading into the top of the sphere.

As he watched his unit enter the sphere, Chamberlain realized that it was going to be a close call for his craft to land before the sphere was submerged as the bottom of the large ball had now touched the water and it wasn't slowing.

. . .

Inside the pilot pod, Amelia Earhart was also aware of the two rates of progress—her descent of the sphere and the landing of the military craft inside. She was following Dane's orders, but it seemed as if he were thinking many different things at once.

The sphere was in the water and she kept it going down. Only three more of the strange planes had to land. She had to trust Dane knew what he was doing, because those planes were going to get wet very soon.

As the last one landed on the cargo deck above her, water began to pour in the opening in the top of the sphere.

. . .

"Everyone sealed?" Chamberlain asked as his Nighthawk was buffeted by a stream of water cascading down.

All answered in the affirmative.

Chamberlain put his helmet against Eddings'. "What the hell is going on?"

"Look," Eddings said, pointing up, through the window in the top of the cockpit.

It appeared that the sphere was no longer moving as the water level had stopped halfway up the large circular cargo bay. Just at the point where the bottom of the splits were.

A killer whale appeared, swimming in through the gap of one of the splits. Then another and another. Soon a dozen of the creatures were inside, swimming just above the parked Nighthawks. The top of the sphere began to close, each petal sealing against the one next to it until it was completely closed.

Chamberlain staggered as his mind was filled with a vision that came unbidden. A beautiful city inside a clear shield. A golden tower extending upward. In the top of the golden tower a large room filled with small golden globes all connected together.

He didn't know where the vision came from; he'd never had one before.

"That's the target," Eddings said.

Chamberlain looked at her in surprise.

"I saw it too," Eddings said. "Those globes. That's the Shadow. That's what we have to destroy."

• • •

"Where now?" Earhart asked.

Straight down.

26

EARTH TIMELINE—XIV
Southern Africa, 21 January 1879

Ahana got as close as possible to the Isandlwana Gate
without entering it. She shrugged off the pack of gear
she'd brought and tossed it on the ground. The sound of
the Zulu chant and the British singing echoed this far,
even though she knew the sound should not carry the distance.

She knew there was something stronger at work than
the physics she understood. Just as this gate was beyond
her, so was whatever was now occurring at Isandlwana.
And she knew with certainty that just as this gate had been
formed and exploited by the Shadow through the power of
the massacre, formed into something evil; she knew that
what was happening at Rorke's Drift was the opposite.

Ahana stared at the devices and instruments trying to decide what to do, feeling a terrible sense of urgency.

. . .

At Rorke's Drift the outer stone wall was now lined with warriors, chanting and slamming the haft of their spears against their shields. Unlike earlier though, this chant was not martial. There was a slow and mournful cadence to it.

Inside the inner wall, the British survivors stood to, looking out at the Zulu warriors, the butts of their rifles on the ground, red-stained bayonets glinting in the remaining firelight, singing hymns under the direction of the sergeant major.

Eyes grew wide on both sides, but none stopped singing, as a bluish glow appeared in the air above Rorke's Drift. A tendril of the strange glowing blue cloud began to move against the wind toward Isandlwana.

. . .

"Stop." Ahana said the word out loud. She moved back slightly from the machines. She'd had many theories about the Shadow, about the edge of science, about physics, but she realized that throughout it all, Dane had been more right about everything than she and Professor Nagoya.

Forget the machines. The thought came unbidden, but she trusted it. She had graduated number one in her class at every level of schooling. She had always used her mind but she knew she had never really trusted it unless machines and formulas agreed with it.

Now it was time to move past that.

Ahana unsealed the Valkyrie suit and stood on the stony ground just short of the top of Isandlwana. She really felt the true evil of the gate drawing power up from the planet and sending it on. She recoiled from it, stepping back several spaces, almost falling down the side of the mountain.

The hair on the back of her head rose as if a warm hand were brushing along her skin. She halted her retreat. She began to feel stronger, more powerful. And she was beginning to see what she had to do.

A single tear flowed down her smooth skin. Then she thought of Professor Nagoya, her mentor who had been killed outside the Devil's Sea Gate. Of the millions, billions, killed by the Shadow and not another tear flowed.

EARTH TIMELINE—III
Vicinity New York, July 2078

In the control pod Earhart could see what was around the sphere she was piloting reflected on the interior walls around her. She had the sphere going down very quickly, the walls of the tunnel flashing by.

Like a driver going someplace she'd never been before she wanted to ask Dane where they were going but she had to trust that he would tell her when necessary.

There was a glow below. A blue glow.

The sphere jerked and bumped, and Earhart suddenly realized they were heading toward a gate.

They hit and were through. Into a portal with pulsing blue walls, moving quickly. It took all of Earhart's skills as a pilot to keep them from hitting the walls of the portal. It was a close fit as the sphere raced through the portal. She hesitated as she rounded a curve and saw a flickering black wall ahead. A feeling of dread almost incapacitated her.

Go.

Earhart knew they could not go through the wall ahead. The Shadow had blocked their end of the portal.

She moved the sphere forward.

. . .

Ahana spread her arms wide, her body actually lifting off the ground from the power coming into her from Rorke's Drift. The gate the Shadow had opened at Isandlwana was so close. She felt as if she were being propelled toward it, almost against her will.

It actually was against her will at a certain level. Every human wanted to live. To give one's life willingly was the highest sacrifice.

Ahana gave it as the power coming into her peaked. Her head pulsed, the cells crystallizing, absorbing, and focusing the power.

Bolts of blue hit the Shadow Gate, even as Ahana was pushed forward, into it.

The collision was more than either could take.

. . .

At Rorke's Drift the chanting and singing stopped abruptly because there was a brilliant explosion to the northeast.

Then silence.

. . .

Earhart would never admit it to anyone, but she shut her eyes as the sphere closed on the black ending of the portal. Ever so briefly.

But there was no impact.

Earhart's eyes flashed open. They were in water, moving.

Entering a huge chamber with a five-mile-wide crystal in the center. That was weakly pulsing with gold.

To the right. The tunnel. It leads to Atlantis.

"Where are you going?"

I'm staying right here.

"I will miss you, my friend." Earhart kept up speed and banked hard right into the tunnel.

• • •

Cetewayo did not have to give an order. He simply began walking. Heading home. His warriors filed into place behind him. He noted that Shakan was next to him. "It was a good way to honor the dead and the brave."

She nodded, her eyes toward the top of Isandlwana. As they marched back, a column of British troops appeared, coming in the opposite direction, Chelmsford's column finally heading to Rorke's Drift, much too late. The two columns passed each other on either side of the track, less than five feet apart. Warriors looked at soldiers and the look was returned. But not one of the thousands passing each other made a hostile move.

Shakan broke off from the column and climbed up Isandlwana.

There was nothing except a single crystal skull, from which the blue was fading.

Tenderly Shakan picked it up. Cradling it in her hands she left Isandlwana, chanting a song of passing in a low voice.

• • •

Dane hovered over the crystal core.

There was an invisible wall, a shield, all around it. A shield he could not penetrate. A shield he knew as being projected by the collective consciousness of the Shadow.

Dane probed, and the shield held. He probed again, not with any hope of punching through, but rather to keep the Shadow occupied and focused here, instead of where they were.

Soon. Very soon.

• • •

Earhart pulled the sphere up. They burst out of the earth into the ocean next to Atlantis. The water was filled with Valkyries and kraken.

Earhart hit the command to unseal the sphere. Water poured in, filling the cargo bay. As soon as they were able, killer whales and MH-90s slipped through the cracks and the battle was joined.

• • •

Colonel Chamberlain had has his first real glimpse of Atlantis as his MH-90 exited the sphere. He recognized the city and the tower. His first issue was how to get in. Even as he was taking in the environment he heard his troops over the command net as they made contact with the Valkyries.

An MH-90 exploded as one of the gun platforms manned by Valkyries zeroed in on it and sent a bolt of gold into the craft. Nose guns on the MH-90s returned the fire, rounds smashing into Valkyries and tearing into their suits, killing the maimed humans inside.

Kraken met killer whale. Teeth versus tentacles as the two species ripped into each other.

Chamberlain saw the network for the Shadow spheres attached to the shield. He began issuing orders, directing his forces toward that.

· · ·

Earhart saw the network also. And she saw one of the spheres begin to detach from its moorings. She directed her sphere toward it, accelerating. This time she did not close her eyes just before the collision, accepting the fate that should have been hers many years ago.

The two spheres smashed into each other. Equal in construction, both outer skins gave way, imploding. Water rushed in, not only into the top cargo area but into the control and power sections.

Water hit the control pod, ripping it from its place. Earhart's last thought was of her navigator, Noonan.

In the power section, water poured in, hitting skulls that had been drained of most of the power, turning to steam as it hit their heat. There was more water than power left, and within seconds all the skulls went dark, the power from Pickett's charge gone.

· · ·

Chamberlain saw the two spheres, their outer hulls ripped open, slowly sinking down to the ocean floor. The one that had just detached—there was a pressure hatch where it had been.

"Right in there," Chamberlain ordered the pilots. "Put our nose right through it."

The MH-90 raced toward the hatch. When they were within a hundred meters the nose gun fired, tearing through the outer door.

Chamberlain hit the control that sealed off the pilot's compartment from the rear.

"Flooding," he announced.

The back ramp cracked open and water poured in.

As Chamberlain led the way out of the cargo bay, a tentacle shot by him, snatching the soldier next in line. Chamberlain dove forward, firing rounds at the creature. Designed to work on the Valkyrie armor, the specially adapted ammunition tore through the soft body of the kraken with little damage, the charge inside exploding harmlessly well after it had passed through.

A killer whale darted up and with one snap of its teeth severed the tentacle. The kraken turned its attention to the whale, and Chamberlain led his soldiers to the gap in the outer hatch. He paused there and did a quick check of the battle behind him.

Half the MH-90s were destroyed, floating derelicts. He saw numerous Valkyrie and Earth Battalion combat suits floating lifelessly in the water. He had a dozen soldiers with him as they placed a waterproof charge on the inner door. The charge exploded and Chamberlain was the first one in, swept in with the water that surged through. He kept his weapon at the ready as the corridor went up and pressure equalized.

He surfaced in the corridor, the pressure from the Atlantis dome keeping the water at bay. He moved forward, checking his rear view, seeing what was left of his battalion following. He focused back on the front.

The walls of the wide corridor were made of black metal, and the corridor went straight ahead, toward a golden glow. A figure was silhouetted against that glow for a moment, about twenty meters ahead, and Chamberlain's training kicked in. He fired automatically, his rounds hitting dead on target.

The Valkyrie was knocked back, tumbling in a heap.

Chamberlain came out of the corridor inside the dome and was momentarily stunned by the display that was projected on the interior surface. This pause allowed the rest of his group to catch up with him. Chamberlain ordered them to deploy tactically, and they moved forward toward the center tower, their suits allowing them to make large leaps and bounds over the terrain between.

They were engaged several times by Valkyries, and four of his surviving soldiers were killed, but there was no solid defense. Chamberlain realized that the Shadow had deployed most of the Valkyries outside of the dome, perhaps being warned by sensors or some other means as to what direction the attack was coming from.

A wide staircase, over a hundred meters in width, led up to massive doors set at the base of the tower. Chamberlain bounded up the stairs and through the open doors. To his right, a ramp went upward along the outer wall of the tower, and he headed in that direction.

· · ·

Memories flooded Dane's essence.

Being a child in a field. Feeling the bright sun and cool breeze on his skin. The smell of the freshly cut hay.

On board a helicopter with his team returning from a particularly dangerous mission in Cambodia, where the exhilaration of being alive mixed with exhaustion as the adrenaline rush of combat wore off.

Sin Fen and the connection his mind had shared with hers.

He could sense how close Chamberlain and his troops were.

It was all coming to an end.

. . .

Chamberlain led his troops through wide doors into the room filled with the latticework of globes.

Destroy them. They are the Shadow.

Chamberlain didn't hesitate. "Charge," he ordered over the battalion net.

The survivors of the First Earth Battalion dashed forward, firing as they did so.

Globes shattered under the barrage.

Chamberlain felt a wave of pain sweep through his brain and he staggered, blinded.

. . .

Dane probed the shield around the crystal sphere. It was weaker. He pushed harder, forcing the surviving members of the Shadow into a difficult decision: defend the source of their power, or defend themselves.

Unaccustomed to being attacked, having destroyed so many timelines with impunity, they failed to act decisively and tried to do both.

They failed in both.

. . .

Chamberlain was the last member of the First Earth Battalion still standing. Barely. Blood was streaming from his nose, mouth, ears, and eyes from hemorrhages in his brain. There was one last Shadow globe still intact.

With great effort Chamberlain tried to aim his weapon,

but he couldn't lift it. He fell to his knees, the image of the last globe flickering on his helmet screen.

. . .

Dane could feel the essence of the last Shadow still trying to shield the crystal. He focused his power and punched through, pouring his essence into the crystal. It was as if he dove into hot lava as he felt the immense power of the globe.

He saw it then—that this crystal supplied the power that made all the portals work. He absorbed that power, drawing it in, feeling it build around him.

He remembered Sin Fen's smile as she lay on top of the black pyramid, focusing its power against the Shadow. A similar smile crossed his face as he realized he was fulfilling his destiny.

The crystal sphere exploded.

Across multiple parallel worlds portals snapped out of existence.

epilogue

As President Lincoln helped Mary into the carriage, she cried out in anguish. He gripped her wrists, keeping her from falling out.

"What is it?"

As he put her on the seat next to him, she put her hands to her head. It had been a long day, perhaps the best and worst week of his life. Just five days ago General Grant had accepted Lee's surrender at Appomattox. Lincoln had traveled to Richmond where he had been wildly cheered by troops and freed slaves. He'd been asked by the ranking Union officer how to treat the people of the former Southern capital. He'd told the general to "let them up easy," in accordance with his policy of integrating the South back into the Union as smoothly and quickly as possible.

General Grant and his wife were supposed to be joining them for the trip to Ford Theater this evening, but at the last minute the general had begged off, citing other responsibilities.

Then Mary had had two visions during the day: one of which showed Sherman's army winning a final victory; the other showing her husband's body laid out in the East Room of the White House and a voice saying "Lincoln is dead."

The president had been uncertain how to interpret these two visions. Perhaps she had had another vision. He leaned close. "What is it?" he repeated.

Mary lifted her head and surprisingly there was a wide smile on her face. "They're gone."

"What's gone?"

"The voice. The visions. They're gone. I'm free."

Lincoln wrapped his long arm around his wife. Her body felt loose, the tenseness that had always been present was gone. She lifted her face toward his, and he kissed her.

"Let's skip the play," she whispered.

Tom Clancy's Power Plays

Created by Tom Clancy and Martin Greenberg
written by Jerome Preisler

TOM CLANCY'S POWER PLAYS: Politika

0-425-16278-8

TOM CLANCY'S POWER PLAYS: ruthless.com

0-425-16570-1

TOM CLANCY'S POWER PLAYS: Shadow Watch

0-425-17188-4

TOM CLANCY'S POWER PLAYS: Bio-Strike

0-425-17735-1

TOM CLANCY'S POWER PLAYS: Cold War

0-425-18214-2

TOM CLANCY'S POWER PLAYS: Cutting Edge

0-425-18705-5

TOM CLANCY'S POWER PLAYS: Zero Hour

0-425-19291-1

AVAILABLE WHEREVER BOOKS ARE SOLD
OR TO ORDER CALL:
1-800-788-6262